Bitter Alpine

AN EMMA LORD MYSTERY

Bitter Alpine

Mary Daheim

THORNDIKE PRESS
A part of Gale, a Cengage Company

Thorndike Press, a part of Gale, a Cengage Company.

Bitter Alpine is a work of fiction. Names, places, and incidents either are products of the author's imagination or are used fictitiously. Any resemblance to actual events, locales, or persons, living or dead, is entirely coincidental.
Thorndike Press® Large Print Mystery.
The text of this Large Print edition is unabridged.
Other aspects of the book may vary from the original edition.
Set in 16 pt. Plantin.

LIBRARY OF CONGRESS CIP DATA ON FILE.
CATALOGUING IN PUBLICATION FOR THIS BOOK
IS AVAILABLE FROM THE LIBRARY OF CONGRESS

ISBN-13: 978-1-4328-6672-3 (hardcover alk. paper)

Published in 2020 by arrangement with Ballantine Books, an imprint of Random House, a division of Penguin Random House, LLC

Printed in Mexico
Print Number: 01 Print Year: 2020

AUTHOR'S NOTE

This story is set in 2007.

Chapter 1

I've never been called a prima donna, but as editor and publisher of *The Alpine Advocate,* I, Emma Lord Dodge, am entitled to be annoyed when I enter my office on the second Monday in January and find a chicken clucking on my desk. Never mind that the Bantam Red hen was staring at me with beady-eyed indignation. I stared right back.

"Whoa!" The masculine voice behind me belonged to Leo Walsh, my ad manager. "How'd that get in here?"

"That's what I want to know," I said. "Where's Alison? I didn't see her at the reception desk when I came in."

"The back shop, maybe?" Leo leaned down to pick up the hen, but she flapped her wings and skittered away to land on my chair. "Hey!" he shouted as he clapped his hands. "Out! Now!"

Apparently the chicken didn't like loud

voices. She turned her back on us and pecked at the draft of an editorial I'd started Friday afternoon. It wasn't one of my better efforts, so maybe that was her way of offering criticism. Before Leo or I could react, our office manager ran toward us.

"So that's where the chicken went," Alison Lindahl muttered. Diving across my desk, she grabbed the hen. But the chicken wasn't giving up without a fight. She tried to flap her wings, but Alison's grip was firm as she carried our intruder through the newsroom and to the reception area.

Leo chuckled. "I'll bet that hen followed the new county extension agent in here. I think he brought a news release."

"And a chicken," I muttered. "I haven't yet met the guy, though Alison pointed him out to me on the street. Boyd Lanier." I smiled at Leo. "He's fairly young and good-looking. Quite a change from his predecessor."

My ad manager nodded. "Single?"

I nodded. "According to the official Skykomish County news release, Lanier is thirty, from Wenatchee, and a graduate of Washington State University. I suspect Alison would let him lead a herd of goats into the office. She and I must talk."

"And I," Leo said, turning toward the

newsroom, "must talk local merchants into buying ads so we *Advocate* staffers can afford food. My wife is fond of both cooking and eating. I'd gotten used to meager meals during the years we lived separate lives. Liza didn't. Now we find two Walshes can't live as cheaply as one."

"But you're both happy about that," I pointed out.

"True. Incredible, but true." Leo's walk was almost a swagger as he headed through the newsroom.

I smiled as he put on his trench coat. It was raining, which was good, since Alpine is at the three-thousand-foot level of the Cascade Mountains. Old-timers recalled as much as eight feet of snow on the ground during winters when they were young enough not to be hampered by having to tunnel their way to school on Tonga Ridge. Recent winters had been more benign. Global warming has had its effect during my sixteen-plus years in Alpine.

I'd arrived with a college-bound son, a used Jaguar, and the ownership of a small-town weekly newspaper. Back then I was more intimidated by failure than hoping for success. The resident ad manager, Ed Bronsky, was a lazy, gloomy dud. I never had the heart to fire him, but after a frustrating three years he'd inherited money and quit. That's when I hired Leo. Thanks to his hard work, the *Advocate* was still solvent. While newspapers were in peril all over the country, there was an advantage to living in a small town. The eight thousand residents of Skykomish County knew most of their neighbors. They liked reading about their fellow Alpiners — and themselves.

I was mulling other topics for this week's editorial when our former House & Home editor tromped into my cubbyhole of an office. "Well now," said Vida Runkel, settling her majestic self into one of my two visitor chairs, "Alison tells me you were invaded by a chicken. Don't argue. I'm putting that in my 'Scene Around Town' column."

"That's fine," I assured her. Not that Vida ever needed my approval. She'd worked for the newspaper long before I arrived in town. But in the fall, she had finally announced her retirement. Vida had been a staple of the *Advocate* for over ten years before I bought the newspaper. Naturally, there were occasional problems about which of us actually ran the show. Now in her late seventies, she was entitled to take her ease, but I'd had trouble imagining the newspaper without her. As it happened, I didn't have to. Vida had retained her right to "Scene" with its snippets of Skykomish County residents' daily lives, along with her advice column and an occasional feature about senior citizens. She'd been replaced — not quite the right word, since nobody really could replace her — by Leo's wife, Liza, who had once held a similar job on a Los Angeles–area newspaper. In fact, that was how the Walshes had met some thirty years ago.

"I'd hoped," Vida went on, "to interview the sheriff's new deputy, since she's female, but my nephew Billy told me Mitch Laskey has already gotten the assignment."

Bill Blatt was one of Vida's numerous relatives on her mother's side and thus duty bound to tell all to his redoubtable aunt. He was also one of Milo Dodge's deputy sheriffs.

I shrugged. "County law enforcement is part of Mitch's beat. I could hardly *not* give him the interview."

Vida adjusted the single pheasant feather of her broad-brimmed hat. "I suppose that's so. But I've already met her."

"So has Mitch. He introduced himself on her first day of work last Monday."

"So did I." Vida's gray eyes were glittering behind her gold-rimmed glasses. "She's rather nice-looking."

"Is she?"

"Didn't your husband say so?"

"No," I replied. "Milo mentioned that she was qualified and seemed sharp. There were four other candidates, but he considered her the one best suited for the job. She'd worked for law enforcement in Tacoma but wanted a change. Having only one female deputy until now, the sheriff felt Doe Jamison has been overworked dealing with abused women, especially during the holidays with so much drinking."

"Yes. I'm sure she'll find Alpine a wonderful place to live. And work." Vida turned thoughtful. "Consuela De Groote. What can she be?"

"Milo's new deputy?" I smiled when I said it.

Vida wasn't amused. "I meant her nationality. She looks French to me. But the name doesn't suit her."

"She's probably gotten used to it."

"Perhaps." Vida paused, then shrugged her broad shoulders. "I must get to work on 'Scene.' " She made her splayfooted way out of my cubbyhole.

I returned to my editorial. After my standard — and dull — hope for everyone in SkyCo to have a healthy, happy, prosperous new year, I needed something fresh. What I really wanted was to demand that County

Manager Jack Blackwell put streetlights on Fir Street where the sheriff and I resided in what was now *our* log cabin since we'd finally gotten married last spring. I could also push for sidewalks, but knew that'd break the budget. If there was one. But whatever I suggested, Blackwell would dismiss. He and Milo had never gotten along since Jack first came to town thirty years ago, when my future husband was still a deputy. I couldn't stand Jack, either. Yet he ran Blackwell Timber as an efficient, safe operation and treated his employees fairly. He had even survived a public tirade against him by a woman who blamed him for her husband's death in an Idaho logging operation. Being our second-biggest employer after the community college, I had to tread lightly around Black Jack.

Alison brought in the mail a little after ten-thirty, which was later than usual. "Marlowe Whipp's limping," she said in a cheery voice. "He was hit by a car."

Our regular mailman was a chronic complainer, but this news jarred me a bit. "But he's doing the route? What happened?"

"The car had started to back up and only bumped him," she replied. "But you know Marlowe. He likes to gripe. I'm surprised he didn't ask the post office to relieve him for the rest of the day."

I was, too. But before I could say anything, Alison went on. "The new county extension agent is a hottie. He's not married."

"So I understand from the news release. Has he asked you out yet?"

The cheer faded a bit. "No, but I'll figure out something. Maybe I'll ask him if he could teach me to churn butter." Alison didn't quite dance out of my office, but she came close.

By eleven o'clock, I'd finished with the mail. There wasn't anything of interest except for two cranks who criticized my editorial wishing everyone a happy holiday season. One insisted I was a Communist atheist because I hadn't mentioned that Jesus was born on December 25. The other informed me I was pandering to the religious right and should have talked about the winter solstice instead. Neither letter was signed, so I didn't have to run them in the paper.

Addressing the editorial conundrum, I decided to go for the streetlights. Nobody should be against being able to see better in the dark. I was tempted to include the paving of Fir Street but held off, as readers who knew where I lived might criticize me for being self-serving.

By eleven forty-five, I noticed that Vida had left. I'd intended to ask her to have lunch with me, but I assumed she had other things to do. Picking up the phone, I called Milo to see if he was free. His receptionist, Lori Cobb, answered.

"He's out on the highway," she replied in her pleasant voice. "I'm not sure when he'll be back."

Every so often my husband likes to hit the road to, as he puts it, air himself out. "He's patrolling?" I asked, not having heard any sirens that might indicate a traffic accident.

"No," Lori replied. "We got a call from someone who moved into that cabin at Baring. You know, the one with the hot tub that the crazy guy tried to burn down about a year ago."

I remembered the incident all too well. Not only had the "crazy guy" set the cabin on fire, but he'd also murdered a federal marshal who was trying to track him down for other crimes. Shortly before his arrest, he'd gotten into it with the county extension agent, Dean Ramsey, who'd ended up stabbing the perp in self-defense. Dean had taken a leave of absence from his job and was still recuperating. Alison's latest romantic target might not stick around too long. The perp had recovered much faster and was doing time in the penitentiary at Walla Walla.

"What's with the Baring cabin now?" I asked, having more distant memories of Crystal Bird, the onetime wife of Dean Ramsey, who had been found murdered in the cabin's hot tub not long after she and I had exchanged harsh words over her newsletter's criticism of me as a tool of Alpine's anti-feminists.

"You know that the cabin finally got repaired," Lori reminded me. "An elderly couple moved in and they thought they heard a prowler. The boss man decided he'd have a look for himself. I think he was getting bored reading up on the latest fishing and hunting regulations. Do you want to leave a message for him?"

"No." I didn't want to admit I was only calling about lunch. "I'll find out when he gets home tonight. Thanks, Lori." I rang off.

Liza Walsh appeared in the doorway, apparently having come from the back shop. "Leo had to take my Nissan to the Chevron station. There's something wrong with the automatic door opener. I wonder if we need two cars here in Alpine. I can walk everywhere I need to go. Leo usually does. If I have to drive, I can use his Toyota. Besides," she went on with a smile that revealed her dimples, "I can use the exercise, especially with all these hills here in town."

I smiled back. Liza was pretty, with silvered black hair and eyes so dark that they looked like jet. She's a couple of inches taller than my five-four, but she also carries at least fifteen more pounds. Like her husband, she obviously enjoys her cooking. The best thing about the Walshes was that they had reconciled after many years apart. Working as an ad salesman in the L.A. area had involved long liquor-fueled lunches and dinners. Leo had finally been fired and Liza threatened to divorce him. I'd been along on that ride to reconciliation after I hired Leo when the feckless Ed Bronsky inherited money and quit without notice to start spending his newly acquired wealth on expensive family trips and the mansion once known as Casa de Bronska. Within a few short years, the Bronskys were broke. Ed wanted his job back, but Leo was an aggressive ad manager who kept us on the positive side of the ledger. He had also acquired something that was better than money — sobriety.

I posed a question for his wife. "How's the house-hunting coming?"

"We may finally have found one that isn't

either about to fall down or overrun with vermin," Liza replied, no longer smiling. "Do you know the Swensons?"

"I know the name. They're an elderly couple who live in the Icicle Creek Development, where Milo's former home is located. In fact, Mrs. Swenson died not long ago. Vida wrote up her obituary."

"I saw that," Liza said. "In fact, Vida told me that their daughter was moving Mr. Swenson to wherever she and her husband live. Monroe, I think it was. Alison just got a listing for the house from Doukas Realty to run in the classified ads."

I sat up straighter in my chair. "Have you seen the house? I only gave it a passing glance when I was in the neighborhood."

"No, I think Leo and I should take a look at it. I suspect it needs some serious updating. But the price might be right, especially when compared to homes in the L.A. area."

"Or Seattle," I said. "One of the advantages of living in Alpine is that housing is so much cheaper. By the way, if you need a lawyer when you do buy a house, I can introduce you to Marisa Foxx."

"I know Marisa from seeing her at church." Liza's dark eyes sparkled. "As you may have noticed, I'm trying to get Leo to go to Mass more often than Christmas and

Easter. He actually likes Father Kelly. I was surprised to find a black priest up here."

I laughed. "So were a lot of Alpiners when Father Den showed up here over ten years ago."

Liza laughed, too. "I can imagine. I've seen a few other minorities, but mostly college students. It's really a culture shock to be in such a small town that's so predominately . . . white."

I agreed. "It was even less . . . dare I say the word 'integrated'? When Leo arrived here, the college hadn't yet opened. Believe it or not, Martin Luther King Jr. Day is honored only by the state and federal agencies in SkyCo. That stunned me when I moved here. It was a shock to Leo, too."

"Maybe the small-town atmosphere and the slower pace helped Leo stop drinking so much." Liza's expression turned serious. "I owe you."

I shook my head. "No. He did it on his own. Really. It took him a few months, but he succeeded."

"But you took a chance on him," Liza pointed out. "That made an impression on Leo."

"Maybe," I allowed. "I think just my hiring him made Leo realize he had to get sober. I was his last chance, but he did it by himself."

Liza smiled. "The main thing was that Leo did it."

I agreed.

The newsroom was now empty. On the job, Liza and Leo made a point of going their separate ways to avoid too much togetherness. Mitch always had lunch at home with his wife, Brenda, who had emotional problems. Whether this state had occurred before or after their son, Troy, had been imprisoned for drug dealing, I've never been quite sure. But despite escaping twice and both times getting caught, Troy was scheduled to be released in September. The Laskeys' move to Alpine had been motivated by their desire to be close to Troy while he served out his sentence at the Monroe Correctional Complex some thirty-five miles west on Highway 2.

It was now noon and I was alone. That meant a visit to the Burger Barn for takeout. *The excitement never stops,* I thought as I put on my red hooded jacket.

I didn't know that it was about to begin. And then I'd wish it hadn't.

CHAPTER 2

By the time I got home that evening at five-thirty, it was raining. The drops that covered my Honda's windshield were heavy, a sign that the temperature was dropping and we might get snow. After coming in from what was now a garage instead of the not-so-snug carport, I went through the kitchen into the living room and opened the front door to take in the mail. Junk. Not even a bill. I retraced my route as far as the recycling bin next to the kitchen door. I didn't bother changing my clothes, but went directly to the refrigerator to contemplate the items I'd picked up at the Grocery Basket on the way home.

I decided to keep it simple — as usual. My husband liked basic cooking, especially if it was steak. The phone rang in the living room. I managed to grab it on the third ring. Alison erupted into my ear.

"Lori just told me Boyd Lanier is staying

at the ski lodge, but he plans to move in here at Pines Villa as soon as all his stuff arrives from Wenatchee. Can you believe I could be so lucky?"

Lori Cobb is not only the sheriff's receptionist, but Alison's roommate. "I thought the apartments were all filled up," I said. "You probably know Leo and Liza are house-shopping, but that could take a while."

"Somebody else gave notice," Alison informed me. "The Ostranders. You know, the weird couple who have the pet hedgehogs, Laverne and Shirley. He's being transferred by the state highway department, and she's a freelance artist who can work anywhere. Vida wrote them up a year or so ago when they first came to Alpine."

I vaguely remembered the article. Vida had left out the hedgehogs. She told me they were repulsive creatures and not worthy of an extra inch of copy. I'd felt she was being a bit harsh.

Alison's voice dropped a couple of notches. "Is there any way . . . I mean, I know you suggested this a couple of times, but . . . do you think I could interview Boyd for the paper?"

"So already he's Boyd?" I tried not to sound critical.

"Why not? He called me Alison."

I hesitated. "I'll give you the same advice I'd give Mitch. Give Boyd a chance to settle into the job, at least a couple of weeks, maybe even after he's moved into his apartment. Okay?"

"Well . . . I guess."

"You'll probably run into him once he's living at Pines Villa," I reminded her. "You may not even need an excuse to get him . . . interested."

"Maybe." She sighed. "He's really good-looking. Tall, too, over six feet, I figure. Of course, I was sitting down."

I thought it was a wonder Alison hadn't fallen out of her chair. "We'll need a photo," I said. "They didn't send one with the news release. Could you do that without drooling on the camera?"

"I'll try. You saw some of the pictures I took on that cruise I went on last year, right? I thought they turned out fairly good."

"They were very nice," I said, hearing the kitchen door open. "Got to go. Milo's here."

"You've got your man. Lucky you. Bye."

My man loped into the living room. "What's for dinner?" he asked, tossing his regulation hat onto a peg by the front door before he leaned down to kiss me.

"Gruel," I replied. "You want it cold or

warmed up?"

"Funny Emma," he muttered, looking at the end table next to his easy chair. "You haven't made our drinks yet?"

"Jeez, Milo, I just got home about five minutes ago, and the phone rang before I could do anything. I had to grocery shop after I left work. Do you want to change clothes while I make the drinks?"

He shook his head. "I'll take over the bartending. I just want to crash first. It was kind of a crappy day."

"Tell me about it when we both sit down," I said as we went into the kitchen. "It was a dull one for me. I want to hear about your new hire. What kind of steak do you want?"

"Any kind," he said, getting out the glasses and putting ice into them. "Just don't serve it half-raw."

I glared at him. "Do I ever?"

"You do it with yours. It's a wonder you don't get some kind of mad cow disease."

"Your steak must taste like a catcher's mitt. All the juices and flavor are lost in the cooking."

"It tastes the way I like it, damnit. Why do you care?"

I started to open my mouth to snap back at him, but instead, I set the frying pan down and put my arms around him. "I only care about you, you big jerk."

Milo held me close and leaned down to kiss the top of my head. At six foot five, he was over a foot taller. "I *am* a jerk. Why did you marry me?"

"Because you tricked me into it," I said against his chest. "It was something I'd never done. Marriage, I mean."

I felt him sigh. "For somebody who was married before, I can tell you it's sure as hell better the second time around."

I looked up at him. "I'm never going to find out if a second marriage could be better. I like this one a lot."

He leaned down again to kiss me on the lips. It was a very intense kiss. What it led to meant that I didn't start dinner until after six-thirty. When we finally sat down to eat, I asked Milo why his day had been, as he'd put it, "crappy."

"For starters, Jack Mullins was late getting to work," he explained after downing a large chunk of steak. "It wasn't his fault. Their furnace went out last night and the repairman was supposed to show up at seven, but he didn't get there until seven-forty. Then Jack had to stick around to make sure it got fixed. Nina's not into household repairs."

"Probably not," I agreed. "She's the

delicate type."

"Right." Milo paused to eat a Brussels sprout. "Breaking in a new hire is always a pain in the ass. I'm going to let Bill Blatt take over after I give Consi — that's what De Groote likes to be called — the basics. He's good at that stuff and has more patience than I do."

"I'll have to introduce myself," I said. "I'll wait a few days. I remember what it was like when I came to Alpine. I swear I met at least fifty people in the first couple of days. I was overwhelmed."

Milo gave me an arch look. "I wasn't one of them."

I smiled. "I told you later why I waited to introduce myself. I'd seen you a couple of times on the street and you looked intimidating."

"That's how a sheriff is supposed to look."

I laughed. "You did. But then you took me to the Venison Inn and bought me drinks. You loosened up, so I decided I liked you."

He ran a hand through his graying sandy hair, and his hazel eyes were faintly reproachful. "It took you long enough to figure out how much."

"I know. You know, too." *Almost sixteen years,* I thought, *despite a false start with*

Milo that lasted over a year and a half. And all because I was determined to finally marry the father of my illegitimate son, Adam. I was an idiot.

"What else happened today?" I asked.

Milo polished off his last bite of potato. "That call to the cabin was a false alarm. No sign of an intruder."

"Who's living there now? And who legally owns it?"

"Don't ask me about the ownership," my husband replied. "The old coot I talked to is Waldo Danforth. I didn't see his wife. She was lying down. I guess she was still overcome by the so-called intruder."

"Mitch will get it off the log tomorrow," I said. "What else happened?"

Milo gazed at his empty plate. "Where's the pie?"

I sighed. "I almost didn't buy one at the store. It's peach. I'm full. You can get it yourself."

My husband headed to the fridge. "When I started back from the cabin some idiot was going too damned fast in an old beater and I decided to chase him down. He accelerated and skidded into the guardrail. Two of his tires blew out, so I had to send for help to get him off the highway."

"Was he hurt?"

"No, but he was higher than a kite. I cited him for that and for speeding. Dustin Fong took him to the ER. The dink's from Colville, so I guess he was heading home over the pass." Milo began devouring a very large chunk of pie.

"Anything else?" I asked, in what I hoped was a voice of wifely concern rather than that of an overbearing newspaper editor.

"Yeah." Milo attacked another bite of pie. "Dwight Gould's got a cold. He may not make it in tomorrow. Hell, Gould's never sick. If we get snow, we'll be shorthanded, even with the new deputy. She's just breaking in and I don't want to put too much pressure on her."

"Consi's had some experience being a cop, though," I said.

"In Tacoma," Milo replied after he'd swallowed the elephant-sized chunk of pie. "She knows zip about winter road conditions in the mountains. I don't like having a snow-and-ice rookie on highway patrol."

"Have her stay in town. They should sand around here if it gets bad. By the way, Vida met Consi." I kept my voice neutral. "She says your new hire is very good-looking."

Milo scowled at me. "I didn't hire her for her looks. Hell, I'm old enough to be her father. Which reminds me," he went on, having finished his pie and putting the fork down, "Bran called to say I'm going to be a grandfather. Solange is expecting a kid."

"When?"

"Sometime in the spring," he said. "April, May. I guess."

I'd gone to the wedding with my husband, which had been held on Seattle's Eastside. Solange's parents had been there along with Milo's ex-wife, Tricia. I couldn't help but feel like an outsider. I'd never be a grandmother. And because my son, Adam, is a priest, unless the Catholic church changed the rules, he would never give me grandchildren. The thought always made me a little sad.

"That's great," I said, hoping to sound enthusiastic as we got up from the table. "Has he told Tanya? I haven't seen her since she and Bill Blatt came here for our New Year's Day get-together."

Milo shrugged. "Probably. If he hasn't, Tanya spent Christmas in Bellevue with Mulehide, so she probably found out then."

Tanya was Milo's daughter, and "Mulehide" was a reference to his ex-wife. Tricia and Milo had been divorced for over twenty years. The first Mrs. Dodge had been involved in an affair with a high school teacher who also had a spouse. After the move to

Bellevue, Tricia and Jake Sellers got married as soon as their divorces became final. Tricia had taken the three Dodge children with her. But cheaters don't change. The second marriage ended in divorce as well. The ex–Mrs. Dodge/ex–Mrs. Sellers now had a new man in her life. I suppose I couldn't blame her to never stop trying.

After we sat in our usual places, I stopped thinking about Tricia. I should be grateful to her. If she hadn't left Milo, I would never have ended up married to him.

Milo looked up from his book. "What are you smiling about?"

"You."

He smiled back.

Only a dusting of snow had fallen during the night. Milo had checked the forecast and been informed that by early morning the snow clouds were blowing westward out over Puget Sound. Our outdoor thermometer sat at exactly thirty-two degrees when I headed for the office. By noon the temperature would be in the high thirties and the snow would be gone later in the afternoon. Yet as I drove down the steep hill to Front Street, I smiled at how pretty the town looked in its coating of winter white. Even the homeliest, dumpiest houses and buildings were transformed. An illusion, of course. But I was reminded of how small and mean Alpine had seemed to me when I first moved here after leaving Portland. I'd never planned to stay in the town. Then marriage changed all that. Now I'd spend the rest of my life here. I kept on smiling.

But my mood was dampened as I walked into the office. I heard Ed Bronsky's voice whining to Leo. "Why do I have to pay for a subscription to the paper? Wasn't I the one who kept it from going under back in the day?"

Leo was accustomed to his predecessor's bitching. "That was then," Leo replied calmly. "This is now. You haven't worked here in the last ten, twelve years, Ed. Alison tells me you're six months behind in your subscription payment."

Ed waved a dismissive pudgy hand. "I can't keep up with everything." He shot me a wary glance. "Emma — did I forget to tell you about my new project?"

I was blank. "I don't recall you mentioning it when you and Shirley dropped by on New Year's Day."

He shook his head and made a face. "That wasn't the right setting for talking about something serious like what I've got in mind. In fact, I'm here now to give you and

Leo a heads-up. It's only fair that I . . ." Ed stopped talking as Alison appeared with the Upper Crust bakery's goodies. "What kind of pastry did you get today?"

Alison assumed a sweet smile. "Date bars and fig rolls. We're all trying to keep a healthy style of eating in the new year. In fact," she went on, now frowning, "I wonder if I should put everything in the microwave to warm it up. It might taste a little dry." Our office manager and the pastries moved on to the back shop.

All three of Ed's chins dropped. "What happened to sugar doughnuts and cinnamon rolls?" he virtually bleated.

Leo gestured at his wife's vacant desk. "It's my wife's idea. Now that we're back together, she wants us to eat healthier so we can live longer to enjoy each other's company."

The concept appeared to flummox Ed. "You don't enjoy eating?"

"Moderation in all things," Leo replied. "What's your project, Ed?"

Ed assumed a serious expression. Mitch had just come into the office and knew Ed well enough to merely nod before going to his desk. But that didn't stop my former ad manager from insisting that our reporter had to hear about The Project. "You'll like this, Laskey," he said. "You're from a big city. Cleveland, right?"

"Detroit," Mitch responded. "Actually, a suburb — Royal Oak."

Ed nodded vaguely. "Okay, here's the deal. Mayor Baugh isn't in very good shape these days, and he's officially out of office with the new government change. That leaves only Jack Blackwell as county manager, and face it, he's not a warm and fuzzy guy. We need somebody around here who can put some serious warmth into Alpine, especially for visitors. I'm thinking *billboard.*"

"Billboard?" I echoed. "On Highway 2? I'm not sure they're legal."

The comment was dismissed with a wave of Ed's pudgy hand. "We can worry about that stuff later. But you bet your boots it'd bring in the tourists."

Leo was trying to hide his dismay and almost succeeding. "What would be on the billboard?"

Ed beamed. "Me. I'll be the spokesperson for the town and for all of Skykomish County, for that matter. I'm a native son and nobody can ever say I haven't done my share to boost my hometown. Do you think I should wear a costume?"

My phone was ringing and I'd had enough. I excused myself and practically ran into my office. The last thing I heard from Ed was ". . . maybe a trench coat like yours, Walsh, to add some kind of intrigue . . ."

The only intrigue I was interested in was finding a topic that might induce subscribers to actually read my editorial. Paving was probably out; it sounded too expensive. Streetlights throughout the town might be worthwhile, since January had the longest dark days of the year. By the time February rolled around, I always felt like a mole. I'd use the analogy in the lead and maybe in the headline. "Mole People of Alpine." Why not? Some of our readers might actually read at least the first couple of sentences.

I'd just reached the not-so-exciting conclusion when I saw Postmaster Roy Everson come into the newsroom. He paused by Mitch's desk, but shook his head and came into my office. I had a premonition of what was coming next.

Roy fumbled with the chair before parking his unimposing body in it. "I didn't mean to put off your Mr. Laskey," he said by way of greeting, "but this is something you should hear first." He swallowed in a way that made his Adam's apple jump. "It's about Mama."

It always was with Roy. Going on twenty

years ago, his widowed mother, Myrtle, had disappeared while on a blackberry-picking expedition. No sign of her had ever been found. Roy had become obsessed about Mrs. Everson up to the point of being hospitalized a little over a year ago. In fact, we'd all hoped that episode had cured him. Apparently it hadn't. I sat up a little straighter to hear him out.

"After Bebe and I take down all the Christmas decorations," he began, "we do what we call our 'sprinter' cleaning." He paused, smiling a bit. "That's a cross between spring and winter. Then we can skip another cleaning when March rolls around."

"Smart," I said, just to let him know I was listening.

"We've got a lot of boxes for our holiday trimmings," he went on, "and sometimes we're not as organized as maybe we should be about which holiday is which. That is, Thanksgiving and Christmas come pretty darned close together some years. And Halloween kicks everything off." Roy paused, frowning, then turned very serious. "It's Halloween that got me wondering about the bucket we found in the basement when we were putting everything away." His expression indicated this was serious stuff.

"How so?" I asked, sensing what was coming next.

Roy had started to perspire. He took out a white handkerchief and mopped his brow. "Mama never liked being bothered by the trick-or-treaters. Oh, she loved kiddies, but sometimes they could be grabby or rude or . . . you know how kids are. Anyway, she'd turn on her porch light and put candy in a bucket on the porch. The bucket Bebe and I found in the basement had what looked like dried berries in it. Nubs, you might say. Do you know what that means?"

I knew what it meant to Roy and Bebe, but I wasn't giving in without an argument. "Haven't you two gone berry picking over the years?"

Roy shrugged and pocketed the handkerchief. "A few times. But that wasn't the bucket we used. It seemed wrong to use hers. It was . . ." He scrunched up his face. "Mama's bucket was sort of like . . . sacred, being the last thing she may've touched. But now it means she came back to the house. So what happened to her after that?"

"I don't know," I admitted. "She obviously went somewhere else."

"Where?"

"If you and Bebe don't know, then nobody does, Roy," I said in a sympathetic voice. "She was what? Sixty-two?" I saw him nod.

"I understand she was in fairly good shape. But accidents can happen to anyone."

"Mama didn't have accidents," Roy declared. "You people don't realize what she was like. You never even knew her."

"No, I didn't," I replied. "I wish I had. Everyone seems to have liked her. She sounds like someone I'd have enjoyed knowing."

"You would have," Roy asserted, clumsily getting up from the chair. "You missed out. Everybody liked Mama."

"I'm sure they did."

Roy hustled off through the newsroom while I wondered if there had been somebody who hadn't liked Mama. Maybe we'd never know. It might be better if we didn't, especially for Roy and Bebe.

Chapter 3

"What's our lead story?" Mitch asked around two o'clock. "We don't have much going on right now."

"The new deputy and the new medical practitioner," I replied. "Did you get much from Deputy De Groote?"

"Enough for about three inches," Mitch replied. "Maybe I can run down . . . what's his name? Janos something, right?"

"Kadar," I said, and spelled it out. "I think he's from Anacortes. You can somehow tactfully write about how relieved Doc Dewey and Doctor Sung are to finally have some backup."

"Good idea." Mitch grinned. "I don't know how those two ever manage to get a full night's sleep with over eight thousand potential patients in Skykomish County. Do you think it's okay to tie the two new hires together?"

"Sure. But see if you can get photos. If

not, we've got headshots."

"Got it." Mitch checked his watch. "I should be able to catch both of the newbies before deadline."

"Go for it," I said. "Oh — if you have time, can you go over to the courthouse and take a picture of the new county extension agent?"

Mitch pulled on one of his long earlobes. "Lanier, right? I remember the name because Bob Lanier was a big NBA star for the Detroit Pistons."

"Right, very imposing. Did you go to a lot of their games back then?"

"Never did," he replied with a touch of regret. "Tickets were too expensive. Besides, Brenda's never cared for sports. I'm off."

I watched him walk away through the newsroom. Mitch might be occasionally gloomy, but he was the best reporter I'd ever had. He'd honed his skills for years on the *Detroit Free Press.* I couldn't pay him as much as he was worth, but being close to their incarcerated son made up for it.

At five o'clock my tepid editorial and the rest of the paper were in the hands of Kip MacDuff, my back-shop guru. He'd started out as one of our teenage carriers, but I discovered early on that, like most of his generation, he was a tech whiz. I'm not, and even in my younger years as a reporter for *The Oregonian* I'd practically passed out when they introduced computers to the staff. I was so panic-stricken on my first attempt that I blew out the entire system. Luckily, I didn't get fired.

By the time I got home, we'd reverted to our usual January rain. Milo wasn't far behind me. After a quick kiss, I noticed he looked befuddled. I asked him what was wrong. He told me to wait until he'd changed out of his uniform and had a drink in hand. Like a good wife, I continued making dinner. My husband could take on the cocktail duty.

"Well?" I said after we were settled in the living room. "What happened?"

Milo lighted a cigarette before responding. He'd cut down on his smoking, and I was going through one of my phases of trying to quit. "Blackwell came to see me this afternoon." He paused, knowing I'd be concerned. "The bastard was all buddy-buddy. You'd think we'd been high school pals."

I'd taken a big sip of bourbon. "What did he want? An apology from you for busting him at the Labor Day picnic after his ex-wife filed a complaint against him for slugging her?"

"No." Milo rubbed his forehead. "That never came up. She dropped the charges, anyway, though I'll be damned if I know why. As for Jack, now that he's county manager, he thinks we should get together every so often to make sure we're in synch when it comes to law enforcement. You know what that really means."

I didn't, but I took a stab at it anyway. "He wants to run your job?"

"He wants to run me out of town," Milo replied. "I figure this is his way of having one of his underlings do some kind of audit or study or whatever the hell he'll call it and come up with bogus reasons to get rid of me. He won't find anything, but the sonuvabitch could plant stuff."

"What did you tell him?"

"I said fine, go ahead. In fact," Milo went on, "I told him he could start tomorrow. Jack waffled, insisting he needed time to put together his criteria. I was tempted to tell him where he could put it, but I didn't."

I laughed. "You as the soul of restraint?"

"Hell, I don't give a damn. But whoever's the bag man for Jack will be watched like a hawk. I bet I know who it'll be." Milo looked at me as if I could guess.

"His number-two guy, Bob Sigurdson, right?"

"Probably. Unless it's Ken McKean, the new hire he brought in last fall." Milo paused. "I only met the guy once, when Alison fled to the McKeans' house to escape the crazy strangler. They seemed like decent people. Too bad he's stuck working for a horse's ass."

"Hey, even you admit Jack treats his employees well as long as they toe the company line."

Milo shrugged his broad shoulders. "If he didn't, they might mutiny. Hell, that guy he fired last fall took a shot at him. He's doing time on a plea bargain."

"Mickey O'Neill came from a long line of feisty males," I said. "Their feud with the Hartquists wiped out not only his father, but his uncles. They ended up dead in the local meat locker."

My husband acknowledged the tragedy with a nod. "Speaking of meat, are we going to eat or are you trying to starve me?"

I took the not-so-subtle query seriously and announced that dinner was probably ready. The rest of the evening was spent watching an NBA game between two teams we didn't care about. The Sonics had gone on the road, but it didn't really matter. They weren't having a very good season. That didn't bother either of us. We were content to snuggle on the sofa and let our eyeballs glaze over as the game wound down with a parade to the free-throw line. By morning, we didn't even remember who'd won.

My first task at work the next morning was to flip through the new edition of the *Advocate.* There had been no calls from Kip MacDuff while he printed out the paper, so there had been no crises and the new edition was on its way to subscribers. Kip would be in later. He stood by until the press job was finished in the wee small hours of the night, always watching for any hint of a press jam. That could halt the process for at least half an hour. Luckily, we hadn't suffered one of those nightmares for over a year.

Alison was looking unusually perky. I asked if she'd finagled a way to meet Boyd Lanier outside of office hours.

"No," she replied, "but I did see him drive by Pines Villa. He's got a Mini Cooper. What could be sexier than that?"

"A Rolls?"

Alison made a face. "I've only seen pictures of Rolls-Royces. They look stodgy to me. Not the kind of wheels you can cuddle in."

"I wouldn't know," I said, starting into the

newsroom. "I'm a stodgy middle-aged matron."

Alison giggled. "That's not what I heard a year or so ago when you and Dodge were making out on a street corner."

I looked back over my shoulder. "I'd fallen down at the medical clinic. Milo had to carry me out to his SUV. He kissed me to make me feel better. And no, I wasn't a patient at the time. Roy Everson was having a Mama meltdown."

Alison was still giggling. I kept going. Mitch was already at his desk, but staring at the coffeemaker as if he could will it to finish perking. He asked me who had the bakery run. I told him it was one of the Walshes, but I couldn't remember which. Leo showed up just as I finished speaking. Except for his briefcase, he was empty-handed.

"Hang in there, Laskey," he said. "My much better half is at the Upper Crust. Her arrival is imminent."

Mitch's shoulders slumped in relief. "Good. I didn't have breakfast this morning. Brenda wasn't feeling well. I hope it's not flu."

"It's that time of year," Leo responded.

I went into my cubbyhole. Brenda had a lot of problems, both physical and mental. I was sympathetic, but I'm never at my best in the early morning. Neither is Milo. To preserve our married state, we barely communicate before he's the first to leave our log cabin.

The morning ran its usual low-key post-pub course. Vida hadn't stopped by, so I assumed she had no complaints about the latest edition. When I went out to get a coffee refill around ten o'clock, Liza was just returning from wherever she'd been and was the only staffer in the newsroom.

"What's with the old guy who's using a telescope to look through the rain for space aliens?" she asked with a bemused expression.

"That's our resident UFO expert, Averill Fairbanks," I explained. "He's harmless. Just humor him if he tells you he's spotted some Plutonians trying to sneak into the Whistling Marmot Movie Theatre."

Liza reacted with her usual gusty laugh. "And I thought Crazy Eights Neffel was an oddball. Last night he was playing an accordion in front of the statue in Old Mill Park. He kept telling your town founder to sing along with him. Carl Clemans — right?" She saw me nod. "Carl didn't seem inclined to join the entertainment."

"He wouldn't," I replied. "Mr. Clemans

was a dignified man and a Stanford grad. Vida once related that after he finished his logging operation here in 1929, he stayed friends with some of the families who had lived and worked here. One evening while he was at Frank and Mary Dawson's house in Seattle they gave him a birthday party. When he blew out the candles on his cake, his dentures landed in the frosting. Mrs. Dawson said he retrieved them without a word and put them back in his mouth. The party continued as if nothing had happened."

Liza laughed again. "That's what I call class. For all of them. Which reminds me — I've got a dental appointment this afternoon at three. It's for a cleaning and to meet Bob Starr. He and his wife just got back from two weeks in Jamaica. I'll do a piece on their trip and hope they got some decent pictures."

"They're good people," I said. "Carrie Starr often takes trips on her own. Bob doesn't feel right about abandoning his patients for more than an annual two-week vacation. And yes, when you need it, he has giggle gas."

"Good. I'm a real chicken when it comes to dental work." She headed back into the newsroom with her usual quick step.

By noon, I'd somehow managed to devour a cinnamon doughnut, a glazed twister, and a chocolate cupcake. That's one of the drawbacks of not feeling pressed to meet a deadline. It hadn't helped that Liza had overbought on the goodies. She'd made as many trips to the pastry tray as I had. Still feeling full, I decided to skip lunch and run household errands instead. I made purchases at Parker's Pharmacy and Harvey's Hardware, but paused outside of Francine's Fine Apparel. She was holding her post-holiday clearance sale, which was tempting. But I had bills to pay, mainly for the presents I'd lavished on my son, Adam, and my brother, Ben. Much to my delight, they had joined us for Christmas. As missionary priests, they'd taken a vow of poverty. After spending so much money on their gifts, I was feeling a bit impoverished, too.

But that was unfair. Adam and Ben had given me a far greater gift. They, along with Father Den, had blessed my marriage to Milo after St. Mildred's congregation had dispersed on Christmas morning. My husband was appropriately solemn during the brief ceremony because he knew how much it meant to me. Milo was a believer, but not a churchgoer. It didn't matter to him who performed the rite.

A little after two o'clock, I was leafing through some older issues of the *Advocate,* trying to come up with fresh ideas that Mitch and I could tackle for a series of articles. In the past year, we'd dealt with physical and verbal abuse as well as the change in county government. Hearing the rain beat on our tin roof, I considered the weather. Global warming was no joke. The milder winters had put a big crimp in the snow sports business, especially up at Stevens Pass and here in Alpine.

Ten minutes later, I heard sirens. Sometimes that signaled breaking news, though it could also be a traffic accident or a minor house fire. I glanced out into the newsroom to see if Mitch was at his desk, but he and his raincoat were nowhere in sight. When he got back from his beat, he'd know if there'd been a fender-bender or a driver with a fifty-dollar speeding ticket.

Another hour passed before I found out that the sirens had nothing to do with traffic. Mitch still wasn't back in the office, but Milo called me.

"If you're wondering where your star reporter is," he said in a gruff voice, "Laskey's here at headquarters. He saw the emergency vehicles — including mine — at the Alpine Falls Motel and smelled a headline." Milo paused, and I could hear him speaking to someone, probably one of his deputies. "Okay," he resumed, "here's your news. A woman's body was found in her motel room. She'd apparently been strangled with her own scarf. ID pending verification. Laskey can give you what few details we've got so far. What kind of steak are we having for dinner?"

Chapter 4

Mitch showed up fifteen minutes later. Predictably, his gloom had been lifted by bad news, which was always good news for journalists. Being hardened by the nature of our jobs, we wished the murder had taken place before, rather than after, the paper had gone to press.

"I'll say this for Dodge," he said as he slid his lanky frame into one of my visitor chairs. "He's a straight arrow when it comes to dealing with a homicide."

I tried not to take umbrage, aware of the tension that existed between Milo and Mitch. When Troy's second escape attempt had failed a year ago, he'd ended up in Alpine Memorial Hospital with pneumonia. The state police had intervened, insisting the patient should be moved to the Monroe Correctional Complex's infirmary. Mitch had demanded that Milo insist that Troy be kept here. But the sheriff was outranked by the state. Mitch had implied that in Detroit there were other ways to make things happen. Assuming he meant bribery or coercion, Milo stuck to his ethics. The two men hadn't been on very good terms ever since.

I acknowledged Mitch's backdoor praise with a nod. "Any ID yet?"

"Yes. Rachel Jane Douglas, thirty-nine, resident of Oakland, California. She drove here from Oakland and arrived around six last night." Mitch glanced at his notes. "Car is a 1998 Kia Sorento, fairly well kept up. Doc Dewey will perform an autopsy after he gets through seeing patients around six. Details of what was in her purse and wallet will come later from Dodge. Maybe he'll tell you when he comes home."

The "maybe" wasn't sarcasm. My husband was notoriously tight-lipped about his investigations. He had loosened up a bit since we were married, but he still didn't allow me to go public until he was ready.

"If Doc confirms it was foul play," I reminded Mitch, "you know he'll send the body to Everett so the Snohomish County lab can do a more thorough job. Maybe someday we'll have enough funding to get one of our own in SkyCo."

Mitch looked dour. "Maybe."

I didn't argue. "By the way," I said as he

started to walk away, "how did Will Pace handle a homicide at his motel? He's not exactly a gracious host."

"What you'd expect," Mitch replied. "The Alpine Falls Motel would never get a second look for a rating from AAA. He took the poor woman's murder personally. I don't envy the sheriff's interrogation of that jerk."

I agreed. Maybe Milo would let Dwight Gould handle Will Pace if the ailing deputy was back on the job. Dwight's social skills were only a few notches up from those of the motel owner. I'd hear about it when my husband got home. Or at least what he'd be willing to tell me "this early in an investigation." Those words weren't music to my journalist's ears.

Mitch went off to post the news on our website. I considered calling the sheriff, but abstained. He'd no doubt be tied up in the aftermath of the murder. In fact, he might be late coming home. Maybe he'd call to let me know. Maybe he wouldn't. When Milo was on the job, he sometimes forgot he had a wife. Since we'd been married less than a year, that was almost understandable.

But to my surprise, my husband arrived only fifteen minutes after I did. Mitch's prediction was right. The first words out of Milo's mouth after a rather perfunctory kiss were to be expected.

"Why didn't the killer off Will Pace instead of some poor woman from California? That asshole is impossible to interrogate. I should nail him for impeding a homicide investigation."

"Why don't you?" I asked innocently.

"Because I don't want him hanging out in our jail," Milo replied. He paused as he hung his hat on the peg by the door. "I could threaten him with it, though. Maybe I will if he doesn't cooperate."

I decided not to ask any more questions until he settled in with a Scotch in hand. Instead, I went into the kitchen and continued getting dinner under way. A big rib-eye steak should improve my husband's mood. I'd boil the potatoes and the asparagus. Since Milo hadn't followed me, I assumed he was changing out of his uniform.

When he showed up a few minutes later in jeans and a plaid Pendleton shirt, I asked if he was officially off duty.

"Yeah," he replied, getting out the glasses and the booze. "De Groote's on the desk tonight. Hell of a way for her to break into the new job. She'll let me know if we hear anything about the vic from the Oakland cops. Fong and Heppner had just about finished going over the Kia when I left."

"I should stop by and introduce myself," I said as Milo handed me my Canadian Club and 7-Up on the rocks. "It's too bad she wasn't here for our open house."

"Consi had some family thing over New Year's. Her parents live in Parkland. I think that's a suburb of Tacoma."

We headed into the living room to assume our usual places — Milo in the easy chair and me on the sofa next to the end table. "Has Consi ever worked a homicide case?"

My husband shook his head. "Only dealing with women and kids who'd been traumatized by someone close to them getting whacked. This should be a real test for her, especially since the vic is female. I'm going to have to keep my eye on her."

"Of course." I felt a flicker of unwonted jealousy. I trusted Milo completely. Just as long as he kept only an eye on her.

After dinner, Dustin Fong called to let the sheriff know the background information from Oakland wouldn't come through until morning. Milo grumbled about why it would take that long to come up with the basics. That meant I couldn't give Kip a name for the murdered woman. I called to tell him he didn't have to stand by the phone to post anything online until morning.

Thursday brought more rain and a sharp wind blowing down through the Skykomish River valley. I made a mental note to listen to Vida's radio program. It had always been broadcast on Tuesdays at seven o'clock, but the time had been changed as of the first of the year. It was her decision, rather than that of KSKY's owner, Spencer Fleetwood. Vida had been appointed chairman of her Presbyterian church's outreach program and they met on Tuesdays. If anybody could reach out to all of Skykomish County, it was my semiretired House & Home editor. She'd been doing it for almost sixty years.

The first thing on my to-do list was to tell Mitch to find out what was going on in the homicide investigation. It wasn't that the veteran reporter needed encouragement; rather, it was because of the rift between him and the sheriff. Despite being my husband, Milo retained an annoying habit of playing things close to his chest.

When the mail arrived a little before ten, Alison wasn't quite as chipper as usual. I asked her if something was wrong.

"No Boyd sightings," she replied, placing the stack of what was mostly junk on my desk. "Maybe he changed his mind about moving to Pines Villa. I should get so lucky, right?"

"Give him time," I said. "You said his belongings hadn't arrived yet. Boyd's probably still at the ski lodge."

Alison considered my words. "I suppose. But most newcomers move in to Pines Villa the first of the month. All his stuff is coming from Wenatchee. That's only a few hours away. Stevens Pass has hardly been closed at all so far this winter."

I leaned back in my chair and smiled. "Relax, Alison. Do you want Milo to bust you for stalking Boyd Lanier?"

She ran a hand through her blond hair, which had grown quite long since the last cut at Stella's Styling Salon. "You think I'm pushing it. But how many really good-looking, eligible dudes in my peer group live here?"

She had a point. Alison had turned twenty-three in the fall. But she was driven to find a marriageable man in Alpine. Maybe that's because her parents' marriage had failed when she was about six. I, on the other hand, had never thought about getting married at all. At Alison's age, I had to make a living to support my son, Adam. I couldn't marry his father because Tom Cavanaugh already had a wife. My youthful folly hadn't given me much spare time for a social life. When Tom was finally widowed, we planned to marry. But instead he ended up getting killed. I was in my forties then and had resigned myself to being a single woman. But Milo had changed my mind — and my life.

Mitch didn't come back from his morning rounds until almost ten. "The sheriff didn't get the victim's ID until about ten minutes ago. Since I had to wait, I went over to the courthouse and introduced myself to the new county extension agent. Lanier seems eager to start the job. I told him I'd give him until Monday to do a full interview."

I refrained from grimacing. The story was Mitch's, of course, but I regretted suggesting to Alison that she might give it a try. Since my reporter was touchy about turf, I had to let him take on Lanier. Our receptionist would be disappointed, but she was resourceful. Where there was a girl like Alison, there was a way.

"Okay," I said. "Now tell me about the murder victim."

Mitch looked faintly dismayed. "The sheriff hasn't called you?"

I rolled my eyes. "Get serious, Laskey. When Milo has a homicide to deal with, he forgets I'm his wife. You have to know more than I do, which is that the woman is dead."

My reporter checked his notes. "Really, I don't. Will Pace isn't the type to get chummy with his guests, which is just as well, considering that a lot of them use the motel for illicit rendezvous. All he told me was that she didn't say much, just wanted a room and maybe for more than one night. If she went somewhere to eat dinner, Will didn't know about it. Of course, Dewey's preliminary autopsy report will show if she did."

"Right." I paused, trying to think if I knew of anyone named Douglas in SkyCo. I didn't think I did. "Was there a mention of a wedding ring?"

Mitch shook his head. "Pace thought not. No jewelry that he could see unless she had studs in her ears. He said her hair was shoulder-length. Or sort of like that. Will does his best to ignore guests."

"I can see why," I said. "They usually want their privacy."

Mitch went off to post his news on our website. I resisted the temptation of calling Milo, though maybe he'd be free for lunch. I glanced into the news office, wondering if Vida would come in to tell us what or whom she'd be featuring on her program. But by eleven-thirty, there was no sign of her.

Shortly before noon, I wandered down to the sheriff's office. The Yukon was parked in its place, so I assumed Milo was in.

Jack Mullins was behind the front desk and the sheriff's door was closed. "You can't be missing the big guy already," Jack said, grinning. "Or are you two still in your newlywed stage?"

"Give me a break," I replied. "We've already had two ceremonies, and after knowing each other for almost seventeen years, we're lucky we're still on speaking terms. In fact, we aren't in the mornings. Who's he got in there? A suspect, I hope."

"Deputy De Groote," Jack replied, looking puckish as he ran a hand through his untamable red hair. "You jealous?"

"I haven't even met her. Don't tell me he's assigning her to the case."

Jack shook his shaggy head. "Your old man's going to have to handle this one himself. Information on our vic is hard to come by. From what we can get out of Oakland, we can't even find out if she had a job."

"She had to have a reason to come to Alpine," I pointed out. "I understand she might've intended to stay for more than just overnight."

Jack's major flaw — besides his wacky red

hair — was that he was lazy. But he was also the sharpest of Milo's deputies, which kept him employed. "If she has any relatives or friends in Oakland, they may know why she came here. But we won't hear from them until they realize she doesn't seem to be coming home."

I agreed. "You've lived here all your life, Jack. Do you recall any Douglases who ever lived here?"

The deputy considered the question. "No. That doesn't mean there weren't, though. As a kid, I wasn't aware of people I didn't actually know. You know how it is — you see people, have a vague idea of who they are, but don't know them by name. Working on this job, we get acquainted with damned near everybody, and usually for all the wrong reasons."

"That's what I figured," I said, but looked beyond Jack to see Milo's door open.

I got my first look at Deputy De Groote. She wasn't beautiful, but she certainly was attractive. Consuela was tall, slim, and had short, simply styled black hair. She wore no makeup, except for pale pink lip gloss. The way she carried herself was purposeful rather than graceful. She glanced at me, and I smiled.

Jack turned around. "Hey, Consi, meet

our stalwart leader's wife. She's Laskey's boss at the *Advocate.*"

Milo had stayed in his office. I stood up and put out my hand. "I'm glad to see there's another female on the staff," I said, noting that her grip was firm and brief.

"I'm glad to be here," Consi replied with a rather tight smile. "I'm afraid I haven't had time to look at your newspaper yet. But I will."

I took that as a promise rather than a threat. Her eyes were very dark, almost jet. "It comes out every Wednesday," I responded, and felt like an idiot. "Have you found a place to live?"

"Yes. I've been staying at the Tall Timber Motel, but I understand there'll be a vacancy soon at that apartment building by the medical clinic."

"My ad manager, Leo Walsh, lived there for many years," I said. "He had no real complaints."

"That's good to hear." Consi's gaze shifted to the window overlooking Front Street. "Excuse me. I have to go on patrol now." She nodded at Jack and moved off in her purposeful fashion.

When I turned around, Milo was leaning against the doorjamb of his office. "What are you doing here, little Emma?"

With his back turned to the sheriff, Jack stifled a snicker. I glared at him — and then at my mate. "Stop calling me little! I should file a complaint against you for verbal abuse. You know I'm almost average."

Milo was unmoved by my protest, while Jack was trying not to laugh out loud. "If you're here," my husband said, no longer leaning but checking out the coffeemaker next to the wall, "you can go over to the Burger Barn and bring back my lunch. I'm eating in today. Cheeseburger, fries . . ."

"I know it by heart," I snapped. "I can't afford to pay for your lunch and mine. I only have ten dollars and change with me."

Milo let out an exaggerated sigh and reached for his wallet. "Here," he said, coming to the front of the office to hand me a twenty-dollar bill. "Get me a cup of coffee. Ours here was kind of off today."

I snatched the Andrew Jackson from my husband. "It's always off. I was hoping your new deputy would be able to improve what you deluded people call coffee. Has she complained about it yet?"

"She doesn't drink coffee," Milo replied, looking a bit smug. "She likes tea and brings her own. Some fancy special brand."

"Then De Groote is even savvier than she looks." I turned away and collided with the counter, uttering an undignified "Oof!"

Jack seemed to be biting the inside of his cheek, but Milo chuckled. "Serves you right, my ornery *little* bride."

I ignored the remark and started to leave the premises. But my aggravating better half called out to me, "Hey, if you want to join me, I'll give you a ten to go with the twenty."

I felt like refusing, but I caved. "Include another five with that," I said. "I prefer my hamburger bun to contain actual meat in it."

"God, but you're fussy," Milo muttered, doling out the money. "The next thing I know, you'll want an ice cream cone for dessert."

"Unlike you, I usually don't eat dessert." I snatched the fiver out of his big paw and refrained from mentioning the word "pie." It might give Milo another idea.

There was the usual line for takeout. I nodded to Del Amundson, one of the ambulance drivers, and to Cal Vickers, owner of the local gas station. Del was at the front of the line. After he picked up his order, he stopped to speak to me in an unusually somber tone.

"We got called in about the dead woman at the motel," he said. "She was sent to the hospital for an autopsy. Terrible thing, really.

Nobody seems to know who she was. Has Dodge got any leads?"

"Not so far," I replied, "but she was from Oakland and he hopes to get more information from there. Her relatives and friends are in for a terrible shock."

Del nodded. "She was good-looking. That is . . . considering what had happened to her. I don't suppose anyone around here claims to know who she was."

"Not so far." I didn't add that somebody might have known her. "Of course, she could have been followed to Alpine."

That idea seemed to reassure Del. "That must be it. Maybe she was meeting up with someone she knew. I mean, from Oakland."

I let Del go on his way. My suggestion was reasonable. But I hadn't convinced myself that it was right. If Rachel had planned to stay for more than an overnight, she had a reason. She'd come to see someone, and whoever it was might have done her wrong in the worst possible way.

CHAPTER 5

Milo griped about the size of his burger. "They're cutting down on the amount of meat they use at the Burger Barn. What's wrong with these new owners? Do they want to get picketed?"

"You could always arrest them for trying to starve you to death," I said innocently. "They're some relation to the Gustavsons, who started the place long before I moved here. Ask Vida. She's probably related to them. Obviously, you didn't read the story Mitch did last October when ownership changed hands."

The sheriff had the grace to look faintly guilty. "I can't read every word that's in the paper. Sometimes I have to sort of skim through it."

It was an old bone of contention between us, so I let it go. Milo certainly could absorb the sports section of *The Seattle Times,* and not just at home, but while he was on the job. I changed the subject. "Tell me more about the victim. I assume you haven't gotten the autopsy report back from the Everett lab."

"Hell, no," he replied after swallowing a large chunk of burger. "We'll be lucky if we hear by Monday. Everett's got too many stiffs of their own."

"True," I agreed. "I gather that nobody's inquired about Rachel?"

Milo shook his head. "Not yet. We've gone through all her stuff. Purse, shopping bag, carryall. She didn't bring a lot of clothes, maybe enough for two, three days. Oh, there was a laundry bag with some underwear in it, probably what she'd worn for the drive up here. It would've taken her at least a couple of days."

I nibbled on a french fry. Talking about the dead Rachel had taken the edge off my appetite. "Somebody must miss her. At least I hope so. Was there anything in her wallet that showed where she worked?"

"If you mean an employee ID card, no," Milo replied after downing two french fries at once. "Driver's license, Social Security card, voter registration card, and some business cards, all in the Oakland area. Four of them were for different real estate companies. Oh — I forgot to tell you that she worked for the city of Oakland, but they didn't say what her job was. I'm guessing she wasn't the mayor."

"Probably not," I said dryly. "The people down there might be making a bigger fuss about what happened to her."

"That depends. Now that the government change here means Fuzzy Baugh is out of office, how many people would miss him if he croaked?"

"I've always kind of liked him. In a way," I added. "He did lay on the southern charm when he wanted something. Of course, he never really had much to do because the three county commissioners had all the clout."

Milo grimaced. "I'd rather have Fuzzy on the job than Jack Blackwell running the county. His chummy act doesn't play well with me."

"Are you really going to meet with him next week?"

"I suppose I have to. The SOB's officially my boss."

That didn't play well with me, either.

As expected, Milo was late getting home that night. We'd barely finished dinner when it was time for *Vida's Cupboard,* as her radio program was called. Spencer Fleetwood did his usual (prerecorded) introduction along with the sound of a cupboard door being opened. Her guest was Cecelia Doukas, wife of retired attorney Simon, whose family had once owned at least half of Alpine. Cecelia was a nice woman, but her mate had been the first person to call me a whore after I'd arrived in Alpine with a grown son and no husband in my allegedly dark past.

The Doukases had spent Christmas and New Year's in England, which made for a reasonably interesting interview, even if Vida had already written it up in the paper. At least I paid attention, though Milo nodded off about the same time that Vida broke for a commercial from Harvey's Hardware.

After I turned off the radio, the lack of sound apparently woke up my husband. "Vida's done yapping?" he remarked, stretching his long arms.

"Vida's never done yapping. Next week her guest will be Karl Freeman."

"Principal Freeman's going to rant about all the high school kids sneaking out to smoke pot over at the cemetery? I wonder if he knows half of what those kids are really up to."

My nose for news twitched. "Do you?"

Milo yawned. "We try to keep track of what they're doing, just in case it might be illegal. Freeman's a damned clam when it comes to what's goes on in his little kingdom. You remember that from when he didn't cooperate about the girls who were being lured into prostitution down somewhere near Chehalis."

I nodded. "And fired Helena Craig for letting me know the truth. Then it turned out that Roger was involved in the procurement of those girls and ended up in prison. Vida still hasn't recovered from her grandson's disgrace."

"Not to mention dealing and using drugs," Milo said. "Vida claimed he'd fallen under evil influences. Hell, I'd been waiting to bust that prick since he was fourteen. I remember when he and the O'Toole kid went up Tonga Ridge to check out the bikers who were growing pot there. I wouldn't be surprised if that's when he started getting high."

"You've got a scar on your forehead to prove it," I reminded him, recalling how the bikers had resisted arrest and hit Milo with a beer bottle before being subdued. "Ted and Amy rarely disciplined Roger, and Vida doted on him."

Milo lighted a cigarette, started to offer the pack, and then thought better of it. I'd quit on New Year's Day. Again. Maybe this time it might actually take.

"Let's check out some NFL action," my better half said. "There should be a game on tonight." He, of course, was in charge of the remote. Never having been married before, I hadn't realized that was one of the perks bestowed on a husband upon taking a wife. Or so Betsy O'Toole and Roseanna Bayard had informed me. Luckily, I liked sports.

But before Milo could aim the clicker, his cell rang. "This better not be one of my deputies . . . . Dodge here," he said. He listened for a moment, then put a hand to his forehead. "Hey, Will, can't whatever this is wait until morning?" Apparently, it couldn't. "No, the room has been processed and I won't get the lab results back . . . Yeah, I know tomorrow's Friday and it's ski season . . . . Because the lab's in Everett, that's why. If you've got a problem, call them." Milo raised his thick eyebrows and stared at the cell. "The SOB hung up on me."

"I gather Will Pace is losing money," I said. "What does he charge for a night in his dump?"

"Too much." He resumed pointing the clicker. "I don't know, but I'd guess maybe a hundred or so for a night. *He'd* have to pay *me* to stay there."

Milo turned on an NBA game between the Lakers and the Cavaliers before getting up to join me on the sofa. "Sonics aren't playing tonight, so we don't have to focus on who wins. Want to snuggle?"

"Sure." I leaned my head against his shoulder. I got the impression that the game was very tight all the way down to the wire. But I couldn't remember who won. Neither could Milo.

Janet Driggers was the first call on Friday morning. "This is your reminder that bridge club will be on Thursday night instead of Tuesday next week. Three of our members are going to attend a bridal shower Tuesday in Startup. You and I aren't invited because we don't know her."

"If we don't know her, how did the other three get suckered?"

"It's a Gustavson," Janet replied. "One of Vida's five hundred relatives. Ask her who it is and why Edna Mae Dalrymple, Linda Grant, and Lila Blatt got themselves invited. Wait — Lila's somehow related to Vida, right? Come to think of it, they may all belong to Edna Mae's book club. They asked me to join years ago, but I told them I only read porn. And look at the pictures, of course. You'd be amazed by some of those shots. Whoever poses for them must be contortionists."

I was accustomed to Janet's bawdy mouth. She was the wife of funeral director Al Driggers, and I figured that was her way of facing death on a regular basis. "Thursday's better for me anyway," I said. "I wish they'd keep it that way. Tuesday is our deadline. Maybe I'll mention it when I come to bridge. Who's hosting?"

I heard Janet sigh. "Edna Mae. Being the head librarian, she likes to keep close to home in the evenings. Do you think she's ever gone on a date with a *man*?"

"How would I know?" I responded. "She was well entrenched in her job when I moved here. The funny thing is, she never seems to age. She's sort of perennially forty-three."

"How true. By the way, is there any chance the motel murder victim could have a funeral here? Al and I need the money. Sky Travel has a package deal later this month for a sexual bondage tour to Tonga. I gather they have some terrific tribal rites. Since I work here part-time, we'd get a discount. Even now I'm staring at a poster of an incredible Tongan hunk. But the trip is still kind of pricey. Nobody's died around here since the end of the year."

"Sorry, Janet," I replied, "but once the

autopsy is a done deal, Ms. Douglas goes back to Oakland."

"Darn." She sighed again. "Oakland. Not on my world tour wish list. San Francisco is another matter. That city was created for sin. Al and I haven't . . . My other line's ringing. Maybe somebody else died. I can but hope." Janet rang off.

Alison showed up with the mail a few minutes later. "Boyd's still at the ski lodge," she announced in solemn tones befitting the death of a prominent Alpiner. It crossed my mind that would suit Janet just fine. "Lori and I went to the ski lodge coffee shop for dinner last night."

"He'll probably move into Pines Villa over the weekend," I said. "You and Lori could offer to help him."

Alison leaned on the back of one of my visitor chairs. "That sounds pushy. His apartment is on the second floor. He's already put his name in the slot for residents and he apparently has a roommate, but Lori and I didn't recognize the guy's name. Jeffrey Nichols. He's not a local, right?"

I admitted the name wasn't familiar. "That doesn't mean he isn't. Even after all these years, I don't know everyone in Alpine. If Nichols is moving here, I wonder if he has a job. We'll have to find out."

Alison brightened. "You mean I should ask about that when I write the story on Boyd?"

I grimaced. "Mitch is going to interview Boyd," I said. "I should've told you sooner. You know how touchy he is about turf, and the county courthouse is part of his beat. You're going to live in the same building, Alison. You'll have plenty of opportunities to . . . get acquainted."

Her crestfallen expression lessened a bit. "I guess. But I don't want to be obvious. Lori might be interested in the other guy. Her long-distance romance with Cole Petersen hasn't turned out very well. He travels too much in his Microsoft job. Last month he was in Tanzania. Or was it Tasmania? I forget."

"Cole probably has forgotten, too," I said as my phone rang.

"Ohmigod! I should be answering the phones out front!" She whirled away through the newsroom.

I took the call, which was from a female voice I didn't recognize at once. "Is it true that there's a madman loose in town? All my poor kitties are afraid to go outside. What should I do?"

I leaned back in my chair. Grace Grundle, retired schoolteacher obsessed with her feline menagerie, was always worried about something. "No such person has been reported in Alpine," I assured her. "Yes, a young woman was killed at the Alpine Falls Motel, but Sheriff Dodge assured us it's an isolated incident." Milo hadn't done any such thing, but it sounded good. "You and your cats are in no danger."

"How can you — and Sheriff Dodge — know that?" Grace asked in a querulous tone. "Milo sometimes assured me he'd studied his homework when in fact he'd merely skimmed through it. If someone has been brutally murdered and nobody knows who did it, what should the rest of us do? I can lock all my doors, but homicidal maniacs break windows. They can even set fire to a person's house. What's worse, it may snow."

I wasn't sure why the weather would have any effect on Grace's homicidal maniac, but I wanted to get her off the line. "I'll ask Milo to send a deputy by to check on you, okay?"

"How soon will he be here? If he sends Jack Mullins, he'll dawdle. I never had a student who could waste time the way Jackie could."

And I never had a caller who could waste *my* time the way Grace could. But she wasn't finished, even if I was now listening with half an ear. After more details about Jackie's miscues, something she said about our mailman, Marlowe Whipp, snapped me back to attention. ". . . late as usual, after six o'clock, but that woman stopped him to ask how to get to Mr. Blackwell's house. He gave her directions, of course, but you know how Marlowe has problems with addresses . . ."

"I'm sorry," I interrupted, "I got distracted for a moment. Who asked for the directions?"

"The woman who managed to get herself killed, of course," Grace asserted impatiently. "Who else but a stranger would need directions? Though I'm afraid Mr. Blackwell spends more time at Patti Marsh's home than at his own. Frankly, for such a successful man, his house is rather shabby. I have heard — though I don't like repeating gossip — that Mrs. Marsh's place isn't much better. Apparently, she's dilatory about housecleaning. Dino — my garbage collector — told me that there are always several liquor bottles to be picked up every week. Quite shocking, really!"

But no doubt true. Patti liked her liquor. And she loved Jack, despite his often abusive way of dealing with his longtime girlfriend.

Luckily for me, Leo entered my office. I told Grace that my ad manager needed my help. After she told me how glad she was that Mr. Walsh had stopped drinking so much and that Milo had hardly ever raised his hand in class, she finally rang off.

I rubbed my ear as Leo shot me a curious look. "Grace Grundle," I said.

Leo merely nodded. He'd dealt with Grace a few times when one of her cats had strayed for more than a few hours and she insisted on taking out an ad complete with a photo of wandering Tiddlywinks or Sweetie Pie Eyes in the classified section. Luckily for Leo — and for Grace's checkbook — the errant felines had always come home the same day.

It was going on eleven when I finally had a free moment to call Milo and tell him about Ms. Douglas's query for Marlowe Whipp about where she could find Jack Blackwell.

"Jesus," he said softly as I pictured him running a hand through his hair. "How could this woman from Oakland have anything to do with Blackwell?" He paused, but spoke again before I could say anything. "Jack came here from California. The vic's not quite forty. Blackwell arrived in Alpine some thirty years ago, when I was still a deputy. That would make the vic a little kid back then. Unless . . ." He paused, apparently in thought.

I couldn't keep quiet. "Unless she's Blackwell's kid?"

Milo didn't respond at once. "Well . . . maybe. The nurse at RestHaven, Jennifer Hood, was his first wife. They were married somewhere in northern California, right?"

"Yes, in Dunsmuir," I said. "It's a logging town — or was back then. But Jennifer never mentioned anything about having a child by him. She was only seventeen when they got married and she can't be more than late forties now."

My husband sighed. "I suppose Black Jack didn't molest little girls. I'll have to give him a pass on that one. Hell, if she's his kid, he might never have known she existed. It could've been a one-night stand. He would've been just out of his teens back then."

"But will you talk to him about Rachel Douglas saying she was going to see him?"

"I suppose I'll have to," Milo replied grudgingly. "Face it, Marlowe Whipp and Grace Grundle aren't exactly the most reliable sources."

I couldn't argue that point.

■ ■ ■ ■

By noon the office was deserted except for Kip in the back shop. His wife always made his lunch for him. We tried not to encourage visitors during the lunch break. Our hours were posted on the glass in the front door as eight to noon and one to five. Needing the quiet time to think about a special edition for the month of January, I called the Venison Inn to order takeout. Fifteen minutes later I was back at my desk with a medium-rare hamburger dip, fries, a small salad, and a Pepsi. The VI, as it was locally known, was only two doors down, with the dry cleaners in between us.

Unfortunately, my mind was blank. Winter sports, keeping homes snug and cars safe, dealing with ice and snow on the roads, off-season getaways — we'd done it all. I was still staring at my Blue Sky Dairy calendar when Vida came through my door.

"So busy today!" she exclaimed, settling her imposing personage into a visitor chair. "All this to-do over our new pastor's innovations. Really, he's been here for over a year and continues to make changes. He's young, of course, so he has what he terms 'fresh insights.' As you might imagine, some of the older parishioners won't adjust well. Presbyterians generally prefer familiar traditions."

"He probably means well," I said, trying to avoid staring at the fur pillbox Vida was wearing at such a rakish angle that one of her eyebrows was partially obscured. "I'm sure he hopes to attract younger members."

"Perhaps." But Vida sounded skeptical. "He did refer to small at-home gatherings. I find those intimate get-togethers suspect, as if he'd be prying into his parishioners' private lives. I'd hate to think his reason for having those gatherings is of a prurient nature. That would be un-Christian."

It crossed my mind that Vida's interest in others might not be prurient, but she was certainly a world-class snooper. She spoke again before I could respond. "The woman who was killed at that dreadful motel," she began with a frown. "Who can she be? And why would she stay at such a wretched place?"

I hated keeping information from Vida, but I wouldn't pass on what Grace had told me. It was hearsay, after all. Instead, I related the official word from Oakland.

"Oakland," Vida echoed, as if the city were on a yet undiscovered planet. "I believe it's near Frisco, isn't it?"

It always galls me when San Francisco is

called by its nickname. It wasn't just because Tom Cavanaugh had made his home there. When I was growing up, my family's vacation travels often led us as far south as the Oregon-California border. Once, my father grudgingly agreed to go all the way to "The City" — as it was known to its residents — but after one look at the traffic on the Golden Gate Bridge, Dad turned our car around and headed north to Seattle. In my young adult years, San Francisco was a magical place, with steep hills, cable cars, and even the omnipresent fog. I'd never suggested that Milo take me there, though. It was in a hotel on Nob Hill that Tricia had told him she was leaving him for another man.

Vida was still rattling on, but I'd missed part of what she had to say. I tuned in when I heard ". . . severe bruises and a possible concussion. Honestly!" She threw up her hands.

I had to save face. "How did it happen?" I asked, hoping I looked as if I knew what she was talking about.

"How do you think?" she demanded, leaning forward and resting a hand on one of the few uncluttered places on my desk. "I suppose Patti and Jack had been drinking. They usually are in the evening. Why she puts up with him, I'll never know."

"He's been her meal ticket since she started working for him years ago," I said. "They were a couple when I moved here. Say, someone mentioned that Patti's daughter, Dani Marsh, was visiting over the holidays. I forgot to follow up on that with so much else going on. Is it true?"

Vida shook her head, causing the pillbox to slip a bit more. "No," she replied, adjusting the hat. "Dani had to stay in Los Angeles for something to do with that TV series she's in. Her father is the . . . producer. I believe that's what they call people who are in charge of such things. I've never watched it on television. Too much sex and violence, or so I've heard from how Patti described it. Of course, she thought it was wonderful. 'So lifelike,' she insisted. I suppose it was — for Patti."

"Too true," I agreed. But Vida never watched much of anything on TV. She was always too busy ferreting out the latest local gossip, which she, of course, considered news. If it didn't happen in Skykomish County, it didn't happen. "Her ex used to be a director," I went on. "That was his title when he made the movie starring Dani up here many years ago."

"I never saw it." Vida dismissed the film

with a shrug of her broad shoulders. The pillbox again skidded a bit. “As I recall, only certain outdoor scenes were filmed here in Alpine.”

That was probably true. By the time *Blood Along the River* had been released I’d lost interest in Patti’s ex-husband and her movie actress daughter. The film crew had only been in town for a couple of weeks, but they’d painted all of the buildings on Front Street, including the *Advocate.* We’d put up with the canary yellow exterior until last September, when someone had thrown hand grenades into the newsroom. Kip and I had been in the back shop putting out the paper. We were unharmed and the damage was surprisingly minimal, but the exterior required a new, brown paint job. I’d never liked the association between yellow and journalism.

Vida removed her majestic self from the chair. “I must attend to those wretched letters from people seeking my advice. If any of them had a shred of common sense, they wouldn’t have to ask for help.” She sighed heavily, sending ripples through her floral-print polyester blouse. “Oh, well.”

By the end of the workday, Leo told me we might be able to go twenty-four pages in the next edition. He’d twisted enough merchant arms to get at least a half-dozen of them to extend their year-end clearance sales. That was good news. But I still hadn't come up with a fresh idea for my editorial. That wasn't news. I told myself that something might come up over the weekend that would inspire me. I knew better, having often held that thought. But at least I could forget about it until Monday morning.

As it would turn out, I had a lot more to worry about before the weekend was over.

CHAPTER 6

By five forty-five, Milo still wasn't home. That wasn't surprising, since he had a murder investigation on his hands. But when the digital clock on the countertop stove showed 6:10, I started getting antsy. Dinner was simple enough — I'd started a rack of spare ribs almost an hour ago, and put potatoes on to boil a few minutes later. The fresh broccoli would take only a few minutes to cook.

A glance out the big front window revealed that the earlier change of snow to rain had now reversed itself with the evening's drop in temperature. The flakes weren't heavy, but they were starting to stick to some of the shrubs next to our log cabin. I saw a couple of cars go by, but no sign of the Yukon. I was heading for my landline phone next to the sofa when my cell rang. It was still in my purse, which was on the floor by the end table. I groped for it and heard my husband's voice at the other end.

"I'm leaving headquarters in about five minutes," he said rather brusquely. "Don't throw the grub into the backyard. Build me a stiff Scotch, okay?" He didn't wait for an answer.

I turned down everything in the kitchen. It'd be at least twenty minutes after Milo got here before he'd be ready to eat. I poured myself a bourbon over ice and added some 7-Up before I went back into the living room and sat down on the sofa. I opened my laptop and dashed off an email to Adam, asking if he'd settled the controversy between Helga Johannesen and Margaret Whitebear over which of them had made the quilt they'd given my son for Christmas. The controversy had been the talk of St. Mary's Igloo for the past two weeks.

It was almost six-thirty before I saw the Yukon's blurry headlights turn into the drive. The snow was coming down much harder. I went out to the kitchen and opened the door to the garage. Milo unfolded all six feet five inches of himself, not including his regulation hat, which added another three inches. He snatched it from the seat next to him and stalked up the four steps that led to the kitchen.

"Bastard," he muttered under his breath before kissing me soundly, if briefly. "Why can't I find a reason to send Blackwell away for twenty years?"

I gave my husband a big doe-eyed stare. "Because he hasn't done anything really illegal lately?"

"I thought maybe we'd finally nailed him last September when Kay Burns filed charges for him eating her up," Milo said, obviously looking around for his drink. I pointed to the refrigerator. He paused long enough to get out both cocktails and handed me mine. "Let's sit down. It's been a long day. Kay should never have dropped those charges."

Once settled in the easy chair, he lighted a cigarette and proffered the pack to me, but I shook my head. "You know why she did. She'd had his baby years ago and gave it away for adoption."

Milo's hazel eyes sparked. "What if that's who came looking for Jack and got herself killed?"

That had never entered my mind. I almost choked on my bourbon. Then I unloaded about Grace Grundle's call. "Not that Grace and Marlowe are always reliable sources," I concluded. "But if she confronted him, would Jack kill her?"

Milo leaned his head back against the chair and gazed up at the beamed ceiling. "No. Blackwell's a lot of things, but he's not a killer." Pausing, he looked at me. "He might hire someone to do it, though he'd be sure to keep his hands clean."

"That sounds right. What did he have to say about the murder victim?"

"He swore he never heard of her and was pissed off when I asked him why she'd be trying to find him." Milo took a sip of his drink. "We sent the body to Everett and I considered telling him he had to go over there to make sure he didn't recognize her; but even if he did, he'd lie. We've got a photo of her, of course. I showed it to him, but he insisted he didn't know her. Of course, she probably looked a lot better when she was still alive."

"Do you believe Jack?"

Milo grimaced and scratched behind his left ear. "I hate to say it, but I think I do. I can usually tell when someone is lying."

I knew that from experience. The few times I'd tried to deceive the sheriff over the years, I'd always failed. Having been in law enforcement for more than thirty years, he'd gone one-on-one with about every kind of liar imaginable, from teenage speeders to hardened killers.

I thought back to what I knew of Kay Burns's background. She was an Alpine native whose first husband had been the dour Dwight Gould, a deputy under Milo's predecessor, the wily Eeny Moroni. But Blackwell had swept her off her feet and into a second marriage that was equally ill-fated. Still in her early twenties, she had fled Alpine and didn't return until over a year ago, when RestHaven opened in Ed Bronsky's former mansion. Kay came back to town as their PR maven. Until then, I had only known of her as the ex-wife of both Gould and Blackwell.

I had a question for Milo. "Is Kay still getting it on with Dwight?"

Milo shrugged. "Could be. I still can't believe it. Gould's about as romantic as a fire hydrant. He kind of looks like one, too. I think you told me she was interested in one of RestHaven's nut doctors."

"She alluded to that a while ago," I replied. Unlike Vida, I really never pry unless it's for a news item. "It was Iain Farrell, who's always struck me as a world-class jerk. When I interviewed him for the special edition we put out for RestHaven's opening, he was extremely rude."

My husband chuckled. "Yeah, I remember you bitching that he was a horse's ass.

Didn't you walk out on him?"

I admitted that I had. "It wasn't one of my more successful interviews." Since then, my infrequent and accidental encounters with Farrell could be described in terms usually reserved for opposing heads of state: contentious, but not openly antagonistic. Milo had run him through the system and discovered that after a seemingly successful career as a shrink at Marquette University in Milwaukee, Farrell had spent several years working in Montana for the state's penal system. The comedown had been triggered by beating up his then-girlfriend. She'd later dropped the charges, but Farrell decided his reputation was sufficiently sullied that he should move on.

"Speaking of jerks and other weirdos," I said, "what happened to the guy from Colville who ended up in the ER? Mitch got his name off your log, but I forget what it was."

"Hell, I don't remember," Milo admitted. "For all I know, he ended up in the hospital. He needed time to come down from his pretty pink cloud. He's probably left town by now, though he'd have to find a way to get back over the mountains. Colville is way up in the northeastern part of the state near the Canadian border. I went hunting there once a long time ago."

"I assume he hasn't paid his fine?"

"No, but he'd better do it or we'll have to put out a warrant on him." Milo frowned and tugged at his right earlobe. "What was the jerk's name? Damnit," he muttered, taking out his cell. "Fong's on the desk tonight. He'll know. Dustman is detail-oriented."

I got up to check on dinner. As soon as my husband got off the phone, we'd eat before everything dried up. He could change his clothes when we were finished.

"Well?" I said when he joined me in the kitchen.

Milo sighed. "The dink was taken into one of the ER's exam rooms, but by the time the new paramedic got around to him, he was gone. I don't know how he managed to do that, but he did."

I narrowed my eyes. "I think you forgot to tell me his name."

"Oh. Janos Kadar. He calls himself 'Yan,' as if it were spelled with a *Y.*"

"That's the new paramedic!" I yelped. "We had the story in the paper. Don't you *ever* read the *Advocate*? I meant the driver of the . . ."

Milo waved an impatient hand. "Right, okay, the goofball driver's name is Nathan Rodolf, twenty-four. Satisfied? Laskey took it off the log the next day. Don't *you* read your own paper? Can we eat now? It's almost seven."

"I guess I forgot his name," I mumbled, and refrained from reminding my not-always-better half that it had been his idea to have a drink first. We always did, but I usually had dinner on the table by six.

It was seven by the time we started eating. He asked me why I was smiling. I told him I was remembering how low-key he'd been when we first met. "Sometimes I couldn't even hear you on the phone. Now I swear I can hear you from almost two blocks away without the phone."

Milo nodded. "I was still recovering from the divorce. I missed my kids. Between Mulehide hauling them off to Bellevue and the demands of the job, I was lucky to see them once a month. I remember one winter when we had a lot of snow and I didn't see them even at Christmas. I think over three months went by before I got down to Bellevue. Mulehide's excuse for them not coming up here was that the roads were too dangerous. That was always bullshit after early February."

"You hadn't lost your sense of humor," I reminded him. "When I came to your office to introduce myself, you bought me drinks and we laughed a lot."

"You were so damned cute, especially when you almost tripped over your own feet coming through the door."

"I was nervous. I've told you that. I'd seen you on the street and you looked intimidating."

Milo set down his fork and put his hand on mine. "You're still damned cute."

"And clumsy."

"But in a cute way." He squeezed my fingers before taking his hand away. "Is there any pie left?"

"I think you ate it for breakfast."

"Oh. Maybe I did."

So much for a romantic moment. That was fine with me. Romance had brought me great grief when Tom Cavanaugh was killed. Tom, in fact, had brought me plenty of grief in the almost thirty years I'd waited to marry him. Looking back, I realized that the grieving had been not only for him, but also for not recognizing how much I loved the big guy who was looking mildly disappointed because he couldn't find any more pie in the fridge.

By morning, there was at least five inches of snow on the ground. I smiled when I looked out the front window. It was still coming down, but in a fitful manner. In the past few years, there had been very little snow in the western half of Washington state, even at Alpine's three-thousand-foot level. Unlike most of the town's residents, Milo could get one of his deputies to mount the county-owned snowplow that was used to clear the streets — and our driveway. Not that I had any plans for the day, but I knew the sheriff might want to check in at headquarters.

He confirmed my belief after I'd finished breakfast. Milo always got up before I did, even on Saturdays. Since it was the only day I could really sleep in, I'd almost overdone it by not waking up until just before ten.

I'd just put my cereal bowl and spoon in the dishwasher when Milo asked if we'd ever done a story on Will Pace at the time he opened his motel almost ten years ago.

I had to think back. "I know we did one on the opening of the motel itself, but as I recall, it was when Scott Chamoud was working for the paper and he told me that Will didn't want to be interviewed. All Pace told Scott was that he had come here from another part of the state."

"He's a weird guy," Milo remarked. "Not exactly the gracious innkeeper type. But he and his guests have kept out of serious trouble over the years. Until now."

"You did run a background check on him, right?"

"Sure, but he came up relatively clean." Milo paused to pour himself a coffee refill. "Frankly, the information we got was sketchy, but he had no criminal record. Driving violations, a couple of misdemeanor citations for getting into fights. But it did say he'd recently moved from Alaska. Ketchikan, I think. My reaction was to wait and see how he went about setting up business here. He got all the permits, passed the inspection, and there were only the usual complaints about ruckuses at the motel, which mostly involved couples. That can happen at any motel or hotel." He took a sip of coffee and then grinned at me. "And no, I didn't slug Mulehide at that fancy San Francisco hotel when she announced she was dumping me."

"She was an idiot," I declared staunchly.

Milo shrugged. "She had her reasons, and I don't mean just the dink she ran off with. We had a smaller staff back then, so I had to put in a lot of long days and weekend overtime. Mulehide had to carry the load for most of the kids' school and other activities."

I knew the rest of the story. When their

children were older and she got her teaching certificate, Tricia wanted to get out of the house. Milo had hired Frieda Wunderlich to clean their house once a week. But the teaching job was where she met Jake the Snake, who had moved his family from the Tri-Cities to take a job at Alpine High. Tricia's affair with him ended both marriages. Jake and Tricia — along with the three Dodge children — had moved to Bellevue. Luckily, Jake's house in the Tri-Cities hadn't yet been sold. The first Mrs. Sellers and their children retreated to their former home in Pasco.

I finished cleaning up the kitchen while Milo settled into the easy chair to read the rest of *The Seattle Times.* Saturday's edition had grown thin in recent years, though the Sunday edition was still robust. But like everyone in the print media, I worried about the future of newspapers in general. A small-town weekly had one advantage, however. There was really no other source for local news except Spencer Fleetwood's radio station, KSKY — and, of course, Vida.

By the time I went into the living room, Milo was on his cell, frowning. "Have you seen Doc?" he asked, and paused. "Then check yourself into the clinic and find out if you really have pneumonia. I can't diagnose you over the damned phone." Another pause. "No, I won't send De Groote on patrol in this much snow. She stays on the desk today. I'll call in Doe Jamison. Just get yourself checked out, okay? You probably came back to work too soon." Milo ended the call.

"Dwight?" I inquired.

"Yeah." He frowned. "I told the dumbass he should have taken more than two days off. Gould was still coughing his head off like a damned seal when he came back to work. It's a wonder he didn't infect all of us. I'll get Doe to fill in for him. Mullins had to take off for the weekend to attend a funeral for his wife's uncle in Longview." He tapped in Doe's number while I went to change our bed and start a load of laundry.

By the time I finished my chores, Milo was on his feet. "I've got to check in at headquarters. Some new information came in from Alameda County about the vic. Whatever she did in Oakland was some kind of liaison job with the county."

"PR, maybe?" I suggested.

Milo shrugged into his heavy parka. "I'll find out when I get to the office." He glanced out the front window before heading to the kitchen and the garage. "Damn! Now I can't tell Gould to get out the snowplow. Maybe Heppner can handle it. It's a good thing the Yukon can deal with snow even without chains."

I sat down on the sofa and had just opened my laptop to write to Mavis Marley Fulkerston, my old friend and former co-worker on *The Oregonian* in Portland, when the doorbell rang. I looked out to see Alison's Nissan parked on Fir Street's verge. Obviously, she had avoided the unplowed driveway.

When I opened the door, I noticed her cheeks were quite pink. "Did you have to push your car partway?" I asked with a smile.

Alison practically hurled herself into the living room before collapsing in Milo's easy chair. "No, but I just saw Boyd. He remembered meeting me at the office, and he talked to me! He's really a nice guy."

I settled back on the sofa. "Was he moving in?"

"Yes, his stuff arrived last night. He didn't think it would because of a lot more snow on the other side of Stevens Pass." Alison was still smiling. "I offered to help him, but he told me his roommate was due to show up any minute. Boyd really seems like a nice guy."

"He probably is," I said. "Did he grow up

on a farm around Wenatchee? An orchard, I suppose, in that part of the state."

"I don't know," Alison replied, the smile fading. "We didn't talk that long. I guess he was anxious to get back to moving in."

"Of course. That's a big job. Would you like some coffee?"

Alison shook her head. "I'm already hyper. From seeing Boyd, I mean." She looked around the living room. "Where's your superstud?"

I flinched at her terminology. "On the job. We had a murder here in town, you know."

"Oh. Right. A woman at that crappy motel." She looked down at her black leather boots. "I hope Boyd didn't notice how I've scuffed up these things. Maybe I should go to Barton's Bootery before I go home. Do you know if they're having a sale?"

"Ask your neighbor and co-worker, Leo," I suggested. "I didn't notice their ad this week. But a lot of stores are having sales now before they take inventory."

"I'll swing by on my way home," Alison said, getting to her feet. "I wish Lori could find a new man. She hasn't heard from Cole since just before Christmas. I don't think they've gotten together in the last two months. He's always in some weird place traveling for Microsoft. Lori turned thirty in October. Her time's running out."

"I didn't get married until I was fifty-two," I reminded Alison. "I survived fairly well on my own."

Alison's expression grew glum. "I told you, that was different. You already had a kid, you had a solid career, you'd been to Europe, you probably even had some kind of social life in a city like Portland. Lori's never been farther than Chilliwack, British Columbia. Her favorite aunt married a Canadian and moved up there. That Alaskan cruise I took last year was the farthest away I've ever been outside of this state. My parents never traveled much except in the Pacific Northwest."

I'd heard most of this before, except the part about Lori's aunt in Chilliwack. "My social life in Portland revolved mostly around Adam. If you count PTA meetings and watching my son play sports with a bunch of other klutzy adolescents as a social life, so be it. Mother Lord didn't have much time to herself."

Alison actually evinced some remorse. "I sort of forget that you had a life before I came to work for you. I mean, I met you when my birth mother was killed over ten years ago, but I was only twelve. Then I didn't see you again until a little over a year ago. Everybody knew that you and Dodge had an affair earlier and broke up, but finally got back together and then got married . . . ." Her voice trailed away as she grasped the doorknob.

"Yes, Milo and I had a rocky history," I agreed. "We'd both had love stories that didn't end happily ever after."

"That happens to some people. It happened to my father and to my birth mother. And then she was killed." She paused, and I wondered if she was thinking of how her mother, Linda Petersen Lindahl, had given custody of her child to her ex-husband, Howard. Linda had chosen to pursue her career in the family-owned Bank of Alpine. Alison opened the door. "I don't want to wait thirty years to get married. Is that so wrong?"

I smiled. "Not if you find the right man."

"I will." Her effort at a smile struck me as feeble. Maybe her determination was stronger. I hoped so, for her sake. And wondered if Rachel Douglas had found the wrong man.

Chapter 7

Milo returned home just after noon, bearing takeout from the Burger Barn. "I was going to eat there before I came home, but then I remembered that my cute little wife might be hungry, too."

"Gosh," I said in mock surprise, "when you're on a homicide case, I'm stunned that you remember you're married."

My husband narrowed his hazel eyes as he shed his heavy jacket and put it over the back of a kitchen chair. "Mulehide thought I didn't remember. We could have found a stiff in the bathtub and she'd have bitched while I was trying to figure out who it was."

I took a couple of plates out of the cupboard. "Really, I think you exaggerate. Vida once told me that when you became sheriff, Tricia bragged all over town."

"She did." Milo had sat down and was removing the contents from the bag with its familiar logo of a cow going into a barn and coming out on the other side as a burger. "But Mulehide never stopped to think what the job would entail. She was too busy counting the digits in my raise. Which, seeing how strapped SkyCo was for money back then, wasn't all that big. And by the way, Heppner should have the snowplow up here in the next half hour."

"I don't plan on going anywhere," I said, joining him at the table. "But I am interested in what you may have found out about the murder. It could be news." I fluttered my eyelashes at him just to see his reaction.

"Right." He was unmoved. "What if I told you I couldn't because it's . . ."

"Part of an ongoing investigation," I interrupted. "Yes, I know. But I need at least some basics to post online. Consider the public's need to know."

Having taken a big bite out of one of the two cheeseburgers he'd bought for himself, he nodded. "We got lucky. Do you remember Lloyd Campbell's younger brother, Eugene?"

Lloyd was the longtime owner of Alpine Appliance. His family had been involved — innocently — with one of the early homicides I'd covered in Alpine. "No," I replied. "I don't think I've ever heard of him."

Milo devoured three fries before he spoke.

"You probably wouldn't. Eugene — Gene, for short — and his first wife divorced. He'd cheated on her with a woman who'd moved here with her husband from California, and they ran off together to the Bay Area. Turns out the son he had by the second wife works for Alameda County. Jason Campbell's visited his relatives up here a few times, so he felt obligated to do some digging for us about Rachel."

I vaguely recalled a couple of mentions Vida had given Jason in her "Scene Around Town" column. "That was a stroke of luck," I said.

"You bet. He knew Rachel and was shocked when he found out she'd been killed. Jason had taken her out for drinks the night before she left Oakland. I got the impression they were seeing each other, at least casually. He knew she was adopted and had been married for a few years in her twenties — no kids — but she'd taken back her original name, which she used on her personnel forms when she started working for the county." Milo paused to polish off the first burger.

"How long had she been with Alameda County?"

"Eight years," Milo replied. "Before that she worked for the city of Oakland for a few years, which is why she handled a lot of the liaison stuff between the two government entities."

I downed my last french fry. "Can you find out what her married name was?"

Milo nodded. "But not until Monday. Jason can't get at the records over the weekend."

"Was he upset? I mean, overwhelmed with grief or just . . . ?"

"Shocked. That's as close as I could come over the phone."

"Do you think he'll follow through and call you back Monday?"

Milo made a face. "If he doesn't call before noon, I'll call him. What are you thinking? He followed her up here and whacked her at the motel?"

"No," I replied. "But it's possible. Nobody in Alpine seems to know who she was."

"So why did she come here? She knew Blackwell's name even if he swore he never heard of her. Maybe he didn't — at least not as Rachel Douglas."

I began clearing the table while Milo took his jacket out to hang on a peg by the front door. When it came to posting news on our website, I didn't have much. Mentioning Rachel's work connection with one of the Campbells' relatives could upset the local family. Lloyd's Alpine Appliance was a good advertiser. Besides, Milo had bought all of the items in our remodeled kitchen at the Campbells' store. If I upset them, they might cancel our warranties. I decided to wait until Monday, when Milo would hear back from Jason in Oakland.

But I did call Mitch Laskey to let him know of the latest developments, since he'd be covering most of the story. My reporter tended to be touchy if he felt he hadn't been kept up to speed on an assignment.

His initial response was, not unexpectedly, a bit gloomy. "We'd planned to drive to Monroe to visit Troy, but Brenda gets so nervous when we drive in snow. I guess we'll have to see if it melts by tomorrow."

"The highway may be cleared by then," I said, even as I looked out the window and saw more flakes coming down. "You must have had quite a lot of snow in Michigan."

"We did," he agreed, "but unless it was a blizzard, our suburb of Royal Oak was very efficient about keeping traffic moving."

In other words, we Alpiners were a bunch of lazy slobs. But even as I spoke, I saw the snowplow approaching. It appeared that Sam Heppner was in charge, though it was hard to tell because he was so bundled up. In fact, he was even wearing earmuffs.

Maybe he was afraid of joining Dwight Gould on the sick list.

I announced the snowplow's appearance to Mitch. As I figured, he wasn't cheered. "That doesn't mean Highway 2 is being cleared by the state," he said. "Maybe I should call someone to find out. They probably won't know. Oh well." He rang off.

I'd migrated only to the sofa. Milo looked up from *The Seattle Times*'s sports TV schedule. "Laskey, right?"

"Not a bundle of fun," I replied. "Speaking of bundles, the snowplow's outside. I think it's Heppner, but I can't tell by looking at his mummy-like state."

"It should be," my husband replied. "I'll ask him if he wants to come in for a cup of coffee. Or are we out?"

"I'll check." There was still enough for at least one full mug. But when I returned to the living room, Milo had gone outside to talk to Sam, who was turning the plow toward our driveway. I waited by the open door, shivering. The temperature had to be in the mid-twenties. My mate hadn't put on his jacket. I fretted that he, too, would come down with a cold.

But not more than a minute passed before he headed into the house and the snowplow started up our driveway. I waved to Sam, but, being Sam, he didn't wave back. Maybe he couldn't, since he was steering the thing with both hands.

Milo shook himself when he came in and closed the door. "It's colder than a well-digger's ass out there," he declared. "Would you believe that Roy Everson showed up at headquarters half an hour ago to inform De Groote that he'd found his mama's foot-prints outside their house on the Burl Creek Road? The damned fool had walked all that way because their car's battery was dead."

That sounded weird even for Roy. "He's going to walk back?"

Milo shook his head. "Bill Blatt had stopped by to pick up his gloves. He'd left them at work yesterday. He gave Roy a ride home. Oh — Sam declined the offer of coffee. He wants to finish the damned job and go home. He's not officially on duty today, but I'll make sure he gets an extra couple of bucks in his paycheck this time around."

Since my husband had parked himself in the easy chair, I sat down on the sofa. "What's new with Bill and Tanya? They've been dating for over a year now. Do you think they have plans?"

The query caused Milo to heave a big sigh. "I'm not sure, but they *seem* serious. Tanya's dealing pretty well with the PTSD."

He paused to light a cigarette. Milo and Tricia's daughter was suffering from post-traumatic stress disorder after her estranged fiancé had shot her and then killed himself a little over a year ago. Milo had spent three weeks away from Alpine, first at Harborview Hospital, where Tanya had been taken by helicopter, and then at Tricia's home in Bellevue while their daughter continued to recover. Milo's ex had done her best to cope with their daughter, but finally she had to bring her to Alpine. The poor girl only felt safe with her father in the family home that Milo still owned. The stay turned out to be permanent. Tanya had gone to work for the Forest Service and Bill had volunteered to help her recover from the traumatic experience. He, too, had recently experienced a romantic disaster.

"The problem," Milo went on, "isn't with Tanya and Bill. It's Lila Blatt, Bill's ornery mother. You know what she's like."

I did. Lila was one of Vida's sisters-in-law and a control freak. She'd been widowed when she was fifty, which had made her obsessive about her two children, Marje and Bill. Both were in their thirties and neither had ever married. A year or so after I arrived in Alpine, Marje's fiancé was murdered. She'd rarely dated since, but Lila had allowed her to keep the apartment she'd rented as a future home for her and the ill-fated fiancé. Bill hadn't been so lucky. Lila had insisted he live at home because she had to have a man around the house. Her sister-in-law Vida thought she was a ninny. Bill had finally found his backbone and told his mother that his intentions were honorable as far as Tanya was concerned. Apparently, the prospect of grandchildren had won him his freedom.

Just as Milo was about to turn on the Seahawks' playoff game against the Redskins, his cell went off again. Seeing him scowl, I stayed on the sofa. "Don't bother Jamison about it," he said into the phone. "If there's a real problem and not another false alarm, she can stop by. Has the highway been plowed?" He paused. "Okay, if they're up past Startup, they should be by the turnoff here in another twenty minutes . . . . Right." He ended the call. "Those old coots reported another prowler. It's probably the wind blowing stuff around. Everything has grown up around that cabin in the last year after the former occupant went away."

"The last time I drove by before Christmas, from what I could see of the cabin itself, it looked okay," I said, "but all the greenery has gotten out of control over the years. Did you ever run a current title of ownership or find out if the property was actually sold?"

Milo nodded. "According to what we found, the ownership had been passed on to the late Crystal Bird's daughter Amber by Dean Ramsey, who was temporarily on leave from his job as county extension agent. As you know, the cabin was owned back then by Crystal and her estranged husband, Aaron Conley."

"The daughter was also estranged from her mother," I said. "Crystal didn't get along with a lot of people, including me. You gave me a rough time after she was killed because you knew I'd been to see her that night. Crystal had been really nasty, and you virtually accused me of having killed her."

"Gosh, I forgot about that." Milo turned thoughtful. "The daughter may still be the owner. Didn't she get married and move away?"

"She did. I think she lives in Seattle or one of the suburbs." I glanced at the SkyCo directory I kept by the landline. "Except for his office at the courthouse, I don't know if Dean's home number is listed. Remember when we had to go see him a while back in

Sultan?"

Milo nodded. "His wife claimed he was at the fairgrounds with their kids. I still think he was hiding in the shrubbery. Don't you have a Sultan directory stashed someplace?"

I did, so I pulled it out of the end table drawer. I found the Ramseys' number, but when I dialed it, I got a recorded message and disconnected without identifying myself. "Drat! I forgot. Liza wrote up a little piece before New Year's saying the Ramseys had bought an RV and were taking a trip to Oregon to visit Mrs. Ramsey's family and then come back north to go around the Olympic Peninsula."

"Somebody at the courthouse should know how to get hold of the daughter," Milo said. "Check it out on Monday."

"Why don't you? You're the sheriff."

"I only ask questions of perps," Milo replied. "You like to nose around in what people are doing. Better yet, have Vida do it."

"Maybe I will," I replied. "She'll find out more about what they're doing than either of us would."

"I don't give a damn what they're doing except to find out who owns the cabin. Hell, Waldo Danforth is living there with his old lady. He must know. He's got a phone to call headquarters and pester us."

I flipped through both directories. "No Danforths. The number must be unlisted."

"Cellphone, maybe," Milo said, and finally turned on the TV.

I took that to mean we were dropping the subject. But I still intended to find out about Waldo Danforth. The good news was that the Seahawks didn't drop the ball. They beat the Redskins by ten points. After the game was over, I could hear firecrackers go off. No danger there — they'd melt in the snow. There are some benefits to living on a mountainside.

By Monday morning, the snow was gone, swept away by a Chinook wind that occasionally brought warmer air to the region on the west side of the Cascade Mountains. Sunday had been a quiet, uneventful day. Milo had checked in on Dwight Gould, who had been treated and sent home from the hospital that afternoon with a lot of antibiotics.

We'd spent the time watching more football, reading the Sunday *Seattle Times,* and just enjoying our own company. Despite our long history, there was still a sense of newness in finally being married.

Chapter 8

Vida showed up shortly after I arrived at the office. She was wearing a hat I'd never seen before — or at least didn't remember. It was another pillbox, but covered in black and white checks with a big black satin bow set at an angle. I rarely made the mistake of asking her if she was wearing a new hat. Several years ago she'd told me that she had a bedroom reserved for her hats and estimated she had at least four hundred of them, all stored in individual boxes. On rare occasions she would buy a new one. I supposed that some of the hats would become unwearable from age rather than use.

"So confusing," she said to me as she loomed above my desk. "I wanted to go to the post office this morning, but discovered it was closed for Martin Luther King Jr. Day. I'm surprised you didn't shut down here."

"I thought about it, but we've got a special

edition coming out next week and we need the time to put it together." We also needed to decide what it would feature, but I didn't want to admit that to Vida. "I'm paying the staff time and a half to work today."

"That's fair. Really," she went on, "people are so silly. Why must Grace Grundle call *me* to find out details about the woman who got herself killed? She knows I rarely covered crime stories. And two of my fellow Presbyterians asked me the same thing after church yesterday. If this poor woman knew someone in Alpine, I would have heard about it."

Of course. "Do you remember if there were ever any Douglases in SkyCo over the years?"

Vida leaned one hand on the back of a visitor chair and fingered her chin with the other. "No," she replied after a pause. "Unless it was before my time. We could check Mr. Clemans's yearbooks, but they only go up to 1929, when he moved his logging operation to the Robe Valley near Granite Falls."

"That would be a big stretch," I pointed out. "Rachel Douglas inquired about Jack Blackwell."

"Ye-e-s," Vida said slowly, now standing upright. "But he *is* in the logging business.

You're right, though. I can hardly see Blackwell as the benevolent kind of logging company owner that Carl Clemans was."

That wasn't quite fair to Blackwell. His employees were generally well treated. Except, of course, for the deluded young man who'd tried to shoot him at last year's infamous Labor Day picnic. That had been a holiday celebration most of us wanted to forget.

Before I could respond, the set of extra eyes we all swore were in the back of Vida's head apparently caused her to turn around as Mitch arrived with the morning's bakery goods. "My, my!" she exclaimed. "I wonder what the Upper Crust has to offer this morning. The holiday season always provides too many temptations, so I'm trying to shed a few pounds. But I skimped on breakfast and might be convinced to have a little something."

I managed not to smile. Vida's diets were a joke to the rest of us, mainly because she really wasn't fat. At five-ten, not counting her sensible chunky heels or her eclectic hats, she had a big frame and an imposing bust. I doubted if her weight had changed more than a few pounds one way or the other since I met her.

Watching her move briskly toward Mitch

and the pastry box, I decided to remain in my office. The Upper Crust sometimes had cupcakes with smiley faces on them. I wondered if my gloomy reporter had ever asked them to make ones with sad faces. Probably not, but he might like them if they did.

Five minutes later, Mitch came into my cubbyhole holding a mug of coffee and a plain doughnut. Like Vida, he remained standing. "I'm off on my rounds. Were there any late developments Sunday on the Douglas woman's murder?"

Mitch slowly shook his head. "Nothing that won't appear in the sheriff's log," I replied. "Small-town homicides still seem strange to me after Detroit. Brenda wonders if we should have stayed back there. But with Troy . . ." He paused, his eyes fixed on a point on the wall behind me. "No use having regrets. We did what we had to do."

"Most of us are like that," I said. "Twenty years ago, while I was working on *The Oregonian,* I never dreamed I'd end up in a small town like Alpine."

Mitch agreed and went on his way. As usual, he hadn't asked why I'd made a similar move. But I would have told him that my parents had been killed in an auto accident on their way back from Ben's ordination. My brother and I had put the family home up for sale and divided the proceeds. Ben had balked at taking his share after taking a vow of poverty as a priest. It had been a small house in a modest real estate market. I moved into student housing on the University of Washington campus. It was there that I met Don, a grad student who'd done his military duty. He fell in love with me and when he proposed, I said yes. I needed to belong to someone, even if I didn't return his stronger feelings.

But when I did my student internship with *The Seattle Times,* I met Tom Cavanaugh, who was the city desk editor. He and Sandra had been married for only a couple of years and had no children. The lovely Mrs. Cavanaugh came from a wealthy California family, but her inheritance wasn't just money. She was also emotionally unbalanced. Tom and I began an affair; Don became collateral damage. When I became pregnant with Adam, Tom said he'd marry me as soon as he could end his own marriage, but Sandra held the trump card: she, too, was pregnant. Tom withdrew his proposal, though he vowed to help me support our child. I was so furious that I told him I never wanted to see or hear from him again.

I spent the next two decades in Oregon,

finishing my degree, working for *The Oregonian,* and raising Adam. Then I learned that Don had died and had never remembered to remove me from his Boeing insurance policy. The $400,000 allowed me to quit the reporter's job and buy the *Advocate* — and a used Jaguar. It also meant moving to a small town. Alpine had little appeal for me. I figured when I retired I'd move back to Seattle. But Milo changed that idea for me.

As for Tom, he had been acquiring weekly newspapers all over California and was now moving into Oregon and Washington. We managed to survive a weeklong visit without ending up in bed, but a couple of months later he showed up at a newspaper conference I was attending at Lake Chelan, and we couldn't resist temptation. A few years later Sandra overdosed on her elaborate menu of prescription drugs. Eventually, Tom and I made marriage plans, and we decided that after Adam's ordination as a priest, he and Ben would officiate at our wedding. Instead, we were all reunited at Tom's funeral in San Francisco. Over the years my former lover had become involved in the Irish cause. A jealous, hotheaded fellow Irish sympathizer decided that Tom had it too easy, merely doling out money and never getting his hands dirty in the process. My future husband was shot during the annual Summer Solstice Festival Parade and died of his wounds.

Ironically, when Tom had suddenly appeared in Alpine a little over a year after I'd bought the newspaper, Vida was much taken with him, despite his married status. She even called him Tommy, which he took with good grace.

"Are you awake?" Leo asked as he leaned on my desk.

I shook myself and laughed. "I started out trying to think of a subject for the special editorial and ended up mulling over how I got to be a newspaper publisher in the first place. It's a new year, after all, and I suppose a little introspection isn't a bad thing."

Leo cocked his head. "No regrets?"

"None. Really." Since Tom had recommended Leo to me despite having fired him for drinking too much, I wanted to reassure my ad manager that I'd made the right decision, including when it came to hiring him.

He laughed. "Now you've got two of us. By the way, Liza and I looked at that house Saturday and it's basically decent, but we're wondering if we should buy a condo instead. No yard to keep up. I was never very good about it, and she figures she's done enough to qualify for a green thumb."

"I'm sure she has," I agreed. "I still like puttering around in my garden. It's good mental therapy, and Milo does all the heavy lifting."

"Your old man keeps in good shape," Leo conceded. "I gather he works out. I'm too lazy."

"Milo works out at least twice a week before he goes to headquarters. I don't work out because I'm also too lazy."

"You don't need to," he declared. "What do you weigh? Sorry, I shouldn't have asked."

"I stay about the same — close to a hundred and twenty. I used to weigh just under a hundred and twenty-five, but I lost weight after Tom was killed. For some reason, the five pounds never came back. It's all because of my weird metabolism. It burns up calories."

"Lucky you." Leo glanced over his shoulder and lowered his voice. "Don't ever tell Liza. Both of us have struggled to keep off the pounds."

"Speaking of weight, I see Vida's still here," I said, noting that she had sat down at Liza's vacant desk and was eating a second doughnut. "I suspect we're all going to be asked for 'Scene' items."

"Guess I'd better check my memory," Leo replied, and headed back to the newsroom.

Reluctantly I got up and followed him. Maybe someone would come up with an item that would inspire my editorial. Maybe I should have focused on that instead of the special edition. Maybe I needed more coffee.

Just then Liza entered from the front office. "Ah!" my former House & Home editor exclaimed to her successor. "You must have noticed some intriguing items while making your rounds. Do give me something I can use in 'Scene.' "

Liza stopped by the coffee urn. "I overheard someone waiting to cross Front Street say that one of the school bus drivers had forgotten to take off his chains after taking the team to Darrington for a basketball game Saturday. That made the kids late for early classes this morning."

"The driver's name?" Vida asked.

Liza grimaced. "I'm not sure. Hal or Al or . . .? Really, I was intent on watching traffic."

Vida didn't hide her disapproval. "As you must know, in a small town, names make news. Perhaps you should call Principal Freeman and find out which driver it was."

But Liza was no pushover. "Wouldn't that

embarrass the poor guy? It might even get him into trouble."

I edged closer to the coffee urn and realized I was watching a turf war. Vida took no prisoners when it came to people who disagreed with her. Over the years, I'd been careful about treading on her toes. So were our readers. There were still some Alpiners, especially senior citizens, who thought she ran the newspaper and I was her dimwitted sidekick. I glanced at Leo, who looked more bemused than alarmed.

"People," Vida began with a lift of her chin, "should be held accountable for their actions. If I run this in 'Scene,' he may very well be reprimanded. It's a safety issue for our children."

Liza cocked her head to one side. "In that case, why don't you write an article about it?" She shot me a quick glance. "I'm sure Emma would run it in the interest of saving lives."

It was time to intervene. "Let's drop the item," I said. "Nothing happened. My next-door neighbors, the Marsdens, had their grandchildren here from Mountlake Terrace over the weekend. They tried to make a snowman Saturday, but there wasn't enough snow and they gave up. Who else has something for 'Scene'?"

Kip volunteered, "Betsy O'Toole found a stray cat in her office at the Grocery Basket Friday. She has no idea who it belongs to. No collar. Maybe the owners will see that in 'Scene' and rescue the little critter."

"Cats." Vida said the word with disdain. She had no time for cats or other animals. Her only pet was Cupcake, a canary that had to be in his dotage by now. "Very well. That will do. Mitch?"

I retreated into my office. Five minutes later Vida tromped in and sat down. "I would've appreciated more support from you, Emma. You stood there like a statue. Are you daunted by this *newcomer*?" She made the word sound obscene.

"Of course not." I smiled. "Let's not get the week off to a bad start. Liza's doing her best to fit in. It's a big change for her."

"She should be elated that she escaped from Santa Fe," Vida declared.

"It's Santa Maria," I said. "Santa Fe is in New Mexico."

Vida shuddered. "So many Santas in the Southwest. How can anyone keep track of them except for the benighted souls who have to live in such places? Even some former Alpiners have retired to Arizona. Imagine!"

She already knew the reasons people —

especially retirees — loved living in the southwestern part of our country. Instead, I asked how she had spent the weekend. Settling into a less contentious mood, she described the visit she and her longtime companion, retired Air Force Colonel Buck Bardeen, had had with friends in Startup. He'd lived near there for several years before buying a Parc Pines condo. The get-together had been a very pleasant evening, Vida asserted. The dinner had been quite good, and she had asked their hostess to give her the recipe for the delicious chicken entrée. I prayed silently that Vida would never try to make it. Her lack of culinary talent was well known all over Skykomish County. When I'd come down with the overnight flu back in early December, she'd insisted on bringing dinner for Milo and me. I'd refused even to taste it, but my husband was braver. After one forkful, he swore it was boiled owl and threw it in the garbage.

Getting to her feet, Vida started to turn toward the newsroom. "Oh!" she exclaimed. "What's going on with that cabin at Baring? Is someone living there? I saw smoke coming out of the chimney when we drove by."

"It's an elderly couple," I replied. "Milo got a call about a possible intruder the other day. There was no sign of anyone trying to get in, though."

Vida frowned. "Who owns it now that the Conley person is dead?"

"I think the legal owner is Dean Ramsey's daughter."

Vida frowned, and I could see her almost vibrating with curiosity. "Dean has always struck me as a bit of a milk toast. Surely Milo knows the name of the people who live there."

I nodded. "Yes, the man's name is Waldo Danforth."

Vida stared at me. Then her knees started to buckle and she reached out to grab a visitor chair. "No!" she gasped before staggering into the chair and passing out.

Chapter 9

Mitch had seen Vida's collapse, and he rushed into my office. "What happened?" he exclaimed.

"Be careful!" I cried, getting up from my chair and coming around the side of my desk. "Her glasses fell on the floor."

Mitch scooped up the glasses and put them on top of some notes I'd made for possible future editions. "Is she . . . ?" Just then Vida emitted a low groan. "Should we call the medics?" he asked.

I was about to say yes when Vida lifted her head. "No!" she gasped. "No, no!" But she allowed Mitch to help her sit up while I handed over her glasses. I noticed she was very pale and her hands were trembling. She put the glasses in her lap, probably not wanting us to see how unsteady she still was. "Who else is here?" she asked, sounding more like herself.

"Alison's in the front office and Kip's in

the back shop," Mitch replied, sitting down in the other visitor chair. "I just got back from my rounds. Can I get you some water?"

"No, no. But thank you for offering." Vida now sounded almost normal. "It's this weather. So changeable this time of year. I felt as if I were coming down with a cold last night." With a now-steady hand, she put her glasses back on and retrieved the pillbox, which had fallen onto my desk. "I really should be on my way. I'm supposed to meet Maud Dodd at the retirement home." She glanced at the Bulova watch that her husband, Ernest, had given her over fifty years ago. Vida always swore that it had never needed repairing. "It's twenty-six after nine. I told Maud I'd arrive at nine-thirty. I'll call from my car to let her know I'll be a bit tardy. I do hate it when people aren't on time."

Mitch stood up. "Let me give you a hand," he offered.

But Vida shook her head, where the pillbox once again resided. "No, I'm fine. One can't give in to a mere cold." She got to her feet, a bit more slowly than usual, but her majestic exit was sheer Vida.

"Amazing old girl," Mitch said under his breath. "How old is she?"

"A few years shy of eighty," I replied, after Vida left the newsroom. "She never mentions her birthday. I think she ignores the aging process."

Mitch had also gotten to his feet. "Did something set her off, or do you think it was a small stroke? A TIA, I think they're called."

I shrugged. "For all I know, she may really be getting a cold. Even Vida can have an occasional ailment."

"I suppose. Oh, well. Back to work."

I watched him walk away to his desk. Then I sat down and wondered why the mention of Waldo Danforth had sent Vida into a tailspin. The name meant nothing to me, but I was sure it meant something to her. It would take a lot of time and a lot of trouble to find out what it was.

The rest of the morning was spent checking copy that Mitch had handed in for this week's edition and going over Vida's feature on a Gustavson relation of hers who had visited family in Wisconsin for the holidays. "Wisconsin!" Vida had exclaimed Friday afternoon when she handed it in. "All that cheese and Green Bay Packers and more snow than we have in Alpine! How can such a flat place have so much snow? At least we have mountains." Despite her gossipy tone and often burying the lead halfway through an article, I rarely made corrections. Our readers — especially the older ones — seemed to like her style.

I'd lost track of time when I checked my watch and saw it was five minutes to noon. Maybe Milo was free for lunch. I dialed his private line, but the call trunked over to Lori Cobb, who told me that her boss had already left.

"He's taking Consi to lunch at the ski lodge," Lori informed me. "It's the first chance he's had to do that since she started work here. Is there a message?"

"No, it was just a whim," I replied. "Say, do you know anybody named Danforth who lives here? And no, I don't mean the guy who called from the cabin at Baring. I wonder if he has relatives in town."

"Gosh," Lori said after a pause. "I don't think so. But it's possible if there was someone a long time ago."

Lori was only a bit past thirty, so her answer didn't surprise me. I thanked her and hung up. I saw Kip go through the newsroom, but he was only a couple of years older than the sheriff's receptionist. Milo might know. I'd ask him when he got home. Suddenly realizing I was hungry, I called the Venison Inn and ordered takeout. If

Milo was taking his new deputy to lunch at the ski lodge, I'd treat myself again to the VI's rare beef dip. It was much better than the Burger Barn's overcooked version. I also ordered a small green salad. For some irrational reason, *I* was feeling a little green, but I told myself it wasn't with jealousy.

Or was it?

Around three o'clock, our retired county commissioner Leonard Hollenberg wandered into the front office, asking for Vida. I heard Mitch tell him that she'd been in earlier but probably wouldn't be back. Since Leonard liked to talk a lot and never could remember my first name, I stayed at my desk and kept my head down. He started to yak it up with Mitch, but my reporter's phone rang. I could hear the former commissioner's heavy tread coming my way.

"Erma," he barked at me as he crossed the threshold. "You got room for Violet's story about our annual trip to Leavenworth to see all the Christmas stuff they put up over there?"

The Hollenbergs had made that trip almost every year for as long as I could remember. Not that the Bavarian-style town wasn't worth repeated visits. I'd gone there once with Tom and we'd spent the night. I still had the hand-carved madonna-and-child statue that he'd bought for me.

Leonard was opening a manila envelope and hauling out what looked like the first chapter of a long Russian novel. "Violet's a pretty danged good writer, if you don't mind me saying so," he asserted. "Maybe that's why she's not much of a talker."

I nodded politely. No doubt Violet never had much chance to get a word in edgewise.

Not needing any further encouragement, Leonard rattled on. And on. The half-million lights on all the German village buildings along the main street, Father Christmas, the roaming Dickensian carolers, the hearty meals, the comfortable motel bed, the good cheer shown by the merchants . . . my eyelids began to droop. It was only when Leonard sneezed that I refocused on him.

"Gesundheit!" I exclaimed, proving that I was still conscious.

"Yeah, thanks," Leonard said after wiping his nose with a red-and-white bandana handkerchief. "Violet knows how to tell a story. Your readers will eat it up."

"I'm sure they will," I said, hoping I sounded sincere. "Thanks for stopping by."

"Glad to do it," Leonard replied, stuffing the handkerchief back in his pants pocket.

"Violet will be tickled pink to see herself in print. Good to chat with you, Elma." He turned to leave, but I suddenly realized he might be able to answer my question about Waldo Danforth.

"Say," I said, standing up to make sure he knew I was leaving my cubbyhole, "do you recall anyone living around here named Danforth?"

Leonard paused in the doorway, stroking his chin. "Danforth . . . I remember some Daniels and a Dandridge and . . . No, not anybody by that name. Are you trying to find somebody?"

I shook my head. "I'm doing some research and a Waldo Danforth was mentioned. I couldn't place him. I thought you might remember someone from way back with that name."

"Dang, but I don't." Leonard paused. "I'll ask Violet. If she remembers the name, I'll let you know."

I figured Leonard wouldn't remember Danforth's name by the time he got home, but it was worth a shot. "Thanks. Give Violet my best."

"Will do. I'm off now to see George Engebretsen. He's in the nursing home, you know." Shaking his head, Leonard meandered out through the newsroom. Both

Leonard and George were members of the now inactive county board of commissioners. The third member, Alfred Cobb — Lori's grandfather — had died only a little over a year ago. His wife hadn't lasted very long without him. If an old-timer like Leonard didn't remember a Danforth, then I couldn't think of anyone who could. Of course, his memory for names wasn't very good when it came to people he knew in the present.

But Vida remembered Waldo Danforth, and apparently not in a good way. Passing out suggested the memory was an unpleasant one.

It was still raining by the time I got home. Milo didn't show up until going on six. I met him at the kitchen door with a quick kiss.

"How was your lunch?" I asked, following him into the living room, where he hung up his hat and jacket.

"Okay. Henry Bardeen had to hire a new cook for the coffee shop. The one he brought in after the holidays turned out to be higher than Alpine Baldy. The guy kept ducking outside to smoke weed. My steak sandwich was weird. Henry's still seeing Linda Grant. What's for dinner?"

"Aren't you going to change first?"

"No. This uniform has to go to Mrs. Overholt for a good cleaning. Barbie or Belinda or whoever the new waitress is spilled coffee on both the shirt and pants. Luckily, it was after we finished eating, so the coffee was cold." Milo was heading back to the kitchen while I trailed behind him.

"Did Consi get upset when the waitress spilled the coffee?" I asked in what I hoped was a guileless voice.

"Hell no," Milo replied, reaching for the Scotch. "She's a cop, for God's sake. Her father and her uncle are cops in Pierce County. In fact, the uncle's a detective in Tacoma." He paused with the bottle in his hand. "What's with you? Did something happen at work?"

"It did," I informed him. "Vida passed out when I mentioned Waldo Danforth. She came to and seemed to be all right, but insisted she was coming down with a cold. I don't believe her. Is the old guy's name familiar to you?"

"No." Milo was dropping ice cubes into a glass. "Where's your drink?"

"In the fridge. I made it when I got home, but wanted to wait until you were here."

Milo opened the fridge and handed me my bourbon and 7-Up over ice. We went back into the living room and assumed our usual places. I told my husband about Leonard Hollenberg's visit and that he'd never heard of any Danforths, either.

"Hollenberg may not remember voters' names," Milo said, "but he never forgets a face. Are you sure Vida didn't have some kind of spell? Hell, she's not far from eighty. She's entitled to have some off days."

"True, but she seemed shocked when she heard the name."

Milo reached for his laptop. "Let me check our official data base. Everybody who ever lived in SkyCo is listed." He paused, apparently searching through the list of Ds. "No. Nothing even close."

Briefly we both sat in silence. "I wonder," I finally said, "if I should call Amy. But Vida is so secretive that she probably won't tell her daughter she's had a fainting spell. The only one who knows besides us is Mitch, and he's not the type to blab, except maybe to his wife, Brenda. She's got her own emotional problems and is borderline anti-social."

"Maybe Brenda will perk up when Troy gets released later this year," Milo said. "When do we eat?"

"Now." I led the way to the kitchen. "I figured you wouldn't be all that hungry after a lavish lunch at the ski lodge."

“I told you, the steak sandwich was weird.” He encircled my neck with his arm. “Damnit, Emma, are you jealous? De Groote is my new deputy, not my future girlfriend. I worked too damned hard to get you to marry me, and that was after sixteen years of waiting for you to come around. Jesus, I can’t believe you’d think I’d even look at another woman now that I’ve finally got you.”

“I know,” I said in sort of a squeak. “But . . .”

He let go and I turned around. “But what?” he asked, frowning.

“I suppose I can’t understand why other women wouldn’t be attracted to you.” I punched him lightly in the midsection. “You’re a very imposing-looking man, Sheriff.”

His hazel eyes sparked. “Turn off the stove. Let’s impose on each other.”

And so we did.

We were finishing dinner a little before eight when Milo’s cell rang. “What now?” he muttered, and answered the phone. “Dodge here,” he said, and frowned as he listened to whoever was at the other end. “Okay, Sam, they should’ve let us know as soon as it happened. What’s wrong with those assholes over in Shelton?" He paused for the answer. "Right, freaking red tape. Thanks. Alert the rest of the troops." He put the cell back in his pocket. "Mickey O'Neill escaped from the Shelton Correctional Facility over the weekend. They knew he was from here, but they'd had calls from people closer to the prison who thought they'd seen him. Maybe that was before Mickey left the area."

"I forget," I said. "How long a sentence did he get for beating up our awful next-door neighbors' daughter-in-law?"

"Two and a half years," Milo replied. "It was a first offense, and otherwise he was clean. Blackwell dropped the charges when Mickey tried to shoot him at the Labor Day picnic. I figure Jack was embarrassed because of his reputation as a good employer, and there was no proof that Mickey poached those trees on protected land. But the woman he beat up, Sofia Nelson, filed battering charges against him."

"Have you heard about anybody around here seeing Mickey since he escaped?"

Milo shook his head. "Hell no, since we just found out about it. Anyway, I figure he wouldn't come back to Alpine. Yes, he still owns the old family house, but that thing is practically falling down. Mickey's father and his uncles damned near wrecked the place over the years."

I knew that, having seen the house after Mickey was arrested. The three older O'Neills, including Mickey's father, had all been murdered by their longtime rivals, the Hartquist family. It was the culmination of a decades-old feud between the two families that had begun before my time in Alpine. If memory served, it had something to do with a goat.

We migrated to the living room. "Nothing new on the homicide investigation?" I asked innocently.

Milo paused in lighting a cigarette. "No. The autopsy report hasn't come back. Don't you think I'd have mentioned if it had, you little twerp?"

I shrugged. "Sometimes you forget that I own a newspaper."

He flicked the lighter. "So that's where you go during the day. I thought you sneaked off to shop at Nordstrom in Seattle."

"I haven't even been to Nordstrom Rack since I married you," I retorted, referring to the upscale store's discount outlet. "I have clothes that are older than Alison Lindahl."

"You've got so many clothes that I had to put half of mine in the spare room's closet."

"That's because your clothes are much

bigger than mine. I could fit a pair of shoes into just one of your . . ."

The phone rang on the end table. By coincidence, it was Alison. "Guess what?" she said in an excited voice. "I ran into Boyd Lanier outside of Pines Villa. He asked me to lunch with him tomorrow! I am so hyped!"

"That's great, Alison," I enthused — and then added for Milo's benefit, "When do you and Boyd announce your engagement?"

"Emma!" she exclaimed. "It's lunch at the VI, not dinner at Le Gourmand. But it's a start."

"I'm glad for you. Really. Are he and his roommate all moved in?"

"I think so," she replied. "Boyd mentioned he's starting to feel at home. Now I have to figure out what to wear." She disconnected.

Milo looked up from the *Sports Illustrated* he'd been reading. "Alison's on the hunt again?"

"I'm not sure she ever gave up. She's been lying in wait for the next eligible guy since the last one fizzled."

"The new county extension agent, right?"

"Right."

Milo went back to reading his magazine. I picked up an Agatha Christie mystery I'd read so long ago that I'd forgotten whodunit. I hoped that Alison would have better luck this time around. Her last attempt at finding romance had almost proved fatal. The last thing I wanted for her was a repeat.

But, I reminded myself, *we don't always get what we want.*

CHAPTER 10

Alison showed up Tuesday morning in an outfit I'd never seen before. The deep blue cowl-necked sweater accentuated her eyes, and the charcoal tights weren't tight enough to be considered overly provocative. Her only jewelry was a familiar silver locket that contained a picture of her birth mother on one side and one of her father and the stepmother who had virtually raised her on the other. Having taught cosmetology at the community college before coming to work for us, she was very skillful about applying makeup. She had a good complexion, used only a minimum of lip gloss, and except for the mascara she'd applied to her lashes, Alison looked like she usually did. Except, of course, for her sense of anticipation.

"Do I look okay?" she asked as I came through the door.

"Drop-dead gorgeous," I replied. "You're a very pretty young woman."

"No, I'm not," she declared. "It's all smoke and mirrors. Even if my class got cut by the college, I benefited from what I taught. How do you like the new outfit? I got it at Francine's Fine Apparel last night. She stayed open late because of her year-end clearance sale."

"Nice. The color of the sweater is very becoming."

She sat down at her desk. "I hope Boyd thinks so."

"I'm sure he will. He's a man and . . ." I shut up as the phone rang on Alison's desk.

Wide-eyed, she hesitated. "What if it's him and he's cancelling?"

"Unlikely," I replied, but waited just in case.

"Hold on, Mrs. Runkel," Alison said after listening for a few moments. "Ms. Lord is going to her office."

Only Mitch was in the newsroom, waiting for the coffee to finish perking and staring hungrily at the otherwise empty shelf. "Liza's turn," I said as I hurried into my cubbyhole.

Vida's voice assaulted my ear as I picked up the receiver. "We must lunch today. I assume you're free?"

"I am," I replied. "The Venison Inn?"

"No," she said. "The ski lodge coffee shop.

It's more private. I'll see you at noon." On that imperious note, she hung up.

An hour later, Spencer Fleetwood strolled through the now-empty newsroom and into my office. As usual, KSKY's owner was impeccably dressed in charcoal tailored slacks, a navy cashmere sweater over an ecru dress shirt, and a black leather jacket slung over his left shoulder. Spence made himself comfortable in one of my visitor chairs.

"I come with possible good news," he said in that smooth radio voice I'd initially resented, because he was the *Advocate*'s competition, but had grown to appreciate. If nothing else, Spence was a professional. "I stopped to get gas at Cal's Chevron this morning. Cal was giving directions to a man representing the Panera Bread cafés. They're apparently considering Alpine as a future site. Did you know about this?"

"No," I replied. "I thought they only operated in suburban malls. There's one north of Everett near the Tulalip Resort Hotel and Casino."

"Yes," Spence agreed. "I haven't been to the café, but I've visited the Tulalip casino a few times. Rosalie enjoys playing roulette."

The reference was to Rosalie Reed, RestHaven's chief psychologist and Spence's main squeeze long before the facility opened in Alpine over a year ago.

"I appreciate you informing me," I said formally, then leaned closer in my chair. "The newsroom's empty. Why are you really here?"

Spence chuckled. "You read me too well." The amused expression fled and he lowered his mellifluous voice. "Vida called last night to say she didn't want to continue doing her radio program."

I jerked straight up. "No! Do you think she meant it?"

Spence shrugged. "She sounded like it. But she didn't seem like herself. Is she ill?"

I was certain that Mitch wouldn't tell anyone about Vida's faint. But Spence and I had a history. Not a romantic one, but a camaraderie shared as the only two media owners in the county. While we were rivals for news, we also did some co-op advertising. I decided to hedge a bit.

"Vida wasn't feeling well yesterday," I said. "She thought she might be coming down with a cold, and she didn't act like herself." That was true, since passing out in my office was something she'd never done before. "Maybe it's more than a cold."

"She's had remarkably good health ever since I've known her," Spence allowed. "The only time I've seen her off her feed was when Roger got busted. Has she ever visited him?"

"If she has, she's never mentioned it." It occurred to me that her grandson had also been sent to the Shelton facility. It was a wonder that Roger hadn't tried to talk Mickey O'Neill into letting him come along on the breakout. "It's been going on a year since he was incarcerated."

Spence nodded absently. "Maybe I should give her a day or two to think over cancelling her program. Vida doesn't have whims, but if she's not feeling good . . . Well, you know what I mean. I'd hate to lose her. She gets the highest ratings of all our live local programs, including the news."

"Her 'Scene' and advice column are the most-read part of the paper. If she's serious, maybe that's why she wants to have lunch with me today."

"Ah!" Spence's expression matched my own feelings. "It appears that the incomparable Vida Runkel has both of us up a stump, as the natives would say. She's literally irreplaceable."

My face turned grim. "That's true. But she *is* mortal."

Spence's hawklike features were also somber. "Physically, Vida's a strong person. I've always figured she could make it to a hundred without stopping for extra breaths. Still . . ." He lifted his hands in a helpless gesture.

Unfortunately, I understood what he meant.

At ten minutes to twelve, I headed for the ski lodge. When I reached the parking lot, I saw one of the valets parking Vida's big Buick. After leaving my Honda in their care, I entered the lodge to find Henry Bardeen coming into the lobby. He stopped to greet me with the professional, gracious smile that befitted him as the longtime manager.

"I understand you're meeting Vida," he said. "She's sitting by one of the pillars. More private, of course, which she requested. Are you two planning a big exposé of the Burl Creek Thimble Club?"

I smiled back. The remark was as close as Henry ever came to being humorous. "Not exactly. It's more work-related. Vida told me that she and your brother Buck had a pleasant visit to friends in Startup last week."

Henry's smile disappeared. "Yes, so I heard." He touched the obvious toupee that sometimes moved a bit on his bald head. "I'd hoped Buck and Vida might eventually marry, but after all this time, I suppose it'll never happen. I think Buck has wanted that, but Vida apparently likes things the way they are. If only . . ." He paused as a worried-looking bellboy approached him. "Excuse me, Emma, there may be a problem. Misplaced luggage, perhaps. Enjoy your lunch."

I went down the hall to the coffee shop, wondering if having his older brother finally remarry would give Henry the green light to propose to his own longtime companion, schoolteacher Linda Grant. Both Bardeens had been widowed. Maybe the younger brother felt the older brother held rank when it came to their love lives. If so, Henry might have a long wait. I couldn't imagine Vida remarrying. But then, I couldn't imagine her fainting — until she did.

I headed straight for Vida. I'd barely settled into my chair before she went straight to the point. "It's Amy," she said, referring to her youngest daughter and speaking in an unusually quiet voice. "She's going through the change, and it's extremely hard on her."

I nodded. "It's no fun. Doc Dewey was a big help. Has she seen him?"

"Yes, but though Gerry is a fine practitioner, he's not a woman." Vida paused to adjust her gray felt cloche with its wide black band. "He can't imagine how difficult it can be for someone as delicate as Amy."

I forced myself to stay solemn. All three of Vida's daughters were built in their mother's image, though none of them had her strength of character. Amy and her husband, Ted Hibbert, were the only ones who lived in Alpine. The other two and their families were in Tacoma and Bellingham. The Hibberts were also the parents of the wayward Roger.

"I'm afraid Amy may have to be hospitalized again," Vida went on. "Ted is beside himself, but again, men have no idea how grueling menopause can be. When I went out of town last summer for the weekend to visit an old friend in Spokane, my addled sister-in-law Ella forgot to tell my daughter where I'd gone, and Amy ended up in the hospital. When I went through the change, I managed without more than the usual minor symptoms. I had to earn my living. I recall you had your own problems."

I shrugged. "I survived. Like you, I had to put food on the table."

The waitress came to take our orders. I didn't need to look at the menu. The daily special was an open-face Dungeness crab sandwich on toast with a small salad, an easy choice for me. Vida asked for the same.

"Amy has never had to work," Vida said, her gaze flickering across the aisle to two men in well-cut suits. I assumed they were from out of town. In Alpine, only bankers, lawyers, and Henry Bardeen wore suits. "Oh, she did some volunteering before she became pregnant. But once she became a mother, she was devoted to her task."

I realized Vida hadn't mentioned Roger by name. It was all I could do to keep from asking if she'd seen him since he'd been in prison. "Amy's lucky that Ted has such a good job with the state," I said.

"Yes. He's a most diligent worker." Vida paused. "Obviously, he can't take time off to care for Amy, which is why I must devote myself to helping her get through this crisis. You understand, I'm sure."

I smiled feebly. "Your readers and listeners will miss you."

"They'll survive," Vida replied with a touch of irony. "Family comes first. Amy had intended to send Dippy to daycare, but I put a stop to that. Donna Wickstrom does her best, but she has five other children to watch. Dippy is used to having all the attention."

That was undoubtedly true, but not necessarily a good thing. I didn't say so, of course. Dippy's birth mother was dead. With his father in prison, the little guy had gotten off to a poor start. Vida's grandson had impregnated Holly Gross, the late and unlamented town hooker. She and her drug-dealing boyfriend had been killed last spring in a high-speed chase when their car went off Highway 2 and plunged into the Skykomish River. Holly had named Roger's son for Leonardo DiCaprio. "Dippy's what now? Three?"

"Yes, and so clever for his age! I went with him to his last checkup with Doc Dewey, who was impressed with his curiosity. Dippy was very intrigued by the skeleton in the examination room. He kept trying to take it apart. Doc indicated he'd rather keep the thing all of a piece, but I reminded him that he shouldn't squelch a child's thirst for knowledge." She paused. "Here comes our food."

Having passed on information about Dippy's current status, Vida studied the salad with a frown. "Goodness!" she exclaimed, eyeing our waitress with dismay. "You can't be running low on crab so early in the noon hour! Or is this not Dungeness, but Alaskan king crab? I know some people like that type, though I find it . . . pallid."

Kerry — or so the young waitress's nametag identified her — looked stunned. "Oh, no, ma'am! It's Dungeness, the only crab we serve here. Should I bring you a side portion?"

"Yes," Vida replied with her cheesiest smile. "You're new here, aren't you, Kerry? I'm Vida Runkel and I write for *The Alpine Advocate.* Emma Lord is the publisher."

"Oh." Kerry's own smile was forced. "I haven't seen the paper yet. I just moved here from Forks. I don't know Ms. Lord."

"You do now," Vida said with a flourish of her hand in my direction. "Ms. Lord puts out a very fine publication. Of course," she added with an attempt at modesty, "I've worked for the paper twice as long as she has. You really must subscribe so you know what's going on here in Alpine."

Kerry shuddered. "I heard a woman got killed only a few days after I moved from Forks. That's really creepy."

"Violence is part of life," Vida declared. "Now do bring the rest of the crab, and I'd also like more sugar packets for my hot tea. After you pour it, of course. I hope it's steeped long enough and that there's real cream and not that anemic imitation."

"I'll make sure everything's okay," Kerry promised. Thus chastened, she all but ran off down the aisle.

I shook my head. "Poor girl. I'll bet she's just out of high school."

Vida was staring at some point beyond

me. "Why did she move here? I'll have to find out. We always mention newcomers." She paused, the gray eyes sharp as lasers as she watched Kerry's progress by the service counter. "Of course," Vida went on, looking again at me, "a brief interview would be up to Mrs. Walsh."

I avoided wincing. For some bizarre reason, Vida refused to call Liza by her first name. I suspected that even though my former House & Home editor had voluntarily retired, she somehow resented her replacement. Fortunately, Liza had heard enough about her predecessor's quirks to not take offense.

Upon returning with the tea and my Pepsi, Kerry was subjected to Vida's inquiry about why she had made the wise decision to move from Forks to Alpine. Kerry merely smiled and said she wanted to see more of the state than the Olympic Peninsula.

Vida harrumphed after Kerry left our separate bills. "She has a lot to learn. Forks indeed! It's not as big as Alpine, and Amy told me the other day that someone was making a television series about the town. Why would they do such a thing?"

I shrugged. "Ask Kerry. Maybe she knows."

"Certainly not. I wouldn't give her the

satisfaction." Vida attacked her meal. "There still isn't enough crab in this dish. So chintzy."

I refrained from commenting. Instead, I asked if her nephew, Deputy Bill Blatt, thought the new hire was fitting in.

Vida looked a bit prune-like. "I haven't spoken to him since last week. Billy spends his free time with Tanya. I wouldn't be surprised if they got married. They'd better, since they're living together at Milo's former home. I understand he's charging them rent, though not as much as he could charge for that place if his daughter and his deputy weren't the ones living there. Of course, he originally intended to sell the house." Vida's gray eyes glinted. "My evil sister-in-law must be wild. Lila swore she'd put a stop to it, but Billy finally rebelled. Only she would have the nerve to go up against your husband!"

"It didn't bother Milo," I said. "If Bill and Tanya do get married, they may want to buy the house. They've both been doing some work on it."

"Yes," Vida murmured. "After Tricia left him and took their children with her to Bellevue, Milo neglected to keep up the house, except for his workshop downstairs. Tanya must be happy to be back here. The

Eastside suburbs are so wearing. So many people, so much traffic! My, my!"

"As you may recall," I reminded Vida, "she wasn't very fond of Bellevue after her fiancé shot her and then killed himself."

"Not surprising that he did that," she declared. "Living in such a place would drive anyone insane. It's a wonder they don't have murder-suicides on a daily basis. I know it would upset me very much. I'm glad I've never been there."

"Bellevue only had two homicides the last time I checked the statistics."

"Nonsense!" Vida huffed. "They obviously lied to keep up their outrageous real estate prices."

I gave up and changed the subject to the weather. That was always a relatively safe topic, even with Vida. But she did have a quibble: we hadn't yet had enough snow to ensure that the ski lodge would have a busy season. Buck worried about his brother's lack of visitors, something that had happened a few years earlier during an unusually warm winter in the Cascades.

Somehow, we managed to keep the conversation on the colonel, a usually safe topic. Yes, Buck's move from the house he'd lived in some twenty miles west of Alpine to a condo at Parc Pines had been a success.

He was closer to shops and services. Very wise of him, of course. No garden to keep up, no big household chores to do. Vida didn't add that Alpine was as close to heaven as Buck would get while he was still alive. She probably thought we were already there.

On the way back from the ski lodge, I saw Milo's Yukon parked in its usual place outside of headquarters. The old cast-iron clock across the street by the bank told me it was a quarter to one. I decided to stop in and see if my husband had any news.

Dustin Fong was at the front desk. Of all the deputies, he was the most polite and unflappable. Dustman, as he was known to his co-workers, had been partially raised by his Shanghai-born grandmother, who had been obsessed with good manners. In all the years I'd known him, he'd never called me by my first name.

"I see the boss has his door closed," I said. "Is he berating one of your fellow deputies?"

Dustin smiled. "No. He ate lunch in his office today. Go ahead, he won't mind if it's you."

I walked through the counter's half-gate, approached the sheriff's lair, and knocked. A gruff "Who's there?" came from the other side of the door.

"Your loving wife," I replied, opening the door. "Why did you eat in?"

"Because those freaking Californians aren't in the fast lane after all," he replied as I sat down in one of his visitor chairs. "First thing this morning we requested a photo of the vic when she didn't look dead. Mullins was assured we'd have it ASAP. It didn't get here until right before noon. That's why I ate in. We'll post it around town and hope for the best."

"Gosh," I said, fluttering my eyelashes just to annoy my husband, "why not run it in the *Advocate*? Quite a few people actually read it."

"Smartass," he muttered. "That might not be as nutty as some of your other ideas. You want to see it?"

"Sure. She must look better than she did in the post-death photo."

Milo removed the photo from its padded envelope. "Don't screw with it."

I glared at him. "I run a newspaper, remember? The only staffer who ever screwed up photos was Ed Bronsky. He thought they made good placemats for his morning pastries."

"Ed probably never thought about much else," Milo remarked. "Hey — I just remembered that you're my wife. Want to make out?"

"No. I'm trying to focus on your victim. She was really quite attractive. Did you find out what her married name was?"

"Chastaine," he replied, and spelled it out. "His first name is Charles, known as Chuck. He remarried and lives with the new wife and their two kids in Basking Ridge, New Jersey. Rachel dropped her married name after the split." Milo leaned forward. "Are you trying to memorize her face or looking for hidden clues to who whacked her?"

I shook my head and handed over the photo. "Somehow she reminds me of someone. Maybe a girl I knew at Blanchet High School."

Milo chuckled. "You and your fancy private Catholic schools. Did they try to turn you girls into nuns?"

"Not even close," I said. "One of my best friends — also Catholic — once asked me if there was any difference between Catholics and Protestants. We had quite a few Prots in our class, even a couple of agnostics. I will admit that the school chaplain, Father Doug, inspired Ben to become a priest, but he also tried to talk my brother out of it, figuring it was an adolescent whim. Obviously, it wasn't."

Milo nodded absently. "How did your parents feel about that?"

"Mom was okay with it," I replied, "but Dad wasn't. He was raised Catholic, but practically had to be dragged to church. In fact, sometimes he stayed home or went fishing."

"I think I'd have liked your old man," my husband said, grinning. "He sounds like my kind of guy. I forget — what did he do for a living?"

"Dad was a machinist. He worked mainly on boats that were moored in Lake Union. Mom was an accountant by trade. She stayed home, but kept the books for the neighborhood businesses in the small commercial area a couple of blocks away." I narrowed my eyes. "Come on, Sheriff. I told you all that years ago. You're fobbing me off about the victim."

Milo looked indignant. "No, I'm not. We talked to some of her co-workers, including Jason Campbell. She didn't have an active social life, but she was good-hearted, with a concern for homeless people. Rachel helped get housing for them, especially single mothers with kids."

"I suppose she was close to her adoptive parents."

"They're both dead," Milo said. "The

mother died three years ago of an aneurysm, and the father was a hit-and-run victim last October. No other children, only Rachel."

"Good grief! The Douglas family sounds hexed."

Milo looked unusually solemn. "I can almost believe they were."

Chapter 11

Driving to my office, I considered calling on the Alpine Falls Motel's Will Pace, but Mitch was touchy about any infringement on his assignments. Besides, I figured Will wouldn't tell me anything helpful. I only knew the motel owner by sight. He was a stumpy, gnomelike guy of the antisocial variety. I'd always wondered why he'd gotten into a people-oriented business. What little I knew about him was piecemeal, and if memory served, those pieces often didn't fit together. I decided to leave Pace up to Milo. He had more resources than I did.

Mitch was the only staffer on hand when I went into the newsroom. "Where are we with the homicide?" he asked. "Do you know anything I should know?" There was a hint of reproach in his voice.

"Only that the sheriff got a picture that shows her when she was still alive." I didn't go into details about the connection with the Campbell family. "You should probably take a look at it."

"I will." The faint reproach became self-righteous. "I'll do that now." Mitch grabbed his raincoat and was out the door.

I'd just sat down when Alison came in via the back shop. She didn't look happy. "What's wrong?" I asked.

"Lunch was a bummer," she announced in a doleful voice. "We'd just been seated when his roommate showed up. Boyd couldn't tell him to buzz off."

"Jeffrey?" It was the only thing I could think of to say.

"Jeffrey Nichols." Alison slid into a visitor's chair. "He's trying to find a job here. If he can't, maybe he'll move back to Wenatchee."

"Do you know what Jeffrey does for a living?"

Alison nodded faintly. "He's a graphic designer. Freelance. What if he can do his job no matter where he lives?"

"He might," I said, searching for words of comfort. "Jeffrey won't find much work here, but that means he'd have to travel to meet with clients."

"So? Wenatchee's ninety minutes away. He can do that in a day."

I couldn't cheer up Alison short of running over Jeffrey with my Honda, but I gave it one last shot. "You and Boyd will be living in the same complex. You're bound to see each other when you're both unencumbered. I'm sorry I had to assign the story to Mitch, but you know what he's like if he feels he's being shortchanged. Meanwhile, you're giving up on Boyd before he's settled in."

Alison appeared to think over what I'd just said. But then she asked, "What if he has a girlfriend in Wenatchee?"

"Then you'll have to forget about him." Seeing the hopeless look on Alison's face, I felt guilty. "How about the new paramedic? I think Janos Kadar is single."

Alison frowned. "He's got a weird name. Not," she went on, "that it means *he's* weird. Maybe I should check him out. How old is he?"

I tried to remember what the official announcement had said. I couldn't. Maybe his age hadn't been included. "Why don't you fall down and sprain an ankle? Then you could see him in person."

"I could think of something. Was there a photo with the story?"

"No. We only ran a couple of inches. But his name indicates he's part Hungarian. They're often good-looking. Slavic, dark, and lean."

"Interesting," she murmured as my phone rang. "Oh! I'd better get back to the front desk!" She sprang out of the chair and rushed away.

"Alma?" the male voice said, and I wondered if the caller had misdialed. But when he spoke again, I realized it was Leonard Hollenberg. "Violet told me she never heard of anybody named Danforth around here. My better half is pretty danged good about remembering names." That was a good thing, since her husband couldn't.

"It was a long shot," I admitted. "But thanks for checking with her."

"Not a problem," Leonard responded. "Say, when are you running Violet's story and the pictures of our trip to Leavenworth?"

I'd forgotten all about them, but in a flash, I realized that the former county commissioner had given me an idea for our special edition. "We're organizing a big section about SkyCo residents' recent travels and where they're planning to go this year. You and Violet will fit right in."

"I'll be danged! Glad to hear that, Erma. So will Violet. I'll tell her as soon as I hang up. If you need any more stuff from us, give me a ring."

I assured him I would, despite already hearing more than enough from Leonard. But having revealed my off-the-cuff idea, I'd actually have to do it. At least it might bring in enough advertising to cover the time and a half I'd paid my staff for working on MLK Jr. Day.

Shortly after four-thirty, I held an impromptu staff meeting to inform them of my idea. "We'll run a front-page boxed item in this week's edition asking readers to let us know of future travel plans and to submit photographs from their previous trips."

Mitch was the first to have a quibble. "Most people take color shots or make tapes. Won't that mean we have to spend more on reproduction?"

I glanced at Kip. "Will it?"

My production manager shrugged. "It depends on the quality and what they submit. Remember last summer when Arnie and Louise Nyquist went to Norway and sent us a bunch of fjord Polaroids? They looked like big cliffs. No water. We ran only one. Arnie should know better."

"I suspect Louise took those," I said. "Arnie was in three of them."

Leo laughed. "Maybe she tried to drown him. He can be a jackass."

I wasn't laughing. "Arnie and Milo have

never gotten along. Even when Nyquist Construction remodeled the sheriff's office, they had words, despite the fact that my husband was satisfied with the job."

Mitch shrugged. "I can see why. They're both prickly." He saw me stiffen and held out his hands in a helpless gesture. "No offense, Emma. But you know how I feel about Dodge after Troy was sent back to the reformatory when he had pneumonia."

"That was the state's decision," I declared. "They outranked Milo."

It was Liza who intervened, putting a hand on Mitch's arm. "You and Brenda must be looking forward to Troy coming home. Will he live with you or find a place of his own?"

The gesture and the words seemed to signal a truce. Leo was the first to turn away before Kip, Alison, and I moved on to our respective places. I wanted to hug Liza, but she was still talking to Mitch. It was now five minutes to five. There was no point in dwelling on my editorial, but I made a few notes that might kick-start me in the morning.

I drove home through part rain and part snow, focused on what to make for dinner. Meatballs, maybe. I was in that kind of mood. Almost before I could close the door to the garage, I heard the phone ringing in the living room. Trying not to stumble over my own feet, I rushed through the kitchen, flung myself down on the sofa, and grabbed the receiver.

"Hi, Mom," Adam greeted me. "Are you finished eating?"

"It's only ten after five," I said, panting a bit. "When are you going to remember the time change between here and St. Mary's Igloo in Alaska?"

"I won't have to," he replied. "The Home Missions are sending me to Michigan. I move to Gaylord, up on the Great Lakes, February third."

Managing to get myself into a more comfortable position, the only thing I could think of to say was "Michigan?"

"Right, way up north on the peninsula." He chuckled. "After being in this icebox, it'll seem like Florida."

"It sounds . . . remote," I said, then realized that Adam wasn't calling via radio relay from the isolated village less than a hundred miles from Asia. Our conversations from there were marred by frustrating delays between our exchanges. "Wait! Where are you? I can hear you just fine."

"Fairbanks," he replied. "I'm here for two days, winding up the business stuff. Then

I'll meet my replacement, Joe O'Leary. He's originally from Boston, but he knows Uncle Ben somehow. How is that rascal? I should call him after I finish talking to you. He's still on the Delta, right?"

"So far as I know. I haven't talked to him since the two of you were here for Christmas."

"I haven't either." Adam paused, and I could hear voices in the background. "Got to run. I didn't charge the call to your VISA this time. Say hi to Dodge for me. I'll stop over in Alpine on my way to Gaylord. I have to change planes in Seattle anyway. Love you, Mom." He hung up before I could say goodbye.

Adam. My son. My sole companion in the younger years of my adult life. Since he entered the priesthood, I was lucky to see him more than once a year, and rarely for longer than a few days. I was fighting back tears when the kitchen door banged open. A moment later, my husband thumped into the living room.

"Are we eating out?" he asked in a gruff voice.

"No." I hauled myself up from the sofa. "Adam just called. Are you going to kiss me or just bellow?"

"Damn." He tossed his hat onto the peg

by the wall and took me in his arms. "Is Adam okay?"

I nodded, locked my arms around his neck, and kissed him. "He's being transferred to Michigan's Upper Peninsula."

Milo kept his arms around me. "There's supposed to be some good fishing up there. Want to go visit him this summer?"

The suggestion surprised me. "There's good fishing in Alaska, but you never suggested going there."

"That's different," he said, releasing me. "Alaska's so damned big. I've only been up there twice, and the first time it was out of Juneau, in the southeastern part, and then over by Anchorage for the second trip. Neither of those places were anywhere near Adam's digs."

"True," I admitted, turning toward the kitchen. "Are you going to change or have a drink first? My initial impression was that you were . . . not at your best when you came home."

"I sure as hell wasn't," Milo replied, following me out of the living room. "Blackwell put Patti Marsh in the hospital this afternoon."

"She was sick . . . or . . . ?"

"Or," he said, opening the door to the

liquor stash. "He beat the crap out of her. Again."

"Why?" It was only a semistupid question, since Jack didn't always need a reason.

"I don't know." Milo paused to get out two glasses from the cupboard. "The only reason I found out about Patti is that Dwight Gould was fed up with hanging around the hospital and decided to liberate himself. Just as he was going out, Patti was coming in via ambulance. He could see that she was all banged up, so he asked her what had happened. All she said was 'Jack' before Del Amundson and Vic Thorstensen hustled her inside." He paused to hand me my drink. "If Patti finally has the guts to rat out Blackwell, that puts me in a helluva position. I'd have to bust my own boss since he's the county manager."

"You busted him once before," I reminded my husband.

Milo's hazel eyes regarded me with irony. "That was before his job was official. Even if two of the three original county commissioners were old as dirt and one of them — George Engebretsen — was already gaga. I suppose Leonard Hollenberg might have had my back, but so what?"

I looked up from peeling potatoes. "Leonard submitted a story today about their annual Christmas trip to Leavenworth. Violet wrote it."

"Are you going to put it in the paper?"

"I might," I replied, putting the potatoes on the stove. "Edited, of course. I decided our special edition would be about traveling Alpiners."

"That sounds like a folk music group from the sixties," Milo murmured — and headed back to the living room.

He was right. But readers would eat it up. While daily newspapers were fading away like the setting sun in the last scene of an old western movie, small-town weeklies still had a chance for survival. Alpine's semi-isolation was a plus for the *Advocate.* It wasn't quite true that everybody knew everybody else, but they generally knew *of* their eight thousand fellow SkyCo residents. I picked up my glass and was tempted to raise it in a toast to my fellow Alpiners, but the kettle with the potatoes was about to boil over. I had to yank it off the burner before turning down the heat. So much for my uncharacteristic whimsy. Even in a small mountain town, it didn't suit a cynical newspaper editor. I'd seen it all and reported most of it.

Except that it would turn out that I hadn't.

CHAPTER 12

Alison and I showed up for work at the same time Tuesday morning. As soon as we went inside, she informed me that her roommate, Lori Cobb, was coming down with a cold. "She insisted on going to work," Alison said, hanging up her jade-green hooded jacket on a peg in the wall. "If she gets worse, I'll insist on taking her to the clinic. I mean," she went on, not looking me in the eye, "what are friends for?"

"Of course," I agreed, deadpan. "If Lori gets worse this morning, feel free to leave anytime."

"Thanks. I appreciate that, Emma. You're a really good boss."

"I try," I said with a smile — and went into the newsroom.

Mitch was looking impatiently at the coffee urn, which was still burbling away. "Who has the bakery run?"

I had to think about it. "Kip. He's probably there now. His pickup's outside, so he must've nipped in here first to start the coffee."

Mitch gave a jerky nod. "Brenda didn't sleep well last night, so I stuck around to see if she could go back to sleep. She was still awake when I left, which means I didn't have any breakfast. After I go on my rounds, I'll swing by the house to see if she's okay." He paused as the coffeemaker went silent. "Ah! Finally. I didn't get any coffee, either." He kept talking while he filled his mug. "I don't suppose the sheriff has any leads about the Douglas woman's homicide."

Mitch's tone suggested Milo wouldn't have a lead if he caught the killer holding a severed head and sitting on the rest of the corpse. "He's gotten quite a bit of background on her. She seems to be an unlikely victim."

"Random?" Mitch said with a frown.

I wasn't sure how to answer him. Luckily, I didn't have to. Kip arrived with the Upper Crust goodies. He'd done well, bringing cinnamon rolls, two kinds of doughnuts, and sugar-covered twisters. I stepped aside as Leo and Liza Walsh seemed to race each other across the newsroom.

I waited for everybody else — except Alison, who remained at her desk out front plotting how to meet Janos Kadar — before fetching my coffee mug. On my way back to the newsroom, I stopped at Mitch's desk.

"I wonder," I said, "if you should take another shot at Will Pace. He's got to know more than he's admitted so far. Pace might open up with you. Try your Facing-Off-With-A-Detroit-Labor-Leader guise. You could persuade him to talk by saying you're doing a follow-up noting that this is the first time he's had a blemish on his motel."

Mitch turned thoughtful. "Surprising, really. Did Pace or the sheriff say how the killer got in?"

"No. Maybe the vic didn't lock her unit's door or she let the killer in. For all we know, she may have had the killer with her. Pace probably wouldn't have seen her enter the unit. She had a meal earlier, but apparently no one recalls seeing her at any of our local eateries."

"Right." Mitch nodded once. "Blackwell still insists he never heard of her. Do you think he's lying?"

"I don't know," I replied, but didn't add that Milo thought Jack was telling the truth. Mitch's antagonism for my husband would overshadow the admission.

"Okay," he said, having finished his pastry. "I'll head out on my rounds. I probably won't see Pace until after I check on Brenda."

"That's fine," I said. There wasn't much else I *could* say.

I was struggling with my editorial when Milo called just after eleven with the results of the Everett lab's autopsy report. "Nothing really new," he said. "She'd eaten around five-thirty, but it was fast food — burger, fries, coleslaw. That doesn't tell us much. My deputies haven't turned up anything from the local restaurants. She might've gone to a drive-through somewhere before getting to Alpine."

"No reports of anyone else seeing her after she asked Marlowe Whipp about Blackwell?"

"Not so far," Milo replied. "Except for Averill Fairbanks. He claimed he saw her arrive in a space capsule piloted by what looked like a giant purple grasshopper."

I sighed. "I know we have to rule out Blackwell killing her. We also can't consider that he had some underling do it. There was no time for Jack to arrange it. He probably didn't even know she was in town. Or who she was in the first place."

"Right. But," Milo went on, "somebody did."

I couldn't argue with that.

Just before noon, I decided to visit Patti Marsh in the hospital. Although we'd never been friends, she felt that there was some kind of bond between us. She had no other female friends, at least not since I'd known her. Patti's life was entirely focused on Jack Blackwell.

It was still raining, a cold, hard rain, so I drove the Honda up the steep hill to the hospital on Pine Street and turned into the underground parking area. Patient rooms were on the second floor. When I got off the elevator, I grimaced. My longtime nemesis, Ruth Sharp, was at the desk. I had to angle my way around the big stainless-steel container that I assumed held the patients' lunches. Ruth didn't look up at me until I'd been standing in front of her for at least thirty seconds.

"Yes?" Her tone sounded less like a question than a demand.

"I've come to see Ms. Marsh," I said in my most professional tone.

Ruth gently touched the white pleated cap on her graying hair. Doc Dewey followed his father's footsteps when it came to nurses attire. He insisted on traditional uniforms and caps. "I'm sorry. You can only see the patient during regular visiting hours. You do know when they are, Ms. Lord, correct?"

"I do," I replied, "but I'm up against deadline. Newspapers also have a schedule."

Ruth feigned puzzlement. "Doesn't the paper still come out on Wednesday afternoons?"

To be fair, Ruth wasn't the only one in Alpine who assumed it took only a couple of hours to produce, print, and deliver the *Advocate.* "Our deadline is five o'clock this afternoon," I said in my most professional voice. "The paper doesn't come off the press until the wee small hours Wednesday morning. If we have late-breaking news, it's sometimes around six A.M. before our production manager is finished."

Ruth looked unimpressed. "Then you should come back between two and four o'clock, when we have visiting hours. Our patients will be getting their lunches in just a few minutes. We don't like to have them disturbed while they're eating. So many of them have very little appetite, but they need to stay focused on their meals. Distractions are to be avoided."

I pretended to look thoughtful. "Well . . . having known Patti for over sixteen years, I think I know how to encourage her to eat her lunch. In fact," I went on, moving closer to the stainless-steel container, "I'll take it in to her and save you a trip."

Ruth looked almost bug-eyed. "That would violate . . ."

I smiled. "Hey, I know how hard you nurses work and don't get paid nearly as much as you should. In fact," I lied, "I plan to write an editorial later this month demanding raises for all of you here in SkyCo."

The almost bug-eyed look was replaced by shock. "Really?"

I shrugged. "You know you're all underappreciated. Think of what doctors make. It's not fair to you nurses. I should probably not only write the editorial, but do a series on how overworked and underpaid you are." Wondering how I could utter those words with a straight face, I headed down the hall, where I found Patti's name by the second door to the left.

She was slumped in bed with the TV showing a soap opera. Her eyes were closed, but I noticed that one of them was swollen. There was also a bruise on her left cheek and two more on her right arm. I set the tray down on the stand next to her bed before pulling up a visitor's molded plastic chair. I also picked up the TV remote and muted the sound.

After I sat down, I gently put my hand on

her shoulder. "Wake up, Patti. It's me, Emma Lord. Your lunch is here."

Between the damage Jack had caused and the lack of makeup, Patti looked at least ten years older. I'd always guessed her to be a few years younger than her abusive lover, but now I realized she was probably about the same age — sixty, I calculated. Of course, all the booze hadn't helped to retain her looks.

Painfully, she twisted her body under the blanket and forced her eyes open. The bruised eye was bloodshot, of course. I tried to keep smiling. "I delivered your lunch. How are you feeling?"

She was trying to sit up. I reached around to get an extra pillow that was on a shelf behind me. "Here," I said. "Let's use this to prop up your head."

It took some time and effort, but finally Patti seemed more comfortable. "You brought lunch? Where from?" she asked, sounding groggy. "Not here, I hope. Their food stinks."

I grimaced. "I had no choice. The nurse is kind of a hard case."

Patti made an effort at shrugging. "What the hell," she muttered. "I hate hospitals. Talk about grim!" Her effort to scrutinize me was marred by the bloodshot eye. "Why don't you nip out and get me a nip from the liquor store? Some of those little bottles, like they have on planes."

I shook my head, hoping I exhibited regret. "Booze would interfere with your meds and slow down recovery. I assume you want to get out of here as fast as you can."

She sighed, which made her wince. "Damn. I should leave right now. I heard that your big stud's deputy went AWOL from here. Maybe I'll do the same during the night."

"Don't, Patti," I said in a severe tone. "You need to stay here so you can get better." I saw her dubious expression and kept talking. "Do you know why the woman who was killed asked Marlowe Whipp how to find Jack?"

Patti's expression was blank. "I don't know anything about it. Marlowe's an idiot. Maybe he made it up. He's been mad ever since his convenience store went tits up and the wife of one of Jack's employees took it over. I don't know anything about the murder victim. Where did she come from? All I know is that she was offed at the crappy motel by the falls."

"Rachel Jane Douglas was from the Oakland area," I replied. "Is there any way she or her family members could have known Jack?"

"Shit, I can't see how. I don't think he ever lived in the Bay Area, just more up north in California. He left there . . ." She paused, apparently doing some basic math. "Thirty-five years ago, I guess. Jack doesn't keep in touch with anybody down there, not at least as long as I've known him."

"Not even relatives or old friends?"

Patti shook her head, which caused her to flinch. "He cut all his ties when he came north. Except for finding out that his first wife moved up here when that nut job place opened a year or so ago."

It took me a couple of beats to realize she was referring to RestHaven's Jennifer Hood. I wondered if Patti knew Jack and Jennifer had reunited briefly, if unhappily. Their tryst had ended when Jennifer stabbed him in the back in apparent revenge for how he'd treated her during their days in Dunsmuir, California. The wound wasn't serious, but Jack had spent two days in the hospital. He'd been too embarrassed to press charges.

I tried to think of any other reason Rachel might have wanted to see Blackwell. "Is Jack hiring right now?"

Patti shook her head. "He's full up. He hasn't taken on any new people except for some temporary gyppo loggers since he fired that punk who tried to shoot him." She gestured at the tray. "Hand me that slop. I guess I should eat something."

Apparently, Patti didn't know that Mickey O'Neill had escaped from prison. I didn't enlighten her. She had enough to cope with and would find out when she read the *Advocate* tomorrow. *If* she read the newspaper. My recollection was that her reading material consisted of celebrity magazines.

After helping her get settled with the tray, I stood up. "Take care of yourself, Patti. I'll call tomorrow to see how you're getting along."

She looked faintly surprised. "You do that, okay? This place is pretty lonesome."

I agreed that was how it tended to be in hospitals, and went on my way. Ruth Sharp gave me a curt nod as I passed her desk. I nodded back. When I got in the elevator, I wondered why Blackwell hadn't come to visit Patti on his lunch hour. I realized there had been no flowers in her room. By the time I got to the parking area, the answer came to me — I'd always known that Jack only cared about Jack.

But I still didn't know why he'd beaten up Patti.

■ ■ ■ ■

I arrived back at the office a little after one, having ordered more takeout from the Venison Inn. The all-white-meat turkey sandwich seemed a bit dry, but I reminded myself it was probably better than anything Patti had under those steel lids on her hospital tray.

I'd just finished eating when Leo poked his head in the doorway. "I followed through on Fleetwood's rumor about Panera Bread. It's a midwestern outfit, based in a suburb of St. Louis. They've only opened a handful so far in this state, usually in shopping malls. I'll give Spence a heads-up so he doesn't start any rumors."

"He won't," I said. "Just be grateful that he shares even rumors of possible advertisers with us. I stopped thinking of Spence as being our evil competitor after we started doing co-op ads. He's kept his word. And you've been great about returning the favor."

Leo lifted his shaggy eyebrows. "All nine of them in the last year?"

"Nine is better than none," I reminded him. "I still shudder when I think how Ed Bronsky tried *not* to sell ads because it meant that dirty four-letter word — *w-o-r-k* — to him. I really thought the *Advocate* might go broke my first two, three years after I bought the paper."

Leo grinned. "Speaking of Ed, I ran into him at Cal's Chevron this noon. The state won't let him put up his billboard on Highway 2. I guess that stymies his idea of being Alpine's spokesperson. Did he really believe that County Manager Blackwell would shell out big bucks for that?"

"Ed believes many things, mostly about Ed. If Shirley hadn't gotten that teaching job at the grade school, they'd starve. I'm waiting for him to put his two older kids to work. They're both taking classes at Skykomish Community College, but I don't think they have part-time jobs."

"The college *does* have some job openings for students. Don't you read our classified and personals ads?" he asked in mock dismay.

"Honestly? No." I laughed. "Do you read my editorials?"

Leo's grin was faintly apologetic. "It depends."

"Touché. That's what I figured."

"Oh," Leo said, "I got a call a little while ago from some guy who wanted to know what was going on with the murder investigation. Alison must have been away from her desk, but I told him to call you or Mitch. He didn't leave a name or number."

"Better he should call Mitch," I murmured, glancing at my reporter's vacant desk. "He's the best reporter I've ever had, but the prima donna stuff gets annoying."

Leo patted my arm. "You had to put up with me when I started here and was still drinking too much. Liza thinks you should be canonized."

"I'd have to be dead to get the halo," I pointed out. "By the way, was there anything weird or obscene in the personals this time around?"

"No. All one hundred percent pure. Are you still smarting from the one before Christmas that had the typo?"

"I think I'm over it," I replied. But it would probably haunt me forever. The man who had submitted the personal ad had been very upset about his lack of success finding a woman who wasn't after his money. In his apparent haste to finish the ad, he had declared that he was "no longer willing to be a sucker for gold diggers." In our frenzy of putting the paper together the day after Christmas, none of us noticed that "sucker" had been spelled with an *f.* We'd received calls and letters until two days into the new year.

Leo had started to turn around, but stopped. "Say, do you remember if there was any feedback about that personals ad back in early December about someone the writer was trying to track down?"

I had to stop and think. The first week of December seemed like a long time ago. I couldn't even remember the name, though I'd asked Vida, of course. She'd thought about it in her usual conscientious, Alpine-Encyclopedia way, but for once she'd come up empty. "No. Maybe whoever it was got an answer from someone who didn't contact the person via the newspaper. Not knowing who placed it in the first place, I'm guessing it came from a local who was contacted in person or by phone."

Leo nodded. "Probably. Or it was a weird whim on the part of the person who placed the ad. The holidays are a great time for people to wallow in nostalgia."

I agreed, and Leo returned to his desk. It didn't occur to me that the personals submission might return to haunt us.

The heavy rain had some snow in it when I drove home. Approaching our driveway, I saw an old, beat-up Mazda parked on the street's verge with its rear end abutting our property and almost blocking the driveway.

Obviously, the driver was visiting my disreputable Nelson neighbors. Not wanting to take any chances, I slowed down to see if I could spot anyone lurking around our cozy log cabin or in the garage. To my relief, there was no sign of an intruder, so I pulled off the street, drove up the driveway, and parked the Honda in its usual spot.

I had dinner started by the time Milo arrived twenty minutes later. "Snow's coming down harder now," he said after kissing me. "I checked the weather and we could get three, four inches tonight. I hope everybody stays home. Then I can, too."

"Maybe the Nelson women's company will take off," I said, getting down the liquor bottles. "They're crazy enough to party on a weeknight."

Milo scowled at me. "What company?"

"Whoever owns the beater that was parked so close to . . ." I paused, seeing my husband's puzzled expression. "I know it's dark, but didn't you notice that old Mazda?"

He shook his head. "There was no car out there."

"Oh." I shrugged. "Whoever it was must've left. Do you want to change before we have our drinks?"

"No. I'm waiting on the weather. I may get called out. De Groote's on duty this evening, but I want to keep her in town. She doesn't have the experience to chase speeders on Highway 2 in snow. We're shorthanded. If it gets bad, I've got to be ready to roll."

I managed to suppress the urge to say that De Groote should learn to get used to it. We took our drinks into the living room, though I paused to peek around the picture window's drapes, which I'd closed after coming home. "It *is* a lot thicker. The grass is already almost covered. Maybe I should tell Kip to post late-breaking weather warnings."

Milo looked up from the TV sports listings he'd been studying. "Like what? 'It's snowing really hard'? I think most of the folks who live in SkyCo can figure that out for themselves."

"Funny sheriff," I muttered, and flopped down on the sofa. "I did my good deed today and saw Patti Marsh at the hospital."

"How gruesome was it?" he asked — and, to my dismay, he lighted a cigarette.

"Milo!" I screeched. "How many have you smoked today?"

"Four, counting this one." He exhaled and had the gall to form a smoke ring. "Now tell me about Patti."

I did, and by the time I'd wrapped up the

account of my visit, he'd finished his cigarette. "So," my aggravating husband said, "it sounds as if she still won't turn Blackwell in. He's going to have to kill her before we can nail the bastard. Speaking of jerks who beat up women, who's living in the Nelson house these days? I know that Doyle and the oldest son are still in the slammer for the tree-poaching on Blackwell's timber parcel. The two younger ones got off too easy for trying to set this place on fire. Nelson and the older kid won't be released until early spring, but I can't picture LaVerne going very long without a man. I haven't seen any sign of the daughter-in-law and the little tyke, though."

"Sofia and the baby, Chloe — a toddler by now — are still there as far as I know. I wondered for a while if they'd moved in with their relatives in Index, but I noticed after the big maple trees lost their leaves that I could see a light on over there after dark."

"They must get by on welfare," Milo remarked. "Unless they're hooking. But we'd see more cars parked on the verge like the one you saw tonight. They have no garage or even a driveway. That pickup and the old Nova take up all the open space."

I agreed, and stood up. "I think dinner's

ready. Give me three minutes to dish up."

Milo nodded and returned to perusing the sports listings. I'd just gone into the kitchen when I heard the faint sound of a siren. By the time I'd poured the water out of the kettle that held the potatoes, I realized there were at least two sirens and they were coming closer. And closer.

I set the kettle down on the counter and poked my head into the living room. Milo was on his cell but getting to his feet.

"Right," he said in a rueful voice. "I'll meet you there, Sam."

"Where?" I asked, a little breathless as he put on his regulation jacket.

"The frigging neighbors. Who else? Mickey O'Neill was in that Mazda. He beat the crap out of LaVerne and kidnapped Sofia. That's the second time he's hauled her off. Put dinner on hold." He slammed out of the house.

I was left holding the potatoes.

CHAPTER 13

As the local newspaper publisher, it didn't seem right that I should be standing in the kitchen with a bunch of boiled spuds. But I didn't have much choice. Sheriff Go-by-the-Book would kick my butt out of the Nelson house faster than I could say "Who? What? Where? When? and Why?"

I was not without resources, however. I set the kettle on the counter and called Mitch. He answered after four rings. But my reporter's reaction was initially discouraging.

"Damn, Emma, Brenda and I just started dinner. She's better and felt like she could eat something. Aren't those Nelsons your neighbors?"

"Define neighbors," I said through gritted teeth. "At any rate, the sheriff is overly protective of his wife."

"Well . . ." Mitch paused, and I realized that he was speaking for Brenda's benefit and not mine. "If I have to, I'll see what I can do." He rang off.

I was tempted to go outside and try to peer through the bushes, but the snow was really coming down. When I opened the back door — which had been added when we remodeled the previous year — I checked the thermometer that had moved outside after the garage was enclosed. It was twenty-eight degrees. My nose for news was suddenly dulled, and I quickly closed the door before it got frostbitten. Milo would — I hoped — fill me in unless he pulled one of his I-can't-tell-you-because-it's-part-of-an-ongoing-investigation bits on me.

Unfortunately, there was no way I could keep my eye on the Nelson property from inside the house. There were no windows to the west except for the one that looked into the garage. Worse yet, I was getting hungry, but I wouldn't eat until Milo was finished with whatever mayhem was going on next door. What I could do was call Kip to tell him to hold open some space on the *Advocate*'s front page.

Kip's reaction was predictable. "The wild Irishman and your no-class neighbors? You and Dodge should build a wall between your house and the Nelsons'."

"We'd prefer they left town — permanently," I replied. "Move the story about the upcoming college play production to page three. It's not opening until mid-February. If we're still too tight, we can save it for next week."

"Got it," Kip said. "Will Mitch come here or send it from home?"

"No clue." I heard the signal that another call was coming through and told Kip I'd better take it. It might be Milo giving me a heads-up.

I was wrong. It was Viv Marsden, my neighbor to the east. "What's going on, Emma? Val and I heard the sirens, and they were so close that we wondered if you had a problem. It's snowing so hard that we can't see beyond the fence between us. In fact, we can't see the fence."

"It's the Nelson gang," I informed her, and related the bare facts.

Viv groaned. "They've been nothing but trouble since they moved in. I remember when they showed up about five years before you came here. The house had been vacant until then. We never did know who lived there before the Nelsons moved in. For all I know, that bunch may be squatters."

"That's possible," I allowed. "Remember that old house down the other way that had been abandoned in the eighties? I heard that squatters took it over and managed to burn it to the ground."

"I vaguely recall that," Viv said. "Val had just been transferred here by the state fisheries department. We lived in the Clemans Apartments for over a year before we bought this house. We never did know the family that used your log cabin when they came up here to ski in the winter. They spent all their time on the slopes."

Before I could respond, I heard a siren close by. "That sounds like LaVerne's going to the hospital. I'll update you after I hear from Milo."

I'd barely set the phone down when there was a knock at the front door. Checking through the peephole, I saw Mitch shaking snow off the overcoat that had served him well in frigid Detroit winters when he worked for *The Free Press.* Instead of the black fedora he wore on rainy days, his gray hair was covered by a navy-blue cap Brenda had made on her loom. When his wife wasn't ailing, she made a living as a weaver.

Mitch declined my offer of a chair. "I've got to go home, so I'll write the story from there, but I wanted to give you a heads-up. The sheriff is leaving for headquarters to file his report."

I noticed that Mitch didn't call Milo by name, an indication that his ill will toward my husband was still intact. "What about LaVerne?" I asked.

"Broken nose, a couple of loose teeth, a sprained arm, and possible internal injuries," Mitch replied. "Or so Heppner informed me."

In other words, Mitch hadn't talked to Milo. "Nothing about Mickey O'Neill and Sofia? What about poor little Chloe?"

"You mean the little kid?" Mitch saw me nod. "She's fine and will be taken to the Children's Protective Services shelter in the courthouse. No clue about O'Neill and the Nelson daughter-in-law."

I nodded. "Not surprising." I considered mentioning that Mickey had probably taken Sofia to the ramshackle O'Neill home on First Hill, but decided to let my reporter figure that out for himself. It was his story, after all. "Thanks, Mitch, I appreciate you bringing me up to speed."

"No problem. See you tomorrow, Emma."

I stood in the doorway, watching him disappear into the snow. It was still coming down so hard that I could only see the first few footprints he left behind him. Maybe that was just as well. It meant I couldn't see anything beyond the edge of our driveway.

The Nelson house might not have existed. Except for little Chloe, I wished it never had.

I immediately called the Marsdens and brought them up to speed. "It's not fair that we can't watch this in real time," Val said. "Has Fleetwood shown up to do a live broadcast?"

"Maybe," I replied. "He's got a police scanner. I've only got the sheriff and he's not back yet."

Val chuckled. "One more reason we're glad you married Dodge. We don't always have to wait for Fleetwood's breaking news. Stay warm. I think we're really in for it tonight."

Reluctantly, I tuned in to KSKY on the radio in the living room. Spence's engineer was playing country-western classics. Merle Haggard was finishing up "Working Man's Blues," followed by Dolly Parton's "If I Needed You" and Waylon Jennings's "Lonesome, Ornery and Mean." I was starting to feel a little ornery, too, when the songs were followed by Spence's recorded sixty-second ad for Stuart's Sound, our local retail source for all things musical. But then came Mr. Radio, live and direct.

After identifying himself as The Voice of Skykomish County, he told his listening audience where he was: "I'm here at Sheriff Milo Dodge's headquarters, where he and Deputies Sam Heppner and Consuela De Groote have been investigating a domestic incident and possible kidnapping at a home in northwest Alpine. Names have not yet been released, but stay tuned to KSKY, your favorite radio station on the western slope of the Cascade Mountains."

Spence's last words sounded as if he were speaking through clenched teeth. I wanted to laugh, but I quickly realized that if Milo wasn't allowing Spence to name the people involved just yet, he wouldn't want me doing it, either. I dialed Kip's number to tell him to hold off on the Nelson story.

"Why?" was the first word out of my backshop manager's mouth. "Won't it be in the log tomorrow morning?"

I allowed that it would, but I wanted to preserve a happy home. "I assume Mitch has sent it to you?"

"About ten minutes ago," Kip replied. "No names, of course, just the usual vague location unless charges are filed. I was just about to put it on the front page. Mitch's headline is 'Two Women Victimized in Domestic Dispute.' It takes up almost as much space as the story."

"It might go longer if Milo unloads when

he gets home," I said. "He must be really hungry by now." I winced at the prospect of my husband's mood when he finally got here.

"Okay," Kip responded. "Don't worry. I'm right on schedule." With that upbeat note, he rang off.

I decided I'd use the idle time to write a letter to my brother, Ben. I would have called him, but it was well after seven and he was two hours ahead of us on the Mississippi Delta. If he didn't have a meeting, Ben would probably be making an early night of it because he had to get up to say Mass at whichever church he was headed for in the morning.

I was just signing off a little after seven-thirty when I heard the Yukon pull into the garage. Hurrying out to the kitchen, I decided to dish up dinner and put our plates in the microwave. Milo came in just as I set the timer.

"Holy shit," he exclaimed, removing his hat. "I had to call in Blatt and Jamison to check out what's left of the O'Neill house, but Mickey and the girl aren't there. No sign of the Mazda, either."

I followed Milo into the living room, where he was hanging up his jacket and hat on the pegs by the front door. "Where else would they go?"

"Damned if I know. I've got an APB out on them."

"Poor Sofia," I murmured. "She can't be very bright to have gotten mixed up with Mickey in the first place."

"Not your problem," Milo said, grabbing my rear as I led the way back to the kitchen.

I didn't ask any more questions until after I removed our dinner from the microwave and we sat down. "I gather LaVerne will survive?"

"She's built like a Sherman tank. Her injuries weren't all that serious." Milo paused to wolf down a chunk of rib-eye steak. "No names will be given out unless charges are filed. You know the drill."

"What if they find out there are internal injuries?"

Milo shrugged. "Then LaVerne might follow through and want to press charges. Meanwhile, she can stay in the hospital with Patti Marsh and they can commiserate about the macho men in their lives."

"How did Consi handle her first encounter with violence in Alpine?"

"Get serious," Milo shot back. "You think she's not a veteran of that crap? Coming from Tacoma? She's probably dealt with more domestic calls in her eight years on the job than I have in my thirty-plus here in SkyCo."

"I suppose that's true," I said, sounding a bit sheepish. I changed the subject. "Why did Consi decide to come to Alpine?" I asked.

Milo finished chewing a big bite of steak. "Tired of the city. She was raised on a farm somewhere around Puyallup. She's not the type who talks about personal stuff when she's on the job. That's fine with me. I get enough of that stuff when Mullins goes on about the so-called 'discussions' he and Nina have over little things like a burned-out lightbulb."

"That could be a problem if they didn't have a replacement," I said in my most guileless voice.

Milo just stared at me and shoveled in more steak.

By morning, the snow had stopped, leaving almost eight inches on the ground. Milo hadn't set the alarm for his usual six-thirty wake-up call, which meant I was still asleep at seven-fifteen when he came out of the bathroom to get dressed.

"You made me late," I grumbled, struggling with the covers to get out of bed.

"If you weren't tired, you would've woken

up at your usual time," he said in a reasonable voice. "Isn't Wednesday the day the paper comes out?"

I attempted to glare at him, but my eyes were still foggy with sleep. Either my mate enjoyed teasing me about the *Advocate*'s publication schedule or he really didn't know. I preferred believing the former.

"Right," I muttered, staggering toward the other bathroom. During the remodeling, we'd added the second bathroom, which became Milo's, while I retained the original.

"Then you can take it easy at work today, right?"

"Right." I kept going. Neither of us was very social in the morning.

After getting dressed and applying my makeup, I found Milo in the kitchen pouring a mug of coffee. "How am I going to drive to work?"

Milo stared at me. "What did you do last year or the year before or . . ." He peered at me more closely. "You're not awake yet. Get yourself some java and think about what you just said."

"Oh." He was right. "I guess I managed, huh?"

"You did." He began to make his usual hearty breakfast of two fried eggs, bacon, and toast. I always settled for cornflakes, not being sure that I wouldn't set myself on fire in my morning stupor. As I sat down at the table, Milo glanced at me over his shoulder.

"You can go to work with me," he said. "No point in taking two vehicles. Besides, I'm not sure you're fully conscious."

"What if I have to drive somewhere to do an interview?"

Milo flipped his bacon. "Send Laskey. That guy's so gloomy, he needs to keep busy or he might have a meltdown. His wife's already nuts."

"Brenda's not nuts," I declared. "She does have some emotional problems. You might, too, if one of your kids was in jail."

"They're not." Milo dished up his breakfast and sat down. "Despite the divorce, all my kids kept out of real trouble. Mike made that stupid marriage right out of high school, but I figure she did it to convince herself she wasn't gay. Now that she's got a partner, Mike's a lot looser and easier to be around. Tanya's feeling a lot better, and Bran's always been solid."

"Lucky you," I said wistfully. "Your kids are close by. Adam hasn't lived near me since he started college. I'll never have grandchildren."

"You can be a stepgrandma when Bran

and Solange have their baby," Milo said. His hazel eyes sparked. "Mulehide's not thrilled about being a grandmother. She thinks it makes her seem too old."

"That's ridiculous," I declared. "Vida told me that before I bought the paper she once interviewed a thirty-one-year-old woman from Startup who was a grandmother."

Milo shrugged. "Why not? There's not much to do in Startup except screw."

"That," I responded, "is what the young woman told Vida."

CHAPTER 14

The Yukon managed to plow its way through what seemed like a foot of snow in some places, but living on a mountainside could be deceptive. I figured that some three inches had fallen since yesterday, for a total of almost double what we had when I came home from work. When we stopped in front of the *Advocate,* Milo offered to carry me inside, but I declined, reminding him that he'd done that once before and tongues had wagged for days.

Alison greeted me when I came through the door, but she looked a bit glum and immediately announced there had been no further Boyd sightings. "Do you think he's avoiding me?" she asked in a dismal tone.

"I think he's probably busy," I replied. "He's new to the job. Dean Ramsey is probably breaking him in."

"How long should that take?" Alison asked with a sour expression. "I've never known what a county extension agent does."

"Whatever it is, it has to do with farming," I informed her. "I admit, it's not a job that gets into the paper very often."

Alison seemed determined to prolong the conversation. "We don't have many farms around Alpine. I can only think of two."

"There are several smaller farms in the western part of the county. You have to follow Tonga Road out of town to see them."

"I guess I've never been . . ." Alison's phone rang. I escaped into the newsroom.

Liza and Mitch were on hand, waiting for the coffee urn to finish perking. Leo hadn't shown up with the pastries yet. My priority was to check out how the latest edition of the *Advocate* looked. Kip had signed out at four thirty-five A.M. to take the papers to their various distribution points in the county. Most of our carriers were kids, which meant an after-school delivery to subscribers. We also had some former Alpiners who still liked to see what was going on in the town they'd once called home. Kip would put preprinted mailing addresses on their copies and drop them off at the post office. He usually didn't return to the back shop until afternoon. Now in his early thirties, he'd begun as a carrier in his teens only a year or so after I bought the newspaper. He was also the one who posted online updates. If I had to be candid, Kip was probably my most valuable employee. Of course, I could never say that out loud.

Flipping through the pages, everything looked good. Ten minutes later the pastries arrived with a disgruntled-looking ad manager. "My wife," he said with a quick glance in her direction, "isn't fond of snow. She wants you to write an editorial demanding that it be outlawed."

I looked at Liza, who'd been giving her husband the evil eye. "I could write the editorial, but I don't think it would stop the snow. We actually have had a winter or two since I've been here when we hardly had any. Global warming, they tell us."

Liza had moved toward the cinnamon rolls her husband was setting out. "Leo did mention an occasional flurry now and then. But this must be closer to a foot. It comes over the top of my winter boots."

"It drifts," I pointed out. "There's a bit of wind, and because Alpine is located on a mountainside, the ground is sort of . . . uneven."

"So I've noticed," Liza said, but there was a glint of humor in her blue eyes. "Mrs. Runkel told me that many years ago Alpine had as much as eight feet of snow on the ground and the children had to tunnel their way up to the school. Was she trying to make me go back to California?"

I laughed. "No, but that's true of the town's early days. The only way in and out of here was via train. The road wasn't built until the Civilian Conservation Corps came along in the nineteen-thirties."

Liza shook her head. "It's a wonder the people who lived here back then didn't go crazy. What did they do to keep sane in winters like that?"

"They were inventive," I replied. "There were never more than around two hundred residents until the thirties, but they invited speakers, put on plays, had concerts . . ." Pausing, I pointed to the bookcase beyond the door to the back shop. "They also put out an annual booklet to sum up each year's activities. You might want to look through them sometime."

"Maybe I will," Liza said, glancing at her husband, who was on the phone. "Has Leo done that?"

"I don't think so," I admitted. "But he's absorbed the history over the years. Alpiners are proud of their hardy past."

Liza nodded faintly. "I thought he was insane when he took the job up here. But it turned out to be a blessing. Alpine sobered him up. I'm grateful to the town for that — and to you."

I shook my head. "He did it on his own."

She'd taken a bite of the cinnamon roll and looked thoughtful. "Maybe. The important thing is that, one way or another, he did it." Liza smiled softly and moved off to her desk.

I did the same, sitting down and taking a more thorough look at the latest edition. One item I didn't always check before publication was the personals advertising, which fell to Leo, of course. Most of the postings were from love-starved readers seeking romance. Some were amusing, but most were touching. The first was "Lonely widow with few bad habits wishes to meet widower in same boat." I smiled, hoping the boat didn't leak. Another was similar, except the roles were reversed. What caught my eye was a different kind of message: "Anyone in Skykomish County knowing the whereabouts of Piper Erskine please contact J. L. Erskine at P.O. Box 645, Hardin MT 59034."

There was something vaguely familiar in the message, but I couldn't figure out what it was. Vida might know. I turned on the intercom to ask Alison if our former House & Home editor was coming in today.

"Mrs. Runkel just called," Alison informed me. "Her daughter Amy is being admitted to the hospital this morning. Apparently she's emotionally overwrought. At least that's how her mother describes her."

I held my head. "It beats 'crazy as a loon,' " I said — and immediately felt ashamed of myself. "I suppose Vida will stay at their house with Dippy. I imagine Ted's back in town, though he probably can't take more than a day or two off. He must have to catch up with work here. Amy and her sisters may resemble their mother physically, but they lack her backbone."

"Poor Mrs. Runkel," Alison responded. "She's gone through a rough patch lately. I hope she doesn't end up in the hospital, too."

I agreed, and caught myself before I added that Alpine Memorial was in danger of running out of beds. I felt frustrated. The only person I could think of who might know of a Piper Erskine was Vida. But she'd be focused on Amy — and Dippy. I'd try to call her after her daughter was settled in at the hospital.

I wasn't the only one with Vida on my mind. A little after ten, Spencer Fleetwood walked through the now-empty newsroom and parked himself in my office.

"I assume," he said, straightening the creases on his charcoal wool slacks, "you've heard from our favorite absentee. Do you have news of Vida?"

"Only about Amy," I said. "Maybe Vida is hedging her bets. Amy is a weak link in the Runkel chain. I don't know the other daughters, but I suspect they're also shadows of their redoubtable mother."

Spence shrugged and leaned forward a bit. "Dare I be brash and ask you to replace Vida tomorrow night?"

"Me?" I literally fell back in my chair. "No!"

"Is that a refusal or just shock?" He didn't wait for an answer. "You'd be a natural substitute. You can promote the paper and whatever else is buzzing around in your fertile brain. You could even say something laudatory about your brutish husband."

I sat up very straight. "You two should reestablish cordial relations. It's been over a year since he slugged you for making an unsavory remark about him kissing me on a street corner. It all sounds so high school on both sides."

Spence looked faintly embarrassed. "It was. I suppose I was trying to loosen up your beloved. Someone told me after I arrived in Alpine that you and he had been off and on for almost ten years. And then . . ." He stopped. "Never mind. I don't want to upset you."

I smiled. "Mentioning Tom Cavanaugh's name doesn't bother me, Spence. I'm way past that. But you were very kind to me right after Tom was killed. I appreciated that. Thank you again."

"You and I have been through the mill, as the locals say." He, too, was smiling, though a bit ruefully. "You and your bear returned the favor when Rosalie's husband died."

Spence and Rosalie Reed, the head of RestHaven's psych ward, had become lovers long before the facility had opened a little over a year ago in Alpine. Rosalie's husband had suffered from mental illness for many years. Somehow, he'd managed to escape the previous winter. Before he could be found, Rosalie's husband had suffered a fatal heart attack.

Now officially a couple, Mr. Radio and Dr. Reed had bought a house on River Road. I refrained from asking Spence if they planned to get married. Maybe I didn't have the nerve, since it had taken Milo and me almost sixteen years to make our relationship legal.

"It was a sad way to end what had once been his highly respected career as a shrink,"

I said. "Is their son still at UCLA?"

Spence nodded. "Cliff's going for his master's in cinema. He wants to make informational films. We'd invited him up here for Christmas, but his girlfriend insisted he go with her to meet her parents in Santa Rosa."

"It sounds serious," I remarked.

"It does," Spence agreed. "Rosalie wants us to fly down to meet her, but I don't like leaving the station for more than a couple of days." He stood up with an eye on the crease in his slacks. The creases had behaved themselves. "Well? Are you game for tomorrow night?"

I grimaced. "I'll think about it, okay? I'd really prefer not to, but if you . . . Hey, what about Liza Walsh? She's new to Alpine and would be a refreshing change of pace from the usual guests."

Spence lifted one cashmere-covered shoulder. "Maybe. Why don't you approach her first? I've never met Ms. Walsh."

"I will," I promised. "She's smart and has a sense of humor."

"Then I shall leave you to do my dirty work." Spence made a little bow, no doubt checking his creases once more. They were still in place.

■ ■ ■ ■

Liza didn't return to the office until almost noon. Leo was gone and Mitch was on the phone. I asked her to have lunch with me, but she showed off her dimples and turned me down.

"I'm trying to lose some weight," she explained. "All the walking I do on this job helps, but I've still got at least ten pounds to go. When I hit a hundred and thirty, I'll take you up on your offer."

"It's a deal. How would you feel about making your radio debut?"

Liza looked startled. "You've gone multimedia without telling us?"

I laughed a bit feebly. "No, no. Spencer Fleetwood — I don't think you've met him — owns KSKY. He'd like to interview you in what was Vida's Thursday-evening spot tomorrow night." I went on to tactfully explain that our former House & Home editor had a family problem and wouldn't be able to host her show. "Leo took his turn on the program a few years ago," I added, omitting that Liza's husband was not a Fleetwood fan.

"Well . . ." Liza pressed her lips together. "Do you think I should?"

"It's good publicity for the paper, and more to the point, it gives you exposure as Vida's replacement. If she decides to stop doing her show, you'd be a natural to fill the void. Assuming you'd want to, of course."

Liza pondered briefly. "I'll ask Leo what he thinks, okay?" It was her turn to laugh. "I'm still adjusting to our reconciliation. As he puts it, we're on our second honeymoon."

"Fair enough." I was liking our new employee more every day.

I decided to see if my husband would join me for lunch. The sidewalks had been cleared, but a few flakes were still drifting from the low gray clouds. Traffic moved at a slower pace than usual, though there was a lot of dirty slush left by the vehicles' tires. I saw the Yukon parked in its usual place, so I assumed Milo was in his office.

Lori Cobb told me he was indeed there but was a bit grumpy. I feigned disbelief. Jack Mullins, who had just come from the jail section of the building, gave me a sardonic grin.

"Your old man's giving Gould hell for coming back to work when he's still obviously ailing," Jack informed me. "I can't figure out if the boss man's worried about Dwight's health or afraid of our brave deputy collapsing during a traffic stop and letting the perp get away."

"Dwight has no interests in life except his job and fishing," I said. "Any sign of Mickey O'Neill and the Nelson girl?"

Jack had sat down at his desk as Lori put on her jacket and headed outside, apparently for lunch. "No," the deputy replied to my query. "We wonder if that means they never left town. If they're not at that old dump his family owned on First Hill — and we checked, of course — where else would they be? The car hasn't been sighted, either."

"Maybe they found another abandoned dump," I suggested. "There are several around here on the edges of town, especially out on the Burl Creek Road. One or two of them might even have a garage."

"Dodge has De Groote checking . . ." Jack stopped as Milo and Dwight came out of the sheriff's office.

"Saddle up, Mullins," Milo ordered. "You're taking Gould's place on highway patrol. I don't want him having a relapse. He'll take over on the desk."

Jack grimaced before he turned around to salute his boss. "Aye aye, sir. I hope I brought my mittens." He grabbed his jacket, nodded at me, and went on his way.

A wan-looking Deputy Gould eased his short, squat body into the vacated chair. He ignored my presence. That suited me just fine. Dwight always assumed I only visited his boss when I was short of grocery money.

I stood up to address my husband. "Are you eating in or out?"

"In," he replied, approaching me and hauling out his wallet. "The usual. Make sure the bacon on the burger is crisp."

"Hold it!" I shrieked. "I don't work here. Why didn't you ask Lori to get your lunch? She just left. Call her at the Burger Barn and tell her to get your order — and mine. Do you want me to starve to death?"

Milo had the grace to look chagrined. "Okay." He glanced at the phone on Lori's desk. "You call her. I don't know what you want."

"Yes, you do," I muttered, but not wanting to cause a domestic scene, I went over to Lori's desk. Milo retreated to his office. I thought I saw Dwight sneer, probably at me. He respected his boss.

I was checking for Lori's cell number when I heard a distant siren, probably out on Highway 2. Snow had started to fall, which meant there was probably an accident and the state patrol was on the scene. Finding Lori's number, I dialed it — and a nearby phone rang. I looked down at her desk, heard the ringing again, and saw her cell peeking out from under a letter from the state fish and game department. Milo's door was ajar, so I opened it all the way to tell him I'd fetch our lunches in person. He was on the phone, looking grim and motioning for me to come in. "I'm on my way," he said to whoever was at the other end. "Yes, the ambulance should get there before I do. See you at the scene." He rang off.

"What scene?" I asked as he grabbed his jacket and hat before almost pushing me out of the way to get through the door.

"The scene near Baring where Vida wrecked her Buick. She's on her way to the hospital. You'd better be there to meet her. It sounds as if she's in a bad way."

I suddenly felt bad, too. And scared. But Vida was indomitable.

Wasn't she?

All I could do was silently pray as I rushed out of the sheriff's headquarters — and then realized I didn't have a car.

Chapter 15

I had no choice but to walk uphill to the hospital. Fortunately, the sidewalk had been cleared and the snow was still only a few lazy flakes. Better yet, there was almost no wind.

But my hand was shaking when I opened the heavy glass door. The last sound that I heard before I went inside was of a siren as an ambulance approached the emergency entrance on Third Street. I paused, seeing Jenny Bjornson behind the main desk. I knew Jenny and her parents fairly well. Just after Christmas, Vida had noted in "Scene" that Jenny had gotten engaged to a young man from Startup. I had to press my lips together to avoid revealing any sign of my worst fears.

Jenny was on the phone. When she saw me, her blue eyes widened. When she hung up, she said, "You already heard about Mrs. Runkel?"

I nodded. "I was at the sheriff's office when the call came in," I replied. "Did the ambulance attendant give you any information?"

Jenny shook her head. "They never do, really, unless they need a crash cart when the ambulance pulls in. I probably won't hear anything about her status until they put her in a room. Did you know her daughter was admitted just an hour or two ago?"

"Yes. I wonder if they can put Mrs. Runkel and Mrs. Hibbert in the same room."

Jenny grimaced. "That doesn't always work so well. Mrs. Lila Blatt and Mrs. Mary Lou Blatt — Mrs. Runkel's sisters-in-law — were in the same room a year or so ago. They didn't get along very well at all."

I recalled the incident. Lila had slammed a walker into Mary Lou's ankle cast. Mary Lou had retaliated by pouring the water out of a bouquet Lila's son Bill had sent her and then throwing the flowers out the window. Vida couldn't stand either of them and had gloated for days.

"Is Amy Hibbert in a private room?"

"Let me check," Jenny said, turning to her computer monitor. "No, she has a roommate, Mary Smith. I believe she's an older woman who lives farther down Highway 2.

Mrs. Smith was admitted Tuesday night. Her husband is here somewhere. His first name is John. Should we believe that?"

I shrugged. "There could be a dozen Mary and John Smiths in Skykomish and Snohomish Counties. You must have a lot of patients here now," I remarked.

Jenny shrugged. "It's that time of year. We always get overloaded right after the holidays, especially with elderly people. We only have one vacancy left for a woman. If we get any more female patients, we'll have to send them to the hospital in Monroe. Mrs. Runkel will be put in with Mrs. Marsh after her condition is evaluated."

I felt as if a load of TNT had exploded in my head. I didn't want to think about how Vida would react to rooming with Patti Marsh. But then I didn't want to think about Vida having to be hospitalized in the first place. Of course, I had to; that's why I had come. I posed a question to Jenny. "How soon will you know anything about Mrs. Runkel's condition?"

Jenny looked again at her monitor. "I'm not sure. Doc Dewey is still finishing some minor surgery and Dr. Sung is across the street at the clinic. The new medic, Janos Kadar, will see to Mrs. Runkel. He's very good, according to both of our doctors."

I caught a defensive note in Jenny's voice. Maybe Kadar was a medical genius, but I could only imagine Vida's reaction. She respected Doc Dewey — or Young Doc, as he was known before his venerable father, Cecil, passed away a couple of years after I arrived in Alpine. But Vida always believed the son was not quite as sterling as his father, Old Doc.

"Okay," I finally said, realizing I'd come on a fool's errand. I was, however, grateful for Jenny's candor. Unlike big cities, small towns are more willing to share information. The assumption is that everybody knows everybody else, at least in some tenuous way. "Can you call me when you know her condition and when I can see her?"

Jenny assured me she would. I headed out the way I had come, noting that the snow was now coming down harder again. The sidewalk was already covered and I couldn't see the sheriff's office until I was more than halfway down. By the time I got to Front Street, Milo was just pulling into his regular spot. I called to him, but two empty school buses going by drowned me out. When I finally got inside headquarters, Dwight seemed pleased to tell me that his boss had gone to lunch.

"At the Burger Barn?" I asked.

"Could be," Dwight replied, always preferring to give me bad news or no news at all. He resumed reading what looked like another domestic abuse complaint. Maybe that's how he got some laughs. Not that I'd ever heard Dwight laugh. I'd rarely ever seen him smile.

I found Milo already parked in a booth. He was taking out a pack of cigarettes when he saw me. "Where'd you come from?" he asked.

"The hospital," I replied. "Why are you breaking the law by smoking?"

"Because," he began after lighting the cigarette, "I have to. If you've been at the hospital, you know Vida's pretty banged up. She may drive me crazy sometimes, but I still kind of like her."

"Don't we all?" I said softly. "I didn't learn anything other than that her condition isn't very good. Have you got any details?"

"Not much." Milo paused as the waitress, whose name I recalled was Clea, arrived to take our orders. He asked her to bring an extra small plate. Having worked at the Burger Barn for over a year, Clea didn't need to ask why, though the slight twitch in her expression registered disapproval. "Candy-ass," Milo muttered. "Fong caught her with some guy in the library parking lot a month or two ago. He wore a wedding ring."

"What did Dustin do?"

"He told them to get the hell out of there." Milo chuckled. "They did. Dustman's a serious reader. He worried that if he busted the guy for contributing to the delinquency of a minor, it'd upset Edna Mae Dalrymple, who might cancel his library card. Clea's a month shy of eighteen. He didn't recognize the jerk, but noticed a Skykomish County map and a briefcase under the dashboard."

"The old traveling salesman joke," I noted. "Tell me about Vida."

Our salads arrived — along with the extra plate my husband had requested for his ashtray. I tried not to stare at Clea, who suddenly looked seventeen going on thirty.

Milo put out his cigarette. "I don't know all that much. I had only a minute or so with Del Amundson before he had to take the wheel of the ambulance. Vida was already inside. Del thought she might have a broken foot and maybe a broken arm, but he was more worried about internal injuries from the steering wheel. It got jammed into Vida's chest when she went off the road and hit a big cedar tree. The Buick's probably toast."

The rest of our orders arrived. I managed to smile at Clea and thank her. She acknowledged me with a curt nod. Apparently we didn't look like big spenders. I turned back to Milo. "I'm leaving work early and going up to the hospital again. Can you pick me up at the main entrance around five-fifteen?"

"I'll try," he said. "How long has it been since we went to see Vida there after she got shot by the lunatic who killed his parents and almost offed you?"

I shuddered at the memory. "Six, seven years? Maybe more." We both went silent for almost a minute, focusing on our food, even though my appetite had waned. "Any news on Mickey O'Neill and Sofia Nelson?"

Milo shook his head. "No. The APB hasn't turned up anything. They may've tried to go off on one of the logging roads around here, but they wouldn't get far with all the snow. I'd call in a copter from Paine Field, but it's coming down too thick now. I just hope it lets up before dark."

"I worry about Sofia. If she's a hostage, I doubt she's a willing one. She may be a twit, but I wouldn't want anything awful to happen to her."

"Marrying a Nelson is pretty damned awful," Milo declared. "Where did Sofia come from? I checked her maiden name. She was a Doukas, but no close relation I could find to that pain-in-the-ass Simon."

I almost sneered at the mention of the retired attorney's name. When I met him a little over a year after I came to Alpine, his son had just been murdered. I was sympathetic, but Simon had added to the Doukas family's wealth by becoming the first home-grown attorney in town. He took me aside and insisted I ditch the homicide story. It was when I refused that he'd called me a whore. I hadn't spoken to him since.

"We know there aren't any others left here in town," I said. "Simon and Cecelia's other two kids moved away. Simon's father, Neeny, married that woman he'd been living with and they retired to Palm Springs. He died a few years ago. Vida — unwillingly — ran his obit in the paper. There were still some Doukases living west of town on the river where Vida got shot when she was investigating the Rasmussen murder."

"Right." Milo's expression was wry. "And then you went there and almost got yourself killed."

I grimaced at the memory. "Journalists sometimes have to put themselves at risk. Are those Doukases still there?"

"No," Milo replied. "Doe took a call from

there last summer about a possible prowler, but it was a false alarm. I think the name was Ferguson." His cell went off. I heard Dwight's gruff voice at the other end. The state patrol had sent a detailed report of Vida's accident to SkyCo's law enforcement headquarters. "Damn," Milo muttered after disconnecting. "I was thinking about having some pie for dessert."

I narrowed my eyes at my husband. "You don't need pie for dessert at lunch."

"Hey," Milo said, getting out his wallet, "I haven't gained any weight since we got married. I'm still around two twenty-five. I work out, you know."

"Stay that way. I don't want you looking like Ed Bronsky."

Milo gave me a dirty look. "I should make you pay for lunch, but you're always broke." He slapped down three $1 bills for Clea's tip. We parted ways outside of the Burger Barn. As usual, the sheriff jaywalked across Front Street to his headquarters.

Shortly after I returned to my office, Leo told me Liza was willing to fill in for Vida on *Cupboard.* He'd also called the hospital, but Vida was still being treated in the ER. "Helluva thing," he remarked with a shake of his head. "I always figured the Duchess was invincible."

Our ad manager had given Vida the nickname years ago. She'd claimed to hate it, but we suspected otherwise. I told Leo I was going to try to see her at the end of the workday.

He looked skeptical. "I wouldn't. If Vida's in a bad way, she won't want to see anybody. You know how much pride she has."

"True." I paused. "But I wouldn't feel right if I didn't make the effort. Maybe I'll call Doc Dewey to ask what he thinks."

Doc proved unreachable, which was no surprise. The receptionist at the clinic, Marje Blatt, Vida's niece, could only tell me that Doc was still attending her aunt.

"It's awful," Marje declared, her usual dry tone an octave higher with a touch of tremolo. "What was she doing down by Baring? Was she on an assignment?"

I decided not to mention her aunt's decision to withdraw from her contributions to the *Advocate* or the fainting spell. "No. Is there anybody she might've been visiting around there?"

"I don't think so," Marje said after a pause. "I haven't talked to her for a few days. Did she seem to be feeling okay?"

I hedged. "Your aunt *is* getting older. We can't expect her always to be at the top of her game. I don't mean to say she's failing, but it's natural for her to slow down a bit."

"I suppose." Marje didn't sound convinced, and I didn't blame her. "I hope Doc comes back to the clinic before he leaves for the day. Maybe I can find out more from him. If I do, I'll let you know. It'll be after five. What time do you get home?"

I'd already decided not to go up to the hospital. "By five-thirty. If you learn anything sooner, call me at the office." Marje said she would and rang off.

I tried to focus on story ideas for our next special edition, but my brain seemed to have withered. Ten minutes later I saw Buck Bardeen striding through the empty newsroom.

"Emma," the retired Air Force colonel said in a tone that suggested I should salute him, "have you any news of Vida?"

I invited him to sit down. While he settled his tall, imposing self into a visitor chair, I told him what little I'd found out. When I finished, he frowned. "Very worrisome," he murmured, running a hand over his bald head. "You really have no idea why she drove to that part of the highway?"

"None. As I recall, you had some friends in the area that you and she visited occasionally. That's the only thing I can think of."

"They're closer to Startup, where I lived before I bought the condo in town," Buck said. "Anyway, they spend their winters in Arizona. Vida knows that."

I decided to be more candid with Buck than I'd been with Marje. The colonel was an honorable military man and not given to gossip. "Vida hasn't been herself the last few days," I said, and went on to explain that she'd asked to curtail her contributions to the newspaper. "She didn't really give me a reason. Then this morning she told me that Amy was being hospitalized. Of course, Vida was upset."

Buck let out an exasperated sigh. "Amy and Ted are decent people, but they were damned fools when it came to raising Roger. Worse yet, Vida wouldn't listen to me years ago when I told her to stop spoiling the little bastard." He sat up even straighter in the chair. "Not in so many words, of course. But she told me it was none of my business. We had a brief falling-out over that, in fact."

I remembered Vida's allusion to their quarrel. Although she had never mentioned the cause, I'd guessed it was about Roger. "He's always been her blind spot."

"The little punk should've joined the Marines when Vida told me he was dithering around about college. *College,* mind you!" The colonel was turning a bit red in the face. "Roger needed discipline, the old-fashioned kind you get in the service. I told Vida that at the time, but she wouldn't listen. She claimed he graduated from high school, but I'd bet my last two bits he didn't. No wonder he ended up in the stockade!"

I managed not to smile at Buck's military terminology. But he wasn't finished. "Sorry, Emma, I got carried away. I'm upset about poor Vida. I've grown very fond of her over the years. When do you think I could call on her in the hospital? I wouldn't want to upset her if she didn't want me to see her when she wasn't at her best."

"Tomorrow, maybe," I replied. "I was going to see her after work, but I changed my mind. She may not be ready to see visitors."

Buck nodded rather absently. "I'll wait, too." He stood up. "Now I'll go over to Posies Unlimited and have Delphine Corson send a nice bouquet. Roses, at least a couple of dozen. Vida likes roses."

"She does," I agreed. "Vida's lucky to have you in her life."

"Cuts both ways," he said before squaring his broad shoulders and turning around to exit my cubbyhole. There was something touching — even brave — about the octogenarian Colonel Bardeen's military bearing. The urge to salute him returned despite the fact that he couldn't see me. Instead, I smiled to myself. Buck and Vida were a reminder that love is ageless. The thought didn't lift my spirits, though I held it close anyway.

But I couldn't imagine a world without Vida.

Chapter 16

Shortly after four-thirty, I noticed my entire staff was in the newsroom. Alison was dismantling the coffee urn to clean it, and Kip had come from the back shop to ask Mitch a question regarding some copy he'd submitted about road closures. I interrupted to ask if any of them had ever heard of a Piper Erskine from Montana. Everybody looked blank except for Leo.

"You mean the one mentioned in that personals ad?" he responded. "I figured it was a query about a runaway. There was no description given, not even age or sex. The name Piper could go either way."

"That's true," I admitted. "I wonder if we should find out some details. I've never heard of Hardin, Montana, so I assume it's a small town. Maybe we should see if this J. L. Erskine has a phone listing."

Mitch and Kip both looked puzzled, but it was a bemused Liza who asked why I was so curious.

I confessed that I really didn't know. "It's one of those weird things that seems to ring a bell."

"Reporter's hunch," Mitch remarked with what passed for a smile. "Sometimes they actually pay off."

I shrugged. "Maybe it's not the name but the town. When I was growing up, my family took a couple of car trips through Montana. Maybe we went through there and stopped for lunch."

Noticing that my staff was looking as if the subject was of no interest or that they wished I'd evaporate so they could wind up their duties for the day, I beat a measured retreat.

Once I was back at my desk, I clicked a Montana map onto my computer screen. Hardin was a town of a little over three thousand a few miles south of I-90. There was no reason my family would have left the Interstate to take that route. But I couldn't think of any other reason why something about the ad had sounded familiar.

I checked my to-do list. Unlike more organized professionals, I had no daily planner, but jotted down reminders on whatever scrap of paper was available. In this case, it was the back of a grocery list from the previous week. As usual, I had trouble deciphering some of the chicken scratches that passed for my handwriting. My phone rang before I could figure out what "nonse slony" meant.

My husband's voice bellowed in my ear: "I'll be late. Some damned jackass just reported a car floating in the Sky below where the Tye River comes into it." He hung up before I could remind him that I had *no* car, on land or on water.

I practically fell over my own feet rushing out into the newsroom, where only Mitch remained at his desk. "Your boss is without transportation," I confessed. "Is it possible you could give me a ride home?"

My reporter hesitated only a fraction of a second. No doubt he was considering whether Brenda would worry if he was late arriving at their house. "Sure. It's stopped snowing, but I chained up this morning. I'm used to snow, though, being from Detroit, otherwise known as the Big Freezer on the Lake. I'm done for the day. Are you ready to roll?"

I told him I'd grab my coat and purse. And then remembered that "nonse slony" translated as "nurse story," the series I intended to do down the road. *Way* down, given what was happening now in Alpine.

Two minutes later we were in Mitch's Ford Taurus where I broached the subject of the floating car. "This may be something to post online and not a full-fledged story," I said. "It's not a first that a car landed in the river."

Mitch nodded. "I covered the previous disaster. That was a grim one. You were there, too. Almost the same time of year, right?"

"Yes. But we didn't have any snow when it happened." The tragedy had had an impact on Vida, ironically a good one. The hooker who had given birth to Roger's baby was one of the two victims. Shared custody was no longer a problem. But not long after that, her grandson had been sent to prison for dealing drugs and procuring teenage hookers. I was momentarily silent, fretting about Vida's current condition. We were going straight up Fourth Street, which hadn't been plowed except for the first block off Alpine's main drag in the downtown area. I wondered if our own street had been cleared.

It hadn't, but Mitch proved he was a winter weather veteran by plowing through almost to the front door. "I'll check out the floater as soon as I get home," he said. "Do you want me to let you know what I find out?"

"Not unless somebody was in it. The river's running fairly fast, so the car may be halfway to Sultan by now. You may have to call Snohomish County or the state patrol."

Mitch agreed, and I got out of the Taurus, immediately sinking boot-high into the snow. I went to the front door, rather than taking my usual route of coming into the kitchen via the garage. My cell rang just as I stepped inside.

"Where the hell are you?" Milo demanded. "I'm outside your damned office, but it's locked up."

"Mitch brought me home," I replied. "I just got here. I thought you'd be checking out the car that went into the . . ." I realized my husband had hung up on me. As I started to close the door, I saw Mitch reverse on Fir Street and stop. The snowplow was grinding its way past our log cabin.

Ten minutes later, as I was starting to put dinner together, Milo stalked into the kitchen. "Why the hell didn't you call and let me know you had a ride? Did you think I'd forgotten you're my wife?"

I glared at him. "Why the hell don't you prove that I am by kissing me, you big jerk?"

Milo grimaced, took off his regulation hat,

and tossed it in the vicinity of the dishwasher. The hazel eyes sparked as he scooped me up, carried me into the living room, through the hall, and into the bedroom.

Half an hour later he rolled over in the king-sized bed and kissed my nose. "Was that proof enough?" he asked.

"Mmmm. Yes. Yes, it was." I put my arms around his neck and held him close.

We finally sat down to eat dinner a little before seven. I remembered to ask him if he knew what had happened to the car in the river, how it had gotten there in the first place, and had anyone been in it.

"The Mazda was empty when it went in the river and so was the gas tank," Milo replied. "It was probably pushed into the Sky. The plates revealed it was stolen from outside of a tavern in Shelton." He paused to take a big bite of T-bone steak and stared at me.

"Mickey O'Neill!" I exclaimed. "He must have swiped the car and then ditched it. So where are Mickey and Sofia?"

"Not in the Skykomish River," Milo said. "There were no reports of stolen cars in this area for the last four days. My guess is that they're hiding out somewhere around here. I had Heppner check out the O'Neill place again late this afternoon, but no sign of anyone having been around there."

"Everybody has to be somewhere," I murmured. "How many empty houses are there around here? You must have some idea."

"About thirty, thirty-five," Milo replied. "Some of them are no more than shacks. My deputies check them out fairly often, especially the ones by the railroad tracks. They're magnets for bums riding the trains. We hustle them off because they can start fires. That's especially dangerous in the summer when everything's so dry. You might remember last August when we had so little rain that two of those shacks burned down. Luckily, they were out toward the end of the Burl Creek Road and got reported before they could set off more than some bushes and a couple of trees."

I did remember the incidents. We'd run only a couple of inches on page three about the fires. We didn't include Forest Ranger Bunky Smythe's mishap when he'd stopped by to check with the firefighters and gotten bit in the rear end by a chipmunk. Bunky had to visit the ER in case his attacker was rabid.

I switched gears, explaining to Milo about

the personals ad and asking if he'd ever heard of anyone named Piper Erskine. He chewed more steak and reflected. "There was a Bob Piper in my high school class, but the family moved away not long after we graduated."

"No help there," I said. "Somebody around here must know the name. The person who sent in the ad had a reason for thinking he — or she — may've lived here. Vida would know, if anybody does. I'll call the hospital to see how she's doing."

It was after seven-thirty before I was able to get through to someone who could give me any information.

"Mrs. Runkel is finally in a room," Constance Peterson informed me. "She's listed as stable."

Constance wasn't my least favorite of the nurses at the hospital, but she came close. "Were they able to put her in with her daughter, Amy Hibbert? I know she was admitted earlier today."

"No. Mrs. Hibbert is in another room. Mrs. Runkel is with someone else."

I wondered if I dared ask who. Probably not. Instead, I posed a different question. "What exactly does 'stable' mean?"

"That the patient's condition hasn't changed," Constance replied.

I felt like asking if a patient who was dead on arrival would also be described as "stable," but refrained. "Is Mrs. Runkel conscious?"

"No. She's been sedated. Excuse me, a patient is ringing. Check back tomorrow." Nurse Peterson hung up.

Milo looked up from the spy book he'd been reading. "You got Ruth Sharp at the other end?"

"Not quite that bad," I replied, recalling one of the most harrowing nights of my life: I'd almost gotten killed by a nut job at the hospital while Nurse Sharp sat on her butt going over charts. "Constance Peterson. She's an LPN, but another one who thinks she's working for the CIA. Vida's listed as stable and has been sedated, which tells me zip."

"Do you want me to call and tell Nurse Peterson that Vida's condition is part of an ongoing investigation?"

I shook my head. "She can't tell me what she doesn't know. Besides, it's not true."

Milo shrugged. "If you say so." He went back to his spies.

But, I wondered, was it possible that Vida's wipeout with the Buick had occurred during a personal investigation she was undertaking? Why had she been heading away from Alpine when Amy was being admitted to the hospital? Vida never did anything without a good reason. I just wished I knew what it was.

Thursday morning the first thing I saw on my desk calendar was a note I'd scrawled reminding me of bridge club at Edna Mae Dalrymple's house. I'd forgotten all about it. Spence had emailed me to say he was having Leo interview Liza on Vida's program. That was a nice touch on Mr. Radio's part. I'd listen to the program before heading to the bridge bash at Edna Mae's, a block away on Fir Street. Of course, the other members would also tune in. Word might not have gotten out that Vida wouldn't be at the mic.

There had been no new snow during the night and the main streets in the heart of town had been plowed, so I'd driven my Honda to work. At some point during the day I'd go to see Vida. I'd also call to check on her condition, but not until after nine o'clock. I already knew that early morning visitors weren't welcome.

The coffee urn was still perking when I went into the newsroom. Alison always plugged it in before she even took off her jacket. It dawned on me that I hadn't seen her in the front office when I arrived.

Leo apparently read my mind. "Liza started the coffee," he said with a glance at his wife, who was staring at her monitor. "Alison's late this morning. Maybe her car wouldn't start. I don't think she's fussy enough about upkeep on that Audi. They're good automobiles, but they still need maintenance."

Before I could say anything, my phone rang. "Maybe that's her now." I scurried into my cubbyhole and snatched up the receiver. It wasn't Alison, but Lori Cobb, her roommate. As I glanced at the number on the little screen, I saw that Lori was calling not from the sheriff's office but from the condo she shared with Alison.

"Emma?" She sounded breathless.

"Yes, Lori?" I responded.

"Alison slipped on some ice in the underground parking area. I think she may have broken her wrist. I'm taking her to the ER. I'll let you know what happens, okay?"

I heard a click. Lori was off and coping.

The rest of my staff was now staring at the urn as if they could will it to finish perking. I decided to make an announcement about our injured receptionist.

"Poor girl!" Liza exclaimed. "I thought I'd be the one to have that happen. I've never lived in an icy place. I can move to the front office. Somebody should be there to greet visitors."

"It's either you or me," I said. "I don't have any appointments this morning, though I plan to see Vida at the hospital later on."

"I'll take the front," Liza insisted. "You're the boss. How is Vida?"

I recounted what little I knew. Kip shook his head. "I had a bad feeling about her. Where the heck was she going?"

"I don't know," I replied. "Colonel Bardeen came to see me because he thought it was strange."

The urn stopped perking and the red light went on. Leo bowed. "You go first, boss lady."

I did and realized we had no pastries. Apparently it had been Alison's turn. Mitch volunteered to head for the Upper Crust.

As he rushed off, Leo chuckled. "Unfair. The skinniest guy eats the most goodies and never gains an ounce." It was not an uncommon complaint from my ad manager.

The mail arrived shortly before nine-thirty. Liza also brought me a couple of letters for Vida's advice column. "What do we do with these? Just hold on to them?"

I didn't know what to say. "Go ahead and

read them. If the writer doesn't sound as if he or she is about to stick his or her head in a gas oven, we can hold off on answers."

"Sounds good," Liza agreed, and left the usual stack of automatic recyclables on my desk.

A few minutes after nine, I called the hospital. To my relief, Julie Canby answered.

"Emma!" she exclaimed. "How many patients are you checking on? I assume Mrs. Runkel is at the top of your list."

"You got that right," I assured her. "How is she?"

"She broke three ribs on her right side," Julie replied. "The Buick skidded on black ice and crashed into a guardrail. The steering wheel caused the damage, but there's not much that can be done for broken ribs. They usually heal on their own. Since Mrs. Runkel is older, Doc Dewey insisted she stay in the hospital for a day or two."

"Did Vida try to talk him out of it?"

"I don't know." Julie paused. "I shouldn't tell you this, Emma, but I trust you. Doc kept her in the ER because he thought she was in shock. Or maybe had had a stroke. He told me that except for a few isolated words, Mrs. Runkel didn't talk. That struck him as . . . uncharacteristic."

I agreed and admitted Vida hadn't been

herself lately. "Is Doc sure she *hasn't* had a stroke?"

"Yes, he was certain," Julie replied. "It struck him as more like she was suffering from trauma, but Doc didn't put that on her chart."

"Very discreet of Doc," I said quietly.

"I think," Julie went on, "that Doc will try to make other arrangements for Vida since her daughter is also here. He'll probably put them in the same room."

"What's the diagnosis on Amy?" I asked.

"The same as when she was hospitalized a year or so ago." Julie paused. She and I knew each other well enough that she trusted me. "Nerves. Ever since Roger was sent to prison, Mrs. Hibbert has been a regular visitor to Doc Dewey or Dr. Sung. They prescribe medications for her, but she insists none of them work. I suspect she either doesn't give them enough time to kick in or else forgets to take them on a regular basis. I feel sorry for her husband."

"Ted's not a very . . . forceful person," I allowed, deciding that "wimp" would be unkind. "Let me know when or if I'll be able to see Vida today."

"I will," Julie promised, and we rang off.

I'd started going through the mail when I remembered the personals ad. There was something about it that bothered me. On a whim, I dialed directory assistance for Hardin, Montana, and asked for J. L. Erskine's phone number. The phone rang eight times before a recorded message came on: "Jim Erskine here — except I'm not. Check back this evening. Have a good one!"

I didn't leave a message. It was probably a wild-goose chase, something that besets journalists now and then. We, of course, call it a hunch. Once in a while the hunch pays off.

My phone rang almost as soon as I set it down. Alison's voice sounded a little shaky. "I'm coming into the office in a little bit," she said, "but I sprained my wrist. My left wrist, so I can still write. Janos told me it should be okay in about ten days."

Evidently Alison and the new medic were already on a first-name basis. I wondered if she'd taken my advice seriously. I hoped not. "That's okay," I replied. "Liza's filling in for you at the reception desk. Please take it easy!"

"I will. See you soon." She hung up.

I went back to the mail, hoping there might be something that we could use in the newspaper. Usually the sources that provided any local interest came from the state capital in Olympia. But there literally was nothing fit to print. The two letters to Vida were standard fare. They were both from women whose names sounded only vaguely familiar. Ada Schnable thought her husband, Art, might be straying. His wheelchair had mud on the tires and the widow down the road didn't have a paved driveway. Art was spending a lot of time outside lately, despite the threat of snow. The second letter was from Angela Helfinger who wanted Vida's recipe for custard pie. Angela was another innocent who didn't realize that Vida was the most abysmal cook in Skykomish County. Our former House & Home editor was the only person I knew who could ruin hot dogs.

A little after ten, I called the hospital to check on both Vida and Amy. Constance Peterson was on duty again, but she had no real news. "Mrs. Runkel is still listed in stable condition, though I haven't seen her this morning. Dr. Sung has finished making rounds. I believe they may move her daughter in with her later on."

I frowned. "I thought Mrs. Runkel was in with Ms. Marsh."

"She was," Constance replied in her prim voice, "but Ms. Marsh has left the hospital."

"Left?" I repeated.

"Yes. Excuse me. Dr. Sung is motioning for me to join him in Mr. Kubiak's room."

I had no idea who Mr. Kubiak was; I thought the name Kubiak had something to do with pro football, but I doubted that the local Mr. K. was related. I was jotting down story ideas for our special section when Jean Campbell came through the newsroom and entered my so-called office. I greeted the wife of Alpine Appliance owner Lloyd with a friendly smile.

Jean, however, was solemn. I hadn't seen her in some time and noticed that the gray had taken over the brown in her wispy curls. She was tall and very sturdy, almost Amazonian. I felt like an aging elf and was relieved when she sat down in one of the visitor chairs.

"I'm so worried about Vida," she began. "Everyone at the church is."

Jean apparently still worked at First Presbyterian, which Vida also attended. I nodded. "We all are. Even if she officially retired, she still spent quite a bit of time at the office."

"Yes." Jean looked pensive, as if she was having a hard time trying to imagine Vida being confined to a hospital bed. I didn't blame her. "Where was she going when she had the accident?"

"I don't know. But I'm sure *she* did."

Jean smiled faintly, revealing the small gap between her front teeth. "Vida always knows everything. I do hope she can have visitors soon."

I agreed, and asked if she knew that Amy was also in the hospital. Jean did. Vida had called her the previous day, obviously before she took off in the Buick. But to my surprise, Jean had more than our former House & Home editor on her mind.

"I must confess we're curious about that poor girl who was murdered at the motel," she said. "Jason called us yesterday to ask if there was any news about her. Has the sheriff a suspect in mind?"

"Jason?" I said.

"Our nephew in Oakland," Jean replied. "He dated Rachel. He's been quite upset about . . . what happened to her."

"Of course."

Jean grimaced. "It's hard to tell when you're not around a person. We haven't seen Jason for a while. He had a longtime girlfriend — they were living together — but they broke up over a year ago. Then he started seeing Rachel. I have no idea how serious the relationship was. I do know *they* weren't living together." Jean obviously wanted to let me know she didn't approve of unmarried couples sharing the same roof.

"Did Jason say if Rachel had any family in the Bay Area? I understand her parents are dead."

Jean nodded. "That's true. I got the impression that Rachel was on her own. Maybe I should call Jason and ask if he can find out who's making arrangements. Would Sheriff Dodge know?"

"I doubt it," I replied, wondering if she knew I was Mrs. Dodge. "Once his headquarters has sent a body to another jurisdiction, especially in another state, what happens next is out of his hands."

"Oh — I suppose that's so." Jean frowned. "Sad, really. If you see the sheriff, could you ask him, just in case he does know something about what happened to poor Rachel? Jason would want to know."

"I'll try," I said, keeping my expression deadpan.

"Thank you." Jean stood up. "I do hope Vida feels better. She's always so full of . . . news. I must admit I haven't seen her lately, not since before the holidays. Except at church, of course. But that's no time to visit. Besides, Vida's always surrounded by so many of her friends and relatives." She gave me her gap-toothed smile again and went on her way.

Jean's last comment made me smile. Vida would be pumping everybody she could glom on to after the service was over. She had a knack for loosening tongues about even the most intimate matters.

But Vida wasn't going to be doing that now. My smile went away. I worried that she wouldn't ever be able to pump anyone again.

Chapter 17

Feeling antsy, I decided to call on the sheriff, known to those better informed than Jean Campbell as my husband. I marveled that in such a small town, Jean — and probably Lloyd — could be so wrapped up in their own little world that they were unaware of what the rest of us were doing.

Before I could leave the premises, Alison arrived just as I stepped into the front office. I noticed that she had a brace on her left wrist. She saw Liza sitting behind the receptionist's desk and let out a little shriek. "I've already been replaced?"

Liza and I both laughed. "Ms. Walsh is temping for you this morning. Does the wrist hurt?"

"Kind of," Alison replied as Liza stood up. "But Jan — that's what he prefers — gave me some pain meds. He says the *J* is like a *Y* in Hungarian."

"That's right," Liza said, picking up her

coffee mug and making way for Alison, "I have a cousin in Santa Monica who's married to a Hungarian. His name is spelled J-A-K-O-B, but it's pronounced Yakob."

Alison removed her navy quilted jacket. "Is he good-looking?"

"He used to be," Liza replied, "but he's put on a lot of weight and gone bald. At sixty-seven, I figure he's entitled to do that."

Alison frowned. "I suppose that can happen." Her tone indicated a touch of anxiety. Maybe she was picturing Jan in his retirement years.

"Don't get ahead of yourself," Liza cautioned with a smile before returning to the newsroom.

After sitting down, Alison sighed. "Why do we have to get old?"

"Consider the alternative," I said. "I'm off to see my old duffer of a husband."

"He still has his hair," Alison reminded me. "So do Leo and Mitch."

"They're lucky." With that remark, I headed outside.

The snow was starting to melt. I passed Parker's Pharmacy, the Sears outlet store, and the entrance to the VFW Hall before crossing Third Street to the sheriff's headquarters. I'd only gone about ten feet when Jack Blackwell came tearing out of Milo's domain.

He saw me and paused just long enough to yell: "Dodge is the biggest sonuvabitch in the whole frigging state. Put that in your rag of a paper!" He hurtled into his new black Porsche and gunned the engine.

I was still shaking my head when I entered headquarters. Lori looked alarmed, Consi seemed puzzled, and Milo was thumping back to his office. I swore I could see smoke coming out of his ears. He slammed the door behind him, apparently not having noticed my arrival, and I wondered if I should give him time to calm down.

"Hi," I said innocently. "Is your boss in a bad mood?"

Consi started to say something, but deferred to Lori, who said, "The sheriff and Mr. Blackwell sort of got into it. But they didn't come to blows. Patti Marsh finally filed a complaint about Jack beating up on her."

I was stunned. "No kidding! After all these years?"

Lori nodded. "I know. But this time he put her in the hospital. I guess he went too far."

"Not far enough," Consi asserted. "I've seen this kind of crap in Tacoma over and over. The woman calls the cops but then refuses to press charges. They claim to love the guy or that he'll change his ways. Dumb."

I glanced at the closed door. "Dare I go in?"

"Why not?" Lori replied. "You can probably calm him down."

I marched through the reception area. At least Milo hadn't locked the door. "Hi," I said. "I hear you had an unwelcome visitor."

Milo had lighted a cigarette. "Did you see the bastard leave?"

"Yes. He indicated you and he had a disagreement. Has he ever figured out that we're married?"

The sheriff shook his head. "Blackwell is only interested in things that affect Blackwell. It turns out that Patti Marsh got a phone call the other day from somebody in Montana. She inherited a cattle ranch from an uncle. It's about ten thousand acres and worth some big bucks. Patti declined to share with Jack. That's how she ended up in the ER."

I sat down in a visitor chair. "Well! It's a good thing Patti kept her own house all these years. She'd better change the locks. Does he know she left the hospital this morning?"

"He didn't until he went to see her there about an hour ago," Milo replied. "That's when he found out Patti was AWOL. She wasn't at her house, either. He has a key, so he could get in. I wonder if she left town. Maybe she wants to see her big chunk of Big Sky land. If I were her, I'd want to get as far away from Blackwell as possible."

"*You* always do," I said. "Someday Jack might do permanent damage to Patti. He's the type who can get out of control. Did you see her when she came in?"

Milo shook his head. "She called yesterday from the hospital to ask me to send a deputy to take her complaint. I sent Bill Blatt. He's almost as good at calming people down as Fong is. I thought about Jamison or De Groote, but I didn't want Patti going into a tirade about men who beat up on . . ." Milo's phone rang. He glared at it, but picked up the receiver and spoke his usual greeting: "Dodge here." Then his expression changed. "When do you plan on getting to Alpine? . . . Okay, I'll expect you sometime this afternoon. My headquarters is just two blocks from the bridge . . . . Oh, right, you've been here before. Make sure you rent a car with snow tires. This is Alpine, not the Bay Area. See you then." He put down the phone and saw my curious expression.

"That was Jason Campbell. He flew up from Oakland this morning. Apparently he's damned upset about what happened to Rachel."

I told Milo that his aunt had visited me earlier. "It sounds as if Jason and Rachel may've been a serious item."

Milo nodded. "Damned right. You never can be sure about people."

I couldn't argue that point.

I wondered if I should walk up the hill to see Vida in the hospital. My conscience won out. It was after eleven, so I thought perhaps Amy and her mother were already in the same room.

I went straight to the patient floor, where Debbie Murchison was the nurse on duty. She was one of the younger nurses, a pretty, cheerful type who couldn't annoy me if she tried. Of course, my first question was about Vida's condition.

"She's doing much better," Debbie replied, "though she didn't really eat any breakfast. I know hospital food is kind of bland, but Mrs. Runkel runs all those amazing recipes in the newspaper, so I expect she's used to eating much fancier meals at home."

I managed to keep a straight face. "Vida is

careful about what she eats," I replied. That much was true. She had yet to make a casserole with Drano as the main ingredient.

Debbie smiled, revealing her dimples. "She and Mrs. Hibbert are in the same room now, though Dr. Sung feels Mrs. Hibbert can go home today. He diagnosed her as suffering from stress." Debbie lowered her voice. "Of course, she could be menopausal. That does cause a lot of stress. Men — even doctors — don't always understand."

"Probably not," I said. "That's because they're men."

"How true," Debbie said soberly. "They can't help that, can they?"

I assumed the question was rhetorical. "Is Mrs. Runkel in the same room that Ms. Marsh was in?"

Debbie went from sober to somber. "Ms. Marsh shouldn't have left the hospital. She needs to rest and heal. When you fall down and hurt yourself that badly, it takes time to get over it."

So that was the story Patti had told the nurses. Why not? On the other hand, why was she now pressing charges against Blackwell? And where was she? But I merely agreed with Debbie and headed to Vida's room. Before I could get there, a stoop-shouldered elderly man came out of the first room on my left. He bumped into a tray of instruments, swore under his breath, and stumbled off down the hall. I noticed that the room was occupied by Mary Smith, Amy's former roommate.

I squared my shoulders and told myself to prepare for the worst in terms of Vida's condition. But I was surprised. She was propped up on pillows and lecturing her daughter. Her color was off, but her gray eyes were clear. They were easy to see because she wasn't wearing her glasses.

"Emma!" Vida exclaimed. "How nice of you to come. I'm afraid I can't offer you as much as a cup of tea."

I smiled in relief and acknowledged Amy's timid wave from the other bed. "I was here yesterday, but you were not yet in a room. I checked with the hospital last night, though I was told only that you were stable. What happened to your glasses?"

"They were broken in my mishap," she replied. "Ted will bring me my older ones. Very annoying not to be able to read smallish print." Vida gestured for me to pull up the only visitor chair in the room. I decided to put it between the beds, not wanting Amy to feel left out. Vida's three daughters were used to playing second fiddle when their redoubtable mother was around.

After I sat down, I told Vida I'd called the hospital but hadn't been able to learn much. Seeing that she had a bandage on her left arm, I asked if anything had been broken.

"A sprain," she replied. "I twisted an ankle as well and broke three ribs, which heal themselves, of course. Dr. Sung was afraid my spleen was severely damaged, but it was only a bit bruised. I'll probably go home tomorrow." Amy's gaze was riveted on her mother. "Ted is going to pick up Amy on his lunch hour. There's no need for her to stay here with me." She shot her daughter a flinty glance. "You need to be up and doing, dearest. You mustn't mope."

"I can't leave you here alone, Mother," she said in a whiny voice. "And I need to get back my strength."

"Piffle!" Vida exclaimed. "You have a house to keep up and a husband to cook for. Show some spunk! I've no time for lollygagging."

Amy hung her head. I decided it was time to change the subject. "Where were you going when the car went out of control?"

Vida's expression suddenly looked guarded. "Sultan," she replied. "I heard a store there had a wonderful post-holiday sale. I thought I might find some nice items for next Christmas."

"Which store was it?" I asked.

"I forget the name." Vida's gaze didn't quite meet mine. "Now tell me what's going on with the murder investigation."

I got her caught up with whatever she had missed in the last twenty-four hours. Then I told her about Alison's fall and her sprained wrist. She evinced suitable compassion. "Poor girl. This is the time of year for misadventures. The snow, the ice, the extreme cold." She shrugged her broad shoulders.

Out in the hall, I could hear the rattle of trays. "It sounds like they're getting ready to serve lunch. I'd better get out of the way." As I stood up, I smiled at Amy. "I'm sure you'll be more comfortable at home. Ted will take very good care of you."

"He'll have to go back to work," Amy said. "I'll be all alone."

"Then you can sleep in peace," I pointed out. "Hospitals really aren't conducive to quiet nights."

Amy just shrugged. I blew both patients a kiss and left.

Walking down the hill, I wondered why Vida had lied about where she was going when the Buick went out of control. She might dance around the truth, but usually she had a valid reason. I hoped she had one now.

Before I left the hospital, I'd called Milo on my cell to ask if he'd like to have lunch with me. He couldn't. It was Bill Blatt's birthday and he was taking his deputy to lunch at the ski lodge. Rebuffed, I decided to order takeout from the Venison Inn. I'd use the lunch hour to bear down on what we'd run in the special edition. I already had the Hollenbergs' trip to Norway and Dick and Mary Jane Bourgette's Vatican visit on the list. Then I remembered that their daughters, Rosemary and Terri, had gone on a Caribbean cruise in the fall. Rosemary was the Skykomish County prosecuting attorney, and Terri worked as a hostess and bookkeeper at their brothers' fifties-style diner, The Heartbreak Hotel. I also recalled that Superior Court judge Diane Proxmire had spent two weeks in Greece. Maybe I had enough to fill the special edition. I just hoped that all the travelers had taken some decent photos. Except for the Nyquists, the era of fuzzy Polaroids was coming to a close.

Half an hour later, I was finishing my rare beef dip, fries, and salad when I saw Grace Grundle weave her way through the empty newsroom. The old girl had an inner-ear problem that made her look as if she'd had a few too many, but Vida swore that the retired schoolteacher had never touched liquor in her life.

"I'm so glad you're in your office, Emma," she declared, wobbling a bit as she parked her plump self into a visitor chair. "I was afraid you might be out to lunch."

"No rest for the wicked," I said with a smile. "We're planning a special edition on vacations that Alpiners have taken this past year so that we can include advertisers who specialize in travel items. We'll also include those who have trips planned for this year. Have you thought about going anywhere in the near future?"

Grace looked faintly shocked by the question. "My, no! I couldn't leave my kitties by themselves. I haven't been anywhere since my late husband died. Even when he was alive, the one big trip we took was to visit our relatives in Kansas."

The Grundles had been childless, so I'd always assumed the kitties made up for the lack of kiddies. "Milo and I have been thinking about a Canadian trip. We'd like to see the eastern part of Canada."

"It's a very large country," Grace noted. "My students were always amazed to learn that it's much bigger than the United States.

But not as large a population, of course." There was a note of pride in her voice, though her expression quickly changed to a frown. "So surprising that many of them couldn't find Canada on a map. Why, we're so close to it here in Alpine!"

"True," I said, wondering when Grace would get to the point. If there *was* a point. Just to move her on to another subject, I asked if she knew that Vida was in the hospital.

Grace's response was indignant. "That's why I stopped by. She shouldn't be driving at her age. I admit to being a few years older than Vida, but I knew enough to give up my car when I turned eighty-two a couple of years ago. I live close enough to everything that I can walk. Of course, the snow was off-putting. I almost ran out of food for my kitties. I'll stop at the pet store today. I came downtown to buy a new photo album at Buddy and Roseanna Bayard's studio, but they were out of the kind I like. Fortunately, they can order a special one for me." She grimaced. "That awful man from the disreputable motel was there asking Buddy to take pictures of the motel to use for postcard advertisements. Such a shoddy place, though of course I've never been inside."

"He stays in business." It was the only

thing I could think of to say. My brain seemed to have gone dead.

"Milo should shut him down," Grace declared. "Surely Mr. Pace must violate several hospitality codes."

"That's up to the county health department," I said. "The sheriff's office has been called a few times about problem guests, but that happens even in the best motels."

Grace glanced at her gold Gruen watch, which was probably even older than Vida's Bulova. "It's almost one. I should be on my way." She pushed back the chair and held on to the desk as she got to her feet. "I wouldn't put it past Mr. Pace to have killed that poor young woman. You must tell Milo not to let him leave town."

"I don't think Will ever does," I said. "I've never known him to go on a trip. I suppose he doesn't trust anyone to take over his business."

Having gotten upright, Grace moved to the door. "Well, he is now. He wanted those postcards to take with him because this weekend he's leaving for Mexico. Goodbye, Emma, do take care."

Grace wobbled away.

I glanced at my watch. It was ten after one. Milo should be finished with Bill's birthday celebration. Maybe I was overreacting, but I felt that my husband might be interested in Will Pace's travel plans. I put my notes on the special edition in order and went to see the sheriff.

Lori was on the phone and Consi was accepting payment for a speeding ticket from a young man I didn't recognize. Their boss's door was open, so I kept on going.

Milo looked up from something he'd been reading. "What now?" he asked in less-than-husbandly fashion.

I sat down before I spoke. "Your favorite innkeeper is going to Mexico."

"My . . . ?" The sheriff frowned. "You mean . . . Will Pace?"

"Yes. Grace Grundle just told me he's leaving this weekend."

Milo sighed. "Since when is poor old Grace a reliable source?"

"When she heard him say so to the Bayards. He had them making up some postcards of his motel, presumably for advertising purposes."

Leaning back in his chair, Milo picked up a ballpoint pen and clicked it several times. "I'll call Buddy to find out if Pace told him or Roseanna about the so-called trip. Maybe I should send a deputy to the motel to find out if it's true. Jamison's on patrol. She can handle him." He put down the pen and reached for the phone.

I stood up. "Will you be home at the regular time tonight?"

Milo grimaced. "I don't know. It depends on when Jason Campbell gets here. He's supposed to arrive around two, but his flight may not be on time. Why don't we eat out?"

"I'll think about it," I said. "Good luck with the interview." I blew Milo a kiss and left him to deal with his visitor from Oakland.

When I got back to the office, Alison was on the phone and Leo was the only staffer in the newsroom. Unfortunately, he wasn't alone. Ed Bronsky was stuffed into a visitor chair. He saw me before I could scurry down the hall and try to sneak into my cubbyhole.

"Emma!" Ed exclaimed. "Tell this stubborn Irishman why you couldn't use a freelance ad guy to take the burden off him so that he doesn't have to hustle all the time. I know he's been talking about retirement. He can ease his way out with some help, right?"

"Actually," I said, "now that Mrs. Walsh is working here, their plans have changed."

Ed's furry eyebrows shot up. "*Mrs.* Walsh? What do you mean? I thought she was in

California."

I gave him a disappointed look. "Don't you ever read the *Advocate,* Ed? Liza is our new House & Home editor."

Ed ran a beefy hand over his bald spot. "Well . . . sure, right, but that's not the point. I'm talking about adding to the bottom line. What's wrong with some extra help making money for the paper?"

"Nothing," I assured him, "but we're doing okay. As you know, Vida has semiretired and Liza's taken her place. We compensate Vida for her advice column, 'Scene,' and an occasional old-timers piece, but that's it for extra expenses. I didn't realize you wanted to work again."

"I don't," Ed replied. "I mean, I'm not the one to do the job I'm proposing. Joey dropped out of the community college, so Shirley and I thought he might like to get a taste of reality by having a job. The newspaper seemed like a good way to give Joey an idea about real work."

I noticed that Leo had turned away. It was hard for either of us to keep a straight face. "I thought Joey *had* a job," I said.

Ed scowled and waved a pudgy hand. "I don't want him taking a mindless job like slinging Big Macs or pushing a broom at

Harvey's Hardware. Joey needs a challenge."

Like getting up in the morning? But I didn't say so out loud. "I'm sorry, Ed. We're at full speed." I went on, my worst self coming to the fore, "Why not check with Spencer Fleetwood? He often hires college kids."

Ed's squinty eyes widened slightly. "Hey, that's a great idea! I'll head right out to KSKY." He hoisted his considerable weight out of the chair. "That reminds me," he said, putting his hand into his pocket, "I need to get gas. Gee, I left my wallet at home. Either of you got a spare twenty?"

My purse was in the cubbyhole, so I shook my head. Frankly, I wasn't sure I had a twenty. But Leo took out two tens and handed them to Ed. "That should cover it," my current ad manager said.

"Right," Ed agreed. "I'll pay you back, of course." He bustled off through the newsroom.

Leo and I looked at each other. We knew we'd see Ed again — that was unavoidable — but he wouldn't have the twenty bucks.

Back at my desk, I pondered Ed's slothfulness. Shirley was supposed to be substituting at the public and parish grade schools, which I suppose was how they survived. None of the Bronskys were starving to death. They'd finally gotten their money from RestHaven's purchase of Casa de Bronska for its mental health facilities. That had been over a year ago, but I suspected they'd already blown most of the windfall.

My mind was wandering. I forced myself to focus on story assignments for the special edition. Mitch and I could handle most of it, but Liza would take on the retirees. I might let Alison try her hand at writing a story. She could do something about college students planning to travel abroad. If any of them at SkyCo CC were that adventurous.

I considered checking in with Vida to ask if Ted had taken Amy home. But even as I stared at the phone, I remembered the old man who had stumbled in the hospital hallway. John Smith, visiting his wife, Mary Smith. I had one of my rare reporter's hunches. Maybe they really weren't John and Mary Smith. Julie Canby had probably finished her shift, so she should be at home or helping her husband, Spike, run the Icicle Creek Tavern. I tried the tavern first. Julie answered on the third ring.

"Are you busy?" I asked after introducing myself.

"Not really," Julie answered. "Only the serious drinkers are here in the middle of the afternoon. I'm in the kitchen making the edibles for tonight. If you have a question for me, I can guess what it is. The Smiths?"

"If I had a prize to give away," I said with a laugh, "you'd win it. Yes, I am suspicious. Are they aging celebrities who are hiding out in Alpine from their fans?"

"No, nothing that exciting." Julie paused. "But he's very protective of their privacy. The wife has suffered a stroke — she'd already had two mild ones — so if she recovers, she may need physical therapy. But when she was admitted, her husband told Doc Dewey that they knew how Vida often put patients' names into her 'Scene' column to wish them a speedy recovery. He convinced Doc that they should use assumed names. It seemed harmless enough, so that's what they did. Besides, they don't actually live in Alpine. Vida might not even know who they are."

"Where do they live?" I asked.

"Somewhere near Baring," Julie replied. "I think Constance Peterson said it was a log cabin."

An alarm went off in my head. "What are their real names?"

"Waldo and Julia Danforth. Does that mean anything to you?"

"No. Not really." But I knew it meant something to Vida or she wouldn't have passed out after she heard Waldo Danforth's name. I thanked Julie and rang off.

A glance at my calendar gave me a start. I'd forgotten my bridge club date and that Fleetwood was having Leo interview Liza in Vida's programming slot. None of my bridge cronies would miss the show, but they were in for a surprise. I did wonder how Spence would handle his star's absence. Maybe he'd already announced the programming change.

I called Milo to tell him that if he was going to be late, we couldn't eat out. There wouldn't be time to get back before the program came on. The sheriff was on the phone, according to Lori. And no, his visitor hadn't shown up yet. Jason Campbell had called from Sea-Tac to say his flight had been delayed out of the Bay Area. Lori promised to relay my message.

I spent the rest of the workday going over notes that some of our travelers had made about their trips. I tackled Violet Hollenberg's first, just to get it out of the way. Unfortunately, she had written it in longhand. "Spidery" was the kindliest description of her handwriting. Violet might not be much of a talker, but she did go on when she wrote. Nor did she stop when she finished recounting their Leavenworth adventure. One of their children had taken a cruise the past year. I only got as far as where someone "threw up in his lunch" — and after a few puzzled moments realized that she meant the person "drew up in his launch." I quit reading, noticed it was almost five, and called it a day.

Instead of taking my usual route home, I drove along Front Street to see if I could tell whether Jason Campbell had finally shown up. Apparently he had. A new silver Infiniti with a rental sticker on the windshield was parked outside. Milo would be late for dinner. I decided I should meet Rachel's ex-boyfriend. Luckily, Lori was just pulling out, so I slowed down and waved at her. Whoever was behind me honked twice. I didn't recognize the pickup truck or the driver, so I ignored him.

Only Consi was still in the front office. "I'm waiting for Mullins to relieve me," she said. "He's late." The new deputy oozed disapproval.

"Jack's dependable," I responded. "He may not be able to find a parking place. I lucked out and got Lori's."

"Jack can park out back," Consi said. "That's what I did the other day when the spaces out front were full up. Have you come to see the sheriff? He's interviewing Jason Campbell, who only got here about five minutes ago. Dodge was getting impatient."

I'd noted that Milo's door was closed. "Yes," I said. "I know. His aunt, Jean Campbell, came to see me today. She wanted me to meet him, so the sheriff told me I could join them." It was a lie, but journalists have to resort to desperate tactics. Before Consi could say anything, I'd already opened the gate in the counter and was moving past her. My hand was on the doorknob when I heard her say, "I don't know if you should . . ." By then, I was inside Milo's office and was closing the door.

Milo looked startled, if not annoyed. He spoke first to Jason. "Meet my wife, Emma. She owns the local weekly newspaper."

Jason stood up and we shook hands. "Are you here to write a story about me?" His brown eyes were wary.

"No," I replied, sitting down in the other visitor chair. "I'm here to learn more about Rachel Douglas. My reporter Mitch Laskey and I have been covering the story of her murder."

Shaking his head, Jason also sat down. "I still can't believe it. Why would anyone do that to Rachel? It had to be a head case."

Milo leaned back in his chair. "I told Jason we're not ruling it out. Will Pace isn't the kind of motel owner who's fussy about his guests. And yes, he's apparently already left town."

I stared at my husband. "Who's running the motel?"

"Fred Engelman," Milo replied. "He's been out of work since Blackwell fired him after he did some freelance tree-poaching and tried to make Jack pony up. Fred sold the timber to someone in Ferndale."

Jason kept looking from one of us to the other. "I didn't know logging was so controversial except with environmentalists."

"It is in a town that was founded on logging," Milo said. "During the eighties, those environmentalists almost put Alpine out of business. But the state came to the rescue by building a community college." He glanced at me. "Emma moved here while we were still in a slump."

Jason smiled at me. "I noticed the sign for the timber company. At least one mill has survived. You were very brave to move to Alpine."

I shrugged. "I figured I'd live here until I retired and sold the paper, then move back to my native Seattle. Obviously, my plans changed."

"It seems like a nice little town," Jason said. "It looks pretty in the winter. The only snow I've ever seen is when I skied up at Tahoe."

Milo was shifting around in his chair, an indication that he was growing impatient with the chitchat. "Speaking of weather," he said to Jason, "I don't want to keep you here in case it starts to snow again. We've already had a few accidents here in town and out on the highway."

Jason nodded. "I was thinking about staying over to visit my Campbell relatives, but maybe I should make that a quick drop-in and hit the road. I felt I owed it to Rachel to tell you anything that might help you find whoever did such a terrible thing. Being adopted — I suppose it was natural that she'd want to know who her real parents were."

"We appreciate you coming here," Milo said, standing up. "Take it easy. The temperature's dropping, so we may get more snow. Does your rental have snow tires?"

"Ah . . ." Jason looked blank. "I don't know. I never thought about asking at the airport's agency."

"Check the trunk," Milo advised. "They may include them this time of year. And watch out for black ice. It's almost impossible to see."

"Thanks." Jason shook Milo's hand and then mine. "Nice to meet you, Mrs. Dodge. I'll try to find a copy of your newspaper before I take off. I think I saw a newspaper box at the diner by the bridge."

Milo had now moved to the door and opened it. "Ask the on-duty deputy working the desk. There should be one handy. Take it easy with the driving."

"Well?" I said after Jason was out of earshot. "You don't have a spare copy?"

"I don't need one," Milo replied. "I'm married to the publisher."

"You never read it," I asserted. "You never even read it before we got married. You and Fuzzy Baugh and Jack Blackwell get free copies because you're all such big shots."

"I don't read it because you always tell me what's in it. Do you want to stand here and give me a bad time or do you want to go home? It's going on six."

"No. We've got time to eat dinner out. Let's walk to the Venison Inn. Suddenly I don't feel like cooking."

Milo heaved a heavy sigh. "Damnit, make up your mind. When it was my idea, you turned it down."

Jack Mullins was now at the front desk,

and I could see his back shaking with suppressed laughter. Luckily, he was now the only one in the reception area.

"Ohhh . . . fine. I'll make dinner. We have to be home to hear the Walshes fill in for Vida's program. Then I have to play bridge. Let's go."

Milo glanced at his desk, then grabbed his jacket. "Want to race to see who gets home first?"

"Not if the streets are iced up," I said, starting out of his office. "Besides, you'd put on the siren. That's cheating." I paused to greet Jack, who had managed to stop laughing.

"My favorite couple," he said. "Enjoy your evening together."

"I'm playing bridge," I informed him. "Your boss can watch whatever sports are on TV tonight."

The phone rang before Jack could respond. Milo and I made our exit. He grabbed my arm and steered me toward the Honda. "I don't want you falling on your ass," he muttered. "Like I told Jason, the temperature's dropped. It feels like more snow."

I was about to open the car door when Mullins virtually flew out onto the sidewalk, calling to Milo. "What now?" my husband asked in a beleaguered voice.

Jack rushed up to his boss and lowered his voice as a trio of teenagers walked by. "Blackwell wants an APB on Patti Marsh, but he isn't sure she's been missing for forty-eight hours. What should we do?"

Milo lifted his regulation hat, ran a big hand through his graying sandy hair, put the hat back on, and looked at me. "When did Patti leave the hospital?"

"I saw her Tuesday," I replied. "She told me then that she wanted to leave, but frankly, she wasn't in very good shape. Check with Ruth Sharp. She was the nurse on duty that day."

The sheriff turned back to Mullins. "Call the hospital, get Sharp's home phone number if she's off duty. It sounds as if Patti left sometime Tuesday, so go ahead and put out the APB. You know what she looks like. Oh — have Heppner check her house just to make sure she's not there."

"Got it," Jack said, and hurried back into headquarters.

Milo and I got into our respective vehicles. I let him go first. By the time I backed out, he'd already disappeared. That wasn't a problem.

But Patti Marsh's disappearance was more than a problem. It struck me as suspicious.

Chapter 18

I rushed around the kitchen, putting dinner together. Milo was changing his clothes, and I'd let him make our drinks when he was done. When he ambled into the kitchen a few minutes later, he came up behind me and leaned down to kiss the top of my head.

"You got an idea where Patti might have gone?" he asked.

"Probably not to her own house," I replied. "She hasn't got a lot of friends. In fact, none that I know of. If I were her, I'd head to L.A. and hide out with her daughter, Dani."

Milo had let go of me, turning to the liquor cabinet. "She can't be in very good shape. Granted, none of Blackwell's blows were that serious, but Patti must've still been fairly weak when she left the hospital."

"She was in pain when I saw her. If she went home . . ."

Milo's cell interrupted me. "Dodge

here . . . Where was the light inside the house? . . . Okay, Sam . . . Right . . . Tell Mullins to add the car's description to the APB . . . . Keep me in the loop." He pocketed the cell. "Patti went off in her car. Apparently she took some clothes with her. Where the hell would she go? Maybe she *is* heading south."

"That's not a bad idea if she did," I said. "I assume she'd fly down there. But I wonder if she can get as far as the airport in her condition. I suppose she could stop somewhere along the way to spend the night."

Milo was pouring our drinks. "The APB may pay off. But if Patti left town when you think she did, she could be in L.A. by now. I suppose she could pay for the flight."

"Patti has Jack's credit card. I've seen her flash it around. Unless, of course, he's cancelled it."

"He might do that," Milo conceded, handing me my glass of bourbon, 7-Up, and ice. "Are you going to sit down for a few minutes or are you still cooking?"

"Everything's cooking itself," I replied, and led the way into the living room. "By the way, have you turned up anything about the missing Mickey O'Neill and Sofia Nelson?"

Milo shook his head. "Zip. No action on the APB. They've gone to ground."

"If the car was in the river, is there any chance they might have been in the car but tried to get out and were drowned?"

"Dubious." Milo sat down in the easy chair. "It was probably pushed. There were some tire marks farther up on the riverbank that belonged to the Mazda. No usable fingerprints on the car. I'm guessing Mickey pushed it into the Sky. Give it up, Emma. Even if Sofia's a willing accomplice, she may not want to leave her kid. I hear that LaVerne's out of the hospital. There was a light on over at the Nelsons' when I came home."

"Maybe Sofia's there, too," I said after settling onto the sofa.

"Stop, little Emma. You're doing that speculating thing again. I don't want you going near that Nelson house, okay?"

I decided to shut up. We spent the next fifteen minutes speaking of family matters. Milo had heard from his son, Brandon. He and Solange had come up with some names for the baby, who was due in March. They hadn't wanted to know whether the newcomer would be a boy or a girl, so they had three names chosen that would suit either sex.

"Casey, Riley, and Kerry?" I repeated. "They all sound Irish. I thought Solange was French."

"She is," Milo replied, "but only half. The other half is Polish."

"Then . . . ?"

"Don't ask," Milo sighed. "I didn't. At least they're real names and not some made-up bullshit."

"True. Liza told me a couple of weeks ago that one of the Gustavsons had named their little boy Rocket."

Milo laughed. "How did Vida take that? She's somehow related to the Gustavsons, but I've never figured out how."

"Me neither," I agreed as the timer on the stove went off. "Let's eat."

After we finished dinner, it was almost time for *Cupboard.* I turned the radio on a couple of minutes early to hear how Spence was going to deal with Vida's absence. As I should have guessed, he did it with his usual aplomb.

"Your favorite neighbor, Vida Runkel, won't be joining us tonight," he said in his rich radio voice. "Vida was in a car accident, but her injuries were minor and she's on the not-so-dangerous road to recovery." He went on to introduce Leo and Liza Walsh with a plug for the *Advocate*.

Leo announced that he was officially introducing his wife, Liza, who had recently moved to Alpine. Then he used an interview format to get her impressions about making a new home in Skykomish County. Liza was eloquent and full of praise for the town and the newspaper.

"Nice job," I said when the program ended with the usual sound effect of a cupboard door closing. "But Spence didn't say anything about the possibility of Vida quitting the show."

"That's their problem," Milo said. "Want to sit on my lap?"

I'd gotten to my feet. "No! I have to play bridge. Did you forget?"

"Oh. I guess I did." He looked faintly chagrined. "Don't stay all night. Where are you playing?"

"Just a block away at Edna Mae Dalrymple's. Obviously, I'm walking there."

"Be careful. Watch out for ice."

I shrugged into my car coat. "Maybe I should skate there."

"You'd fall down before you got to the sidewalk."

"Probably." I leaned down and, for a change, *I* kissed the top of *his* head. Then I went out the front door.

■ ■ ■ ■

Only half of the eight players had assembled when I got there a little before seven-thirty. Edna Mae greeted me at the door. "Oh, do come in! It's terribly cold outside tonight and the wind has suddenly become very brisk. I'm afraid we're going to get more snow. We were just talking about Vida not being on her program tonight." She paused to glance at Mary Lou Blatt. "Will she be all right? Mary Lou told us she'd been in a car accident before we heard the program."

I could imagine the glee with which Mary Lou had delivered the news. "That's true," I said, taking off my jacket and handing it to Edna Mae. "But she's doing quite well and may be home in a day or so."

Mary Lou's sharp ice-blue gaze pinned itself on me. "My sister-in-law should give up driving. I intend to do that in another few years when I get to be her age."

Having always thought that Mary Lou was a couple of years older than Vida, I merely smiled. "That's up to her. She may decide to replace her car rather than have it fixed. It did suffer some severe damage."

The ice-blue gaze narrowed at me. "I heard it was totaled. A complete mess. Undrivable."

"That's up to her insurance agent," I said, and was saved from any further comments by the arrival of Janet Driggers, who hadn't bothered to knock or ring the bell.

"Just open the wine bottles," she demanded, all but falling through the front door. "Al's leaving me!"

We all stared as Janet braced herself on an armchair by the door.

"No, no!" Edna Mae squeaked, struggling to shut the door as the brisk wind followed Janet into the house. "Al would never do that!"

"Well, he is," Janet insisted, yanking at the sleeves of her faux-fur–lined raincoat. "What will I do without him?"

"What happened?" asked Linda Grant, the high school girls' PE teacher. "Is it a midlife crisis?"

Janet seemed to have regained control of herself. "No," she said, sitting in one of the chairs by the card table closest to the door. "It's actually death."

Edna Ma gasped. "Death? You don't mean . . . ?" She couldn't go on and put a hand to her mouth.

"You got it," Janet said. "It's a weeklong conference in New Orleans. I'd have gone with him, but I'm stuck running the funeral home. That's taking away from my other job at the travel agency. Meanwhile, Al will be wined and dined in typical Big Easy style while I try to be in two places at once." She turned to a bug-eyed Edna Mae. "Uncork one of those bottles, Ms. Dalrymple. I need fortification. I also need fornica—"

Mercifully, just then two loud thumps sounded outside. Our hostess jumped a bit but did her duty. I could see the Dithers sisters stomping their feet in a way that was evocative of the horses they raised on their farm.

"Sorry we're late," Judy Dithers said. "Have to make sure the critters were bedded down. Early for them."

"There's no need to apologize," Edna Mae assured them. "We've been catching up with each other."

Connie had already straddled a hard-backed chair in about the same way I assumed she got on one of their horses. "Ooof!" she exclaimed. "Not as soft as Gray Star. Don't usually put a saddle on him."

"Bareback," Judy murmured. "Best way to ride."

Janet smiled slyly. "I know a few ways to ride, too. Bare everything, of course."

Edna Mae and the Dithers sisters looked puzzled, but Mary Lou spoke up. "Let's start playing cards. That's what we're here for, isn't it?"

Linda agreed. "We'll cut the cards to see who plays with whom. And," she went on with a sharp glance at Janet, "let's stay focused."

I ended up with Dixie Ridley, the wife of the high school athletic coach. Neither Dixie nor Linda had ever warmed to me. I found out a few years later that Linda and Milo had dated for several months before I moved to Alpine. The sheriff broke up with Linda two weeks after I arrived. During my first year in the town, I only ran into Milo occasionally at the Burger Barn or the Venison Inn. But Linda had always felt I was the reason he'd dumped her. She and Dixie were close friends, which was why they weren't keen on my company. Small-town grudges last forever. They seemed to ferment among the rocky crags of Tonga Ridge.

I survived the first round with Connie Dithers, who took card-playing almost as seriously as she took attending her horses. In fact, we made a small slam. I didn't really mind when Connie whinnied in triumph as she recorded our score. I was paired next with Edna Mae, who twittered and fluttered in her usual birdlike manner when playing a hand. Over the years I'd become immune to her idiosyncrasies.

Next came Linda Grant. We were pitted against Judy Dithers and Dixie Ridley. Linda was surprisingly benign except for making a snide remark about all the money Milo had sunk into the remodel of our log cabin. Dixie smirked at the comment but kept her mouth shut.

Last, but certainly not least, was Mary Lou Blatt. To my relief, she seemed unusually benign as we played out the hands. She managed to make a grand slam for us even though I hadn't much point support in my dummy. Of course, I congratulated her when she raked in the final trick.

Our opponents had been Connie and Janet, who got up from the table in apparent despair. I assumed it was an act for Janet, who never took bridge too seriously. Connie looked more glum, though she and Judy were dour by nature. Mary Lou, however, remained seated after putting aside the scorecard and narrowed her eyes at me.

"No Vida on the radio," she remarked. "Is she washed up?"

"She can't broadcast from the hospital," I pointed out.

Mary Lou harrumphed. "It's a wonder she didn't. Why was she driving like a maniac down there by Baring?"

"I don't know that she was," I said. "She probably hit a patch of black ice."

"I heard she was severely injured," Mary Lou responded with a glint in her dark eyes. "Will she walk again?"

"Of course. I saw her at the hospital and she was in quite good spirits. Her injuries were relatively minor."

Mary Lou mulled that over for a bit. "Why was she going to Baring?"

"She was going to Sultan, not Baring."

"Huh." She paused. "She's got you fooled." Mary Lou stood up. "I can guess why she was headed for Baring. But I don't tell tales. Good night, Emma."

I watched her bid Edna Mae farewell and go out the door. Mary Lou, like Vida, was overbearing and opinionated. But the difference between the sisters-in-law was that I'd always sensed Mary Lou had a nasty streak. Vida didn't.

As I walked home in the softly falling snow, I wondered just how nasty Mary Lou might get. Vida's mood at the hospital had cheered me, but I realized that it might have been forced. She certainly hadn't been herself before the car accident occurred. Vida not being Vida was akin to the Skykomish River going dry or Windy Mountain turning to dust. I couldn't imagine Alpine without her.

"Well?" Milo said as I came in the front door. "Did you win?"

"Won some, lost some." I shrugged out of my jacket and brushed off snowflakes before hanging it up on one of the pegs by the door. "Did you survive the evening without me?"

"I managed. No calls from my deputies." He stretched and yawned. "Got any hot gossip?"

I thought of telling him about Mary Lou Blatt's implication that Vida had been on her way to Baring when she crashed the Buick, but Milo would dismiss that as spite on her sister-in-law's part. He'd probably be right.

"Not really," I said after flopping onto the sofa. "The presence of the Dithers sisters tends to put a bit of a pall on loose lips."

Milo chuckled. "You should've met their parents. They were two of the grimmest people I've ever come across. They always wore black. Pa asked their old man once if they were in mourning for someone. Mr. Dithers said they were mourning for the whole world, which would end in the year 2000. He and Mrs. Dithers missed seeing that not happen by over twenty years."

"No wonder their daughters are a bit strange." I glanced at the clock radio, which read 10:42. "I'm beat. It's been a long day." I hauled myself up from the sofa.

"You're not going to bed without me," he said, getting up from the easy chair and taking two long strides to stand next to me. "Did you forget we're married now?"

I leaned against him and looked up into those intense hazel eyes. "No. No. Marrying you was the smartest thing I ever did that I never thought I'd ever do."

Milo looked faintly perplexed. "That almost makes sense. But I'll take it."

"Me too," I murmured, and let him carry me into the bedroom.

CHAPTER 19

Only about two inches of snow had fallen during the night, but the temperature had dropped into the upper twenties. My winter tires seemed to be doing their job, especially since several other vehicles had already left their marks. I pulled in next to Leo's Camry. It was strange not to see Vida's big Buick in front of the office. Stranger still to think that I'd probably never see it again if it really had been totaled.

Alison hadn't yet arrived, but Leo and Liza were at their desks. I told them they'd done a good job filling in for Vida.

Leo was fondling his empty coffee mug. "Did she have a radio in her room last night?" he asked.

"I didn't see one when I was there," I said. "But she might've insisted that someone bring one so she could make sure her image wasn't being tarnished. Maybe Ted exchanged Amy for a radio to please his mother-in-law."

"Not a bad idea," Leo remarked, then glanced at Liza. "Vida's daughters are like tabby cats compared to their lionhearted mother."

The coffee urn's red light went on at the same time Alison arrived. She stopped in the doorway to the newsroom and held up her injured left hand in greeting. "It's better," she announced, though she spoke in a rather doleful manner. I figured our receptionist had been hoping for a relapse — and another visit with Jan Kadar.

Kip, who apparently had ESP when it involved the coffee urn, came in from the back shop. "Guess what?" he said to me. "We're going to a dude ranch this summer in Montana. It was my wife's idea. She's always been nuts about horses."

"That's great, Kip," I said with enthusiasm. The MacDuffs had never ventured far from the state of Washington except for ski trips to Idaho. With two boys and the rather modest salary I paid him, exotic travel plans had been nonexistent. But the mention of Montana reminded me that I should try to call J. L. Erskine in Hardin again to inquire about his relative Piper. That would be my first task as soon as I filled my coffee mug. At that moment I realized that Mitch Laskey hadn't yet arrived. Instead of heading for my office, I went into the reception area to ask Alison if she'd heard anything from Mitch.

"I just got off the phone with him," Alison said, looking subdued. "Mitch will be late, if he can make it at all. Mrs. Laskey had a meltdown. Today's their son's birthday and she's distraught because he's in prison."

"I suppose she is," I allowed. "Brenda's very emotional." I didn't add that ever since Mitch started working for me over a year ago, I'd gotten the impression that his wife had been unstable even before Troy had gone to jail.

Alison nodded. "Mitch is sad sometimes, too. How old is his son?"

I tried to remember. "Twenty-five, twenty-six?"

"Does he have a girlfriend?"

"He did," I replied, noting that my receptionist's eyes lit up. "But they'd broken up long before he was arrested for dealing drugs. He was also using."

"Drugs." Alison frowned. "If . . . Troy, right?" She paused so I could acknowledge his name. "He must be clean now. Being in jail, I mean."

"Not necessarily," I said. "Addicts find ways of getting drugs even when they're behind bars."

"Has Mitch mentioned if his son still does drugs?"

"No. Talking about Troy is very painful for him. I never bring up the subject unless he does it first."

Alison fingered her chin. "Troy only has his parents here, so he must be lonely. I'm trying to come up with some New Year's resolutions, but so far I've only made two — not using Lori's hair conditioner and calling my parents in Everett twice a week unless I drive over there to visit them. Maybe I could visit Troy so he has someone else to keep him from being lonely." She stared at me, obviously waiting for my reaction.

"Well . . ." I couldn't decide if that was the best or the worst idea I'd heard lately. "You should talk to Mitch about that."

"I think I will." Alison smiled. "Maybe I'll just happen to leave for lunch when he does."

I was torn. My initial reaction was negative, but the more I thought about it, Alison's plan might be a good one. Not just for her but also for the Laskeys, including Troy. "Go for it," I said, and went back into the newsroom, where I filled my coffee mug before going into my cubbyhole.

I immediately pulled up the phone number for J. L. Erskine. Montana was an hour ahead of us, which meant it was going on nine-thirty in the small farming town of Hardin. Maybe Erskine would be out in the fields. Or would he? If we had snow, maybe they did, too. I dialed the number — and got the same message. Apparently J. L. spent a lot of his time away from the phone. Or maybe he was out of town. But I decided to leave a message: "Emma Lord calling from Alpine, Washington, regarding the personals ad you put in our newspaper." I left the number for the *Advocate* but didn't identify myself as the editor and publisher. Maybe Erskine would think I'd found Piper.

Shortly after nine, Mitch called. "Emma," he said, and the heaviness in his voice sounded like a doomsday intonation. "I may not be in until this afternoon. I'm afraid Brenda isn't well. Alison probably told you about . . ." His voice broke.

"She did," I said in a sympathetic tone. "I'm so sorry for both of you. Had you planned to visit Troy today?"

Mitch cleared his throat before he answered. "We thought we'd go see Troy tomorrow, but now . . . I'll try to get an appointment today with Doc Dewey or Dr. Sung. Brenda may need a change of medications."

I'd never known what kind of meds Brenda was on. "That sounds like a good idea. Do whatever you have to, but keep me posted, okay?"

"I will." His voice had a tremor. "I hate taking time off, but . . ."

"Never mind," I interrupted. "Family comes first. Good luck, Mitch."

"Thanks, Emma." It sounded as if he fumbled the phone before disconnecting.

I went to his desk, checking to see that he hadn't forgotten any appointments. His daily planner showed only reminders of ongoing story ideas. After refilling my coffee mug, I called Julie Canby at the hospital.

"Mrs. Runkel may be discharged around noon," Julie told me. "She seems fairly chipper. Her daughter was discharged yesterday in the noon hour." She lowered her voice. "Mrs. Hibbert didn't want to leave, but Dr. Sung insisted. She was taking up space for a patient who needed a bed. We're still overloaded."

"Who's taking her home?"

"I suppose Mr. Hibbert," Julie replied. "I assume he can take his lunch hour to collect his mother-in-law."

"If he can't, I'll do it," I said. "Let me know if Ted flunks the job."

"I will. Of course, Mrs. Runkel may have to stay another day. The doctors haven't made rounds yet. If that happens, tomorrow is Saturday and there shouldn't be a problem."

I agreed. "If she does stay on, I may try to see her later today." I thanked Julie and rang off.

It suddenly dawned on me that I'd have to make Mitch's rounds of the sheriff's office and the courthouse. I'd gotten so caught up with Erskine and Vida that I'd put my reporter's duties out of my mind. Grabbing my jacket, I flew through the now-empty newsroom and informed Alison I had to fill in for Mitch.

"What's wrong?" she asked.

"Brenda's sick," I replied, my hand on the doorknob. "He may show up later today. I'll fill you in when I get back."

Once outside, I slowed down. I didn't want people staring at me. Entering headquarters, I was surprised to see Milo talking to Rosemary Bourgette, the Skykomish County prosecuting attorney. My husband didn't look pleased to see me.

"What are you doing here?" he demanded in less than loving tones.

"Filling in for Mitch," I replied. "Naturally, I'm now curious about why our prosecutor is here." I smiled at Rosemary, who smiled back.

Milo didn't respond right away. "Oh, hell," he finally said, "you might as well come into my office." He glanced at Lori, who was on the phone, and at Doe Jamison, who was manning the front desk. "Hold my calls," he told Doe, then led the way into his lair and closed the door behind us.

After we were seated, Milo turned to me. "Rosie's here because Patti Marsh filed battering charges against Blackwell. But Patti has to talk to Rosie first to make the charges official. As you know, Patti's disappeared. And no," he continued, turning to Rosemary, "we have no idea where she went. Neither does Jack."

"But her car's gone, right?" Rosemary said to Milo.

"Right," he agreed. "The APB hasn't turned up any sightings so far. By the time it was issued, Patti could have headed south to her daughter in L.A. We haven't heard back yet from the airlines."

Rosemary nodded absently. "I suppose it's too soon to check with credit card companies?"

"We should hear back this afternoon," Milo replied. "De Groote's working on that.

Patti filed charges against Blackwell a year or so ago, but she dropped them. She might do the same thing again."

"I remember that," Rosemary said with a frown. "I told her to follow through, but she wouldn't listen. Of course, that's not unusual for battered women. They love the jerk no matter how badly they're treated. It's the worst part of my job."

I nodded. "She should call herself Patsy instead of Patti."

Rosemary stood up. "I may leave the office a little early. Evan and I hope to go skiing up at the pass tonight — if it's open."

I smiled to myself. Rosemary and Evan Singer had been seeing each other for going on a year. Maybe the romance was serious. Both Rosemary and Evan were around forty, but neither had ever married. Evan had inherited ownership of The Whistling Marmot Movie Theatre and he also worked shifts as a 911 operator. I made a mental note to include Evan's annual film festival in the next issue of the paper.

Milo ignored the ringing of his phone and turned to Rosemary. "You probably won't know how it is up at the summit until later this afternoon. The last report I got from the state patrol thinks we may be in for it. Hell, Rosie, you could ski right here in town if it gets that bad."

She laughed. "We could, but Evan's already got a college student to fill in for him at The Whistling Marmot. They're showing *Fun with Dick and Jane.* I told Evan I'd pass on that one." Rosemary turned to me. "Evan's sub is one of Vida's relatives, Royce Blatt. How *is* Vida?"

"She seems to be doing well," I said. "In fact, she may be released today."

"Tell her I send my wishes for a speedy recovery." Rosemary saluted Milo and made her exit, closing the door behind her.

"You're not leaving?" my husband asked in a tone of mild surprise.

"Well . . . I guess you aren't glad to see me," I replied.

"I would be if you knew where Patti is," he said. "Nobody just disappears. Oh — I noticed Jason Campbell's rental car parked by the diner when I came to work. He must've stayed over to visit his relatives."

"He may've stayed with them. They've got enough bedrooms in that big house."

"Right." He stood up. "Now go away before I start messing with your face. I need a coffee refill."

I got up from the chair "Brute. I know when I'm not wanted."

"That's the problem," Milo said, holding

his mug and walking to the door. "I always want you." To prove it, he leaned down and kissed the top of my head. I left with my spirits raised a notch.

On my way out I almost forgot to check the log. There wasn't anything really newsworthy, though there had been several minor accidents, mostly weather-related. I made a mental note to have Kip post cautions about driving safely in snowy conditions. Not that locals needed the reminder. In the town's early years, the residents had dealt with snow on the ground from early September to the start of June. I shuddered at the very thought.

By the time I got back to the office, I figured the doctors should have made their rounds. I called the hospital, where Jenny Bjornson answered.

"Mrs. Runkel is on the phone," she informed me. "She wants to go home today, but Dr. Sung told her she couldn't until tomorrow. I think she threatened to call Doc Dewey. She said he had more sense than Dr. Sung."

"Right," I said, "Sung's only been here ten years. Please tell Mrs. Runkel I'll come to see her during my lunch hour."

After hanging up, I went into the front office to ask Alison if Mitch had received any calls that might smack of news. She said he hadn't, just a reminder of his Monday dental appointment with Dr. Starr. I then headed for the back shop to alert Kip to post the weather advisory on our website. I was just returning to the newsroom when Alison came from the other direction to leave a note for Leo.

"It's about that personals ad from Montana," she explained. "A Mr. Erskine called to say we could cancel it. Apparently he found Piper."

"He did?" I was unexpectedly startled. "Did he explain how?"

Alison shook her head. "He didn't go into details. I suppose Piper showed up."

"What number did he call from?"

"I'd have to check our caller ID," Alison said.

"Let me do it." Seeing our receptionist's curious expression, I conjured up a lame excuse. "It's a journalist's hunch. I think I may know someone who came from Hardin."

Alison shrugged. "Sure, go for it."

We both went into the front office, where she clicked on the incoming call number. "Thanks, Alison." I started to turn away, but stopped. "I see your wrist must be better. You only have some surgical tape on it today."

"It is," she said. "I stopped in at the clinic after work last night to have it checked out. Jan thought it was mending fairly fast. He told me to check back with him tomorrow. It's Saturday, of course, but he told me he'd be available in the afternoon."

I managed to keep a straight face. "That's good. You don't want to overdo it."

"Right. Jan insists I should go easy."

"Very smart." I went back through the newsroom.

My phone rang about five minutes later. It was Janet Driggers's husband, Al, calling from the funeral home. "Cubby Pierce's widow passed away last night. Melva — Kitty was her nickname, very fond of cats — would have been a hundred this coming Tuesday." Al's voice was as dry and moribund as if he could see the Grim Reaper beckoning to him.

The names were vaguely familiar. I recalled only Cubby. Vida had mentioned him years ago in connection with some weird hobby he had, which I couldn't remember except that it had something to do with chickens and whiskey. "When are the services?"

"I don't know yet," Al said. "Only one of

the Pierces still lives in Alpine. Nell Pierce Blatt is one of Vida's sisters-in-law. I believe her first name is actually Eleanor. She's trying to contact other family members, but I understand they're scattered all over the country."

"Just let us know," I reminded him.

"Of course." It almost sounded as if Al had put an exclamation point on his words. But not quite. "I have a question for you, Emma."

"Go ahead," I urged him. "I don't guarantee I can answer it, though."

"I got a call this morning from Montana," Al began as if he were reading from a book. "The man asked if we could ship the body of the poor young woman who was killed here to a town called Hardin. I told him the body had already been sent to Oakland. Isn't that correct?"

"Yes. That's where Rachel Douglas was from. Did the man identify himself?"

"No," Al replied, sounding even more dismal than usual. "When I gave him the information, he hung up on me. That struck me as rather rude."

"It was. Do you still have his number?"

"No. I was on the extension in the vault. We only have an older phone there. It belonged to my father and I keep it for sentimental reasons."

"But," I said, "the call would've come to your other phones, right?"

"Yes, yes, it would. Why do you ask?"

I hesitated, not really wanting to explain my complicated reason. "Just curious. You know what we journalists are like."

"My, yes, always seeking the facts." There was a faint hint of humor in Al's voice. Or maybe he had gas. "I must ring off as I have another call. Take care, Emma."

I tried again to phone Vida but got a busy signal. That was a good sign, though I would expect her to be able to talk from the grave. The rest of the morning was spent dealing with some minor stories Mitch would have handled if he'd been in the office. Around eleven I checked in again with the weather service. The snow was accumulating, and they were predicting up to ten inches. I decided I'd drive up to the hospital.

But first I called the sheriff. Lori put me through immediately. "Do you have anything like news for me?" I asked in my meekest fake-wife voice.

"Hell, no," my husband growled back. "The airlines haven't got a Patti Marsh listed on any flight to California. No Marshes of any kind."

"Maybe you should try Montana," I suggested, not quite as meekly. "She may've gone there to check out her windfall of land."

"I wondered about that," Milo said in his normal voice. "But I just heard that they haven't spotted her car in the Sea-Tac underground parking."

I looked up to see RestHaven's PR staffer, Kay Burns, heading my way. "I've got a visitor. Talk to you later." For once, I hung up on Milo.

Kay, who was remarkably well preserved in her late fifties, especially for having been married five times, looked grim. "I've got a news release for you, Emma. It's nothing you need to rush onto your website." She handed me a letter-sized envelope before sitting down.

I removed the single sheet of paper and read the first line. "Iain Farrell is resigning?" I said in surprise.

"Yes, as of February first." Kay's expression didn't change while I skimmed through the rest of the announcement. She'd unzipped her green bubble coat and pulled off the fur-trimmed hood. Farrell's reasons for quitting were summed up as feeling he'd grown stale in the job and needed new challenges.

I stared at Kay. "He's only been at Rest-

Haven for a little over a year," I said. "Have you any idea why he wants to move on?"

Kay sighed. "No. Iain and I are not close. I tried to offer him my friendship, but he remained aloof. He seems to be a true loner."

It occurred to me that Kay might have offered more than just friendship. She wasn't the type of woman who could survive very long without a man. "He gave your boss less than a week's notice. I assume Iain has another job?"

"If he has, Dr. Woo doesn't know about it." Kay looked miffed. "Iain has never concerned himself with the feelings of others."

She made a move on him and he turned her down? The thought stayed with me. "He's always struck me as a very self-centered person. I walked out on my first and only interview with him."

"Good for you," Kay asserted with the hint of a smile. "I remember your article about him was very brief, especially compared with the lengthier and more flattering ones you and your reporter wrote for the rest of our administrators."

"It's not easy turning a jackass into a Shetland pony." I paused. "I shouldn't say that, but he was very difficult."

"I know." Her expression turned ironic. "Yet his methods with patients were quite successful. I always wondered if he related to them because of his own unpleasant personality."

"How did he get along with the rest of the staff?"

"Iain avoided his colleagues as much as he could," Kay replied. "He rarely spoke up at senior staff meetings — or so I've been told. Basically, he was antisocial. He should have been treating himself." She paused to put her hood back up. "When will this run in the paper?"

"In next week's issue," I replied. "I'll call Dr. Woo to get a quote, of course. Will he be around this afternoon?"

"Probably." Kay stood up. "But could you wait until Monday? I imagine Dr. Woo is focused on finding a replacement. Iain should've given more notice. Typical, though — always thinking only of himself." With a shake of her head, she turned toward the door. "Have a pleasant weekend."

I wished her the same. But I noticed that her exit from my cubbyhole wasn't as brisk as her entrance. She walked as if she were carrying something heavy. I wondered if it might be her heart.

Chapter 20

The snow was coming down harder when I left for the hospital. After parking in the underground visitor area, I took the elevator up to the main patient floor. The nurse on duty was again Ruth Sharp. She actually looked up from her ever-present charts to speak to me.

"If you're here to see Mrs. Runkel, she's on the phone," Ruth said with disapproval. "It's a wonder she doesn't wear it out. I feel sorry for her roommate, poor Mrs. Smith. It's a blessing that she's virtually comatose." Without waiting for me to respond, her eyes zipped back to the charts.

As I entered the room, Vida was hanging up. I noticed she was wearing an older pair of glasses. "You can see again," I said in greeting.

"Not as well with these older ones," she replied with a grimace. "I'm due for an eye examination next month. I'll try to see if I can't get in earlier if someone cancels. Do tell me what's new."

I decided not to mention the homicide investigation. Rachel Douglas wasn't from Alpine and Vida had little interest in the deaths of nonresidents. "The big news is that Patti Marsh has disappeared."

"No!" Vida's gray eyes glinted. "I heard from Billy that she filed charges against Blackwell. She did that once before, but didn't carry through. Did Patti disappear as soon as she sneaked out of the hospital?"

Deputy Bill apparently hadn't yet relayed the news to his aunt. "She went home long enough to get some clothes, and her car's gone. Did you hear about Patti's inheritance in Montana?"

"Yes," Vida replied. "You recall that my niece Judi Hinshaw works for Marisa Foxx at what now will be officially called Foxx and Sibley, since Simon Doukas retired a couple of years ago. Patti called to make an appointment, but Marisa was booked until toward the end of next week."

"I didn't know that," I admitted, feeling piqued. Marisa and I had formed a friendship over the years. "Marisa should've told me. I saw her after church last week, but we didn't talk. I'll have to call her."

Vida waved a hand. "Oh, lawyers! My son-in-law in Tacoma is always so wrapped up in whatever case he's working on. He never seems to have time to sit down and visit with me. Patti will spend that inheritance as fast as it comes in. Much of it will go into her liquor cabinet. My, my!"

I was about to say I agreed when I noticed that Mrs. Smith seemed to be twitching a bit in the other bed. She was also trying to say something that sounded like "Wa, wa, wa . . ."

"She must want some water," I said. "Why don't you ring for Nurse Sharp?"

Vida sniffed. "Ruth is a sorry excuse for a nurse. She was in school with my Beth and was always full of herself, fawning over the teachers."

"I'll give Mrs. Smith some water," I volunteered, seeing a glass and an almost full pitcher on the table by her bed. But as I stood up, I saw that she had rolled over and apparently had gone back to sleep. I filled her glass halfway and set it within reach.

"You needn't have bothered," Vida said. "She's always saying 'wa-wa-wa,' but she never seems to take a drink. In fact, the poor woman hardly moves. I don't think she lives in Alpine or I would recognize the name. One of the nurses told me her husband paces the hallway but never seems to come into the room to see her. Of course, men are useless when it comes to illness."

"They feel helpless, I suppose. It hurts their masculinity."

Vida nodded in vigorous agreement. "Speaking of men, it's absurd that Dr. Sung says I need another day here. I need to catch up with my housework and tend to Amy. The main thing is telling her to get some spunk."

Before I could respond, a young, freckled orderly arrived with two lunch trays. He set one in front of Vida but left the other one on a stand between the beds. "I guess she's not ready to eat," he said, then shrugged before leaving the room.

Eyeing the tray with suspicion, Vida made a face. "The food here is barely tolerable. I'll be happy to cook for myself when I get home." She paused to lift up the lid. "A cheese sandwich on whole-wheat bread? Tapioca pudding? Three white mints for dessert? Really now!"

Vida replaced the lid while I wondered if the lunch wouldn't have tasted better than what she made for herself. "I'll wait to eat until after you leave," she said. "It's not as if I have to worry about it cooling off. Now do tell what I may've missed besides Patti's disappearance."

There wasn't much to tell. I mentioned Alison's injuries from her fall, which evoked mild sympathy. Noting that it was almost twelve-thirty and my stomach was growling, I told her I should be on my way.

"I hope to do the same a bit later," Vida declared. "Oh — I forgot to tell you that Jean Campbell stopped by this morning. She keeps track of our Presbyterians who are hospitalized. Jean's what we call our Florence Nightingale. Their nephew Jason called on her and Lloyd last night. He's visiting old friends here. Jason was amazed how much Alpine has grown since his last trip ten years ago. He was, of course, much impressed."

He'd better be, I thought. Vida wouldn't have mentioned his visit if he hadn't been. But I noticed she made no mention of why he'd come here. Maybe Jason had never given his reason to his aunt Jean.

I left Vida to her wretched lunch and drove away from the hospital's underground parking into what was now a thick snowfall. Navigating cautiously, I went straight down Third and turned right on Front to drive the two blocks to the office. As soon as I arrived, I called the Venison Inn and asked them to do takeout for me.

Except for Kip, who rarely went out to

eat, the office was empty. His wife, Chili, made his lunch. On our Tuesday pub night, she brought him dinner. If the MacDuffs were Catholic, I'd ask the Vatican to submit Chili's name for future sainthood. She was also raising two young boys.

I checked my phone for messages, but there were none. We officially close between noon and one, so any calls I receive while Alison is away from her desk trunk over to my phone. I'd gotten so distracted by Kay's news about Farrell that I'd forgotten to ask about the proposed construction of an Alzheimer's patients' wing at RestHaven. I made a note to call her later on. Meanwhile, I sank my teeth into the Venison Inn's Dungeness crab salad sandwich. Such a delicacy wasn't available at the Burger Barn.

Ten minutes later, my phone rang. Mitch's gloom-laden voice informed me he was taking Brenda to visit Troy. She couldn't wait until Saturday, and after all, it *was* their son's birthday. I wished them luck and rang off.

Just after one the phone rang. Milo's voice was on the other end. "Blackwell's skipped town. I can't officially charge the bastard if he's not here. You can't put that in the paper, can you?"

"It's not illegal to leave town," I replied.

"Maybe he's looking for Patti. Who's running his mill?"

"His second-in-command, Bob Sigurdson. I ran into him at the Burger Barn. He swears he doesn't know where his boss has gone, and I figure he's telling the truth."

"He probably is," I agreed. "Why are you telling me this? You often like to keep secrets from your wife."

"Because I want to keep my wife," Milo retorted. "Are you able to drive home with just those snow tires?"

I grimaced. "I did okay getting back here from the hospital a half hour or so ago. I went to see Vida."

"The forecast's pretty grim. I'll call you before five." He hung up.

Alison skittered through the newsroom, waving a phone message. "I forgot to give this to you. It came in just before I left for lunch. Guess what? Jan called and asked me to eat with him in the hospital cafeteria. I walked up there and he drove me back."

"Gee," I said, "I could've eaten there with you two. I was visiting Vida during the lunch hour."

"Emma . . ." But she knew I was teasing. "He told me my wrist was doing really well. The downer is that when it's healed, I won't have an excuse to see him after work."

"If he asked you out for lunch, can dinner be far behind?"

Alison looked uncertain. "I thought maybe he would, but he didn't. Now I wonder if I made a poor impression."

"Dubious," I responded. "Did you hear the story of his life?"

"Not exactly. That's one of the things I like about him. *He* asked *me* questions." Alison all but simpered.

I, however, kept a straight face. "That's a good sign. He's not stuck on himself."

"He's not. I mean, he comes from a big family. Jan has four sisters and two brothers. Yes, his father is Hungarian. He says he's Magyar, not Slavic, but Hungary is surrounded by countries that are. Slavic, I mean."

I agreed that Jan probably knew his roots. Then I asked if I could see the phone message she was clutching. To my surprise, it was from Patti Marsh. "What did she say?"

"Not much," Alison replied. "She sounded kind of strange. But Patti drinks a lot — or so I've heard. She told me she'd try to call back later."

"Okay." Obviously, our receptionist was so wrapped up in Jan that she hadn't heard Patti was missing. I wondered if I should let Milo know that we'd heard from her, but decided I'd wait to see if Patti called again.

Just after three-thirty, Lori Cobb phoned for Mitch, not realizing he wasn't at work. Alison put her through to me. "There've been two bad accidents out on Highway 2," the sheriff's receptionist informed me. "I didn't realize Mitch hadn't come in today."

"He took the day off," I said, not wanting to violate my reporter's privacy. "Any locals involved?"

"Yes, just one, Lee Anne Gustavson. Isn't she related to Mrs. Runkel?"

"Probably. Half of Alpine is. Was she badly hurt?"

"No, only minor injuries," Lori replied. "But a couple from Cashmere were killed when their car crashed into that cabin by Baring. Fortunately, nobody was inside. The car they were driving had no chains and it skidded off the highway. Do you want their names?"

I told her that I did.

Lori continued. "The deceased are Jonathan and Caroline Jacobs, both sixty-seven. The other accident involved Anthony Scarpetti —" She paused to spell the last name. "He suffered chest and leg injuries and was sent to the hospital here. He's forty-two and from Everett. His SUV crossed the center line just this side of Skykomish and hit the car that Lee Anne Gustavson was in. The driver, Tyler Evans of Monroe, suffered chest and head injuries. He was taken to the hospital in Monroe. That's just as well since he's from there and Alpine Memorial is at capacity."

"How did Lee Anne get back to town?"

"Dustin Fong gave her a ride," Lori replied. "He was at the scene with Sam Heppner. The boss and Consi handled the other one. I don't think the sheriff will be in a very good mood when he gets home tonight."

"I'm used to it," I said. "Do you think he'll be able to leave at five? He may insist on giving me a ride home."

"Ohhh . . . I can't say," Lori admitted. "There's a lot of paperwork involved with two bad wrecks. Maybe you'd better walk here if you have to wait for him."

"Okay. I won't bother calling him before I get there. Thanks for the heads-up."

I finalized my story assignments for the special edition. Mitch could take on Janet Driggers — who might annoy him with her bawdy mouth, though he'd probably heard everything and more on his beat in Detroit. She could give him any information on locals who had already booked trips for the coming year. Liza could interview any of the travelers from last year that we hadn't already covered. If Vida was willing, she could interview residents of the retirement home about their vacation plans. If not, Liza could handle that as well.

By three o'clock, the only person in the newsroom was Leo. I went out to let him know how the special edition was shaping up in my mind.

"Sounds good," he said, lighting a cigarette. "I've already put together a list of our advertisers. I can probably talk a few of the businesses farther down the Highway 2 corridor into buying some space. I might even go over to Everett to check with their motels and restaurants. Hell, a lot of visitors to this part of the state come through here on their way to Everett and to Seattle. Why not think big?"

I grinned at Leo. "I like your style, Mr. Walsh. Maybe you should contact the Fairmont Olympic Hotel in Seattle."

He laughed. The prestigious hotel was where I'd dropped him off after we'd met by accident in Port Angeles almost fifteen years ago. Estranged from his family and fired by Tom Cavanaugh for drinking on the job, Leo had aimlessly ended up in Port Angeles. I'd met him on a ferry headed across the Strait of Juan de Fuca, where he was doing a good imitation of someone who was about to jump over the rail and end it all. I'd given him a ride into Seattle without knowing his background and let him off outside of the Olympic Hotel. When I got back to Alpine, there was a letter from Tom with his latest excuses for not coming to see me. He'd added a postscript saying that if I knew anyone who needed an ad manager, they should contact Leo Fulton Walsh at a P.O. box in the Los Angeles area. I didn't need to look far — Ed had just gotten his inheritance and quit without notice while I was out of town.

My phone rang while I was on my way back to my desk. As usual, I answered the phone with my name. Nothing. "Hello?" I said a bit louder.

"It's me," a weak voice said. "Patti. I'm . . . sick."

"Where are you?" I asked.

"At a motel by the fairgrounds. In Monroe."

"How long have you been there?"

"I'm . . . not sure. A couple of days? What day . . ." I heard a rustling sound. Patti must be moving around. I assumed she was in the motel's bed. "Is this Friday or Saturday?"

"Friday," I replied. "Do you have the flu?"

"I don't know . . . ." There were more rustling noises. "I think I'm feverish. Can you . . . come and get me?"

"You need to see a doctor," I said. "Maybe the motel staff can get someone to come see what's wrong with you. If you're ill, you should stay where you are. The hospital here is full up and they're turning patients away."

"Can't you drive down to pick me up?" Her voice was a bleat.

"I can't even drive home," I asserted. "We've got almost a foot of snow." I may have been exaggerating, since I hadn't looked outside in the last half hour. "By the way, Jack's left town."

"That prick!" Patti sounded almost normal. "Where'd he go?"

"I don't know." I considered telling her that Milo was debating putting out a warrant for Blackwell's arrest, but thought better of it. Patti was such a fool about the jerk, she might suddenly forgive him and insist that beating her up was just his way of showing how much he cared. I also wondered if maybe Jack was looking for her, though I doubted it would be to apologize. "Why did you leave in the first place?"

"I was going to Montana," she replied, "to see the ranch I inherited. I . . ." She paused, and I heard her cough several times.

"Sorry. But I started to feel like crap just after I went past Sultan. I stopped at this motel and hung out in the lobby, hoping I'd feel better. But I didn't. That's when I checked in." Her voice had grown stronger.

"Okay, Patti, I'll call the front desk and see if they can help you. I'll let you know what I find out. Give me the motel's number."

More rustling and a sound like something had fallen on the floor. I hoped it wasn't Patti.

"I dropped the phone book," she said. "Hold on. I need to put on my cheaters." After what sounded like a lot of fumbling, she gave me the number. I told her I'd call her back.

"No," she said in a defiant voice. "I'll call you in fifteen minutes. I didn't register under my own name in case Jack bothered to try to find me. I'm in room four-twenty. I'll hang up now."

"How will I know what to tell the front desk . . ." The line went dead.

I dialed the motel and someone named Rose answered. I explained that a friend of mine was the guest in room 420 and needed a doctor. Was it possible to send for someone to see her?

Rose asked if I knew why she needed

medical attention. I explained that she'd just gotten out of the hospital here in Alpine and — sticking to Patti's version — apparently had suffered a relapse from her injuries in a fall. Rose said she'd notify the clinic that the motel used for guests who had health problems. I thanked her and rang off.

But I felt guilty. I couldn't say I really liked Patti, but she'd always struck me as pathetic. Dani's father, movie producer/director Ray Marsh, had left Patti not long after their child was born. That was before my time in Alpine. Everyone assumed he'd dumped her for another woman. Years later when Ray returned to the area to film a movie starring Dani, we learned that he'd left Patti for another man. That didn't faze most of us, but some Alpiners were — and still are — narrow-minded. Vida was not among them. She might vote for any Republican who could breathe without an oxygen mask, but she was remarkably open-minded in other ways.

Since Vida was on my mind, I decided to call the hospital and find out if she'd managed to spring herself out of her uncomfortable bed. Unfortunately for her, she was still there.

"Doc Dewey was most uncooperative,"

Vida informed me in a testy voice. "He insisted I can't go home until tomorrow. Haven't I always said Gerald's not as clever as his father, Cecil? Old Doc would know I'm fine."

It was pointless to argue with Vida. "You'll probably be discharged tomorrow. How's Amy?"

"Still puny. She can't make dinner for Ted, so they're having soup out of a can. Really! The first thing I'll do when I get home is make them a lovely casserole. I saw a recipe in a magazine last week for one with chicken gizzards, onions, parsley, and . . . some other things."

I was glad Vida couldn't see my horrified expression, so I changed the subject. "How's your poor roommate?"

"She's finally shut up with the wa-was. I tried to give her some water, but she turned away. That was a couple of hours ago. She's been asleep ever since. I don't think she's had anything to drink or eat since they brought her in here. I must speak to the nurses about that. In fact, here comes Astrid Overholt now. I must hang up. Take care, Emma."

The phone rang almost as soon as I put down the receiver. Patti's voice was much stronger this time around. "The medic's coming here from the clinic in about half an hour. I hope he's got a jug of pain meds. In fact, I'd like a jug of something else, but . . . to hell with it." She paused, and I wondered if she was holding her head. "I hope nobody's stolen my car. I had to leave it parked kind of half-assed in front of the motel."

"Ask someone at the front desk to put it in a regular guest . . ." I stopped. "If Jack's looking for you, you should mention you want it parked behind the building."

"You think?" Patti paused again. "Well . . . maybe I should. Unless he's not mad anymore."

"What if he is? Play it smart, Patti. He put you where you are in the first place. Okay?"

I heard her sigh. "Okay. I'll call the desk. Bye."

I set the phone down. After talking to Patti, I was getting a headache. But that was a minor problem. If Blackwell had left town to find his girlfriend, Patti might end up with something much worse.

CHAPTER 21

At five o'clock, I started through the newsroom, where the Walshes were arguing over whether they should walk to Pines Villa or take Leo's car. Leo turned to ask if I intended to drive home. I told him I didn't because the sheriff thought the Honda couldn't handle what was now over a foot of snow. The plow had only been able to play catch-up on Front Street and Alpine Way.

"I'd volunteer Milo to drive you there," I said, "but he's probably not going to leave for a while. Blackwell's causing some problems."

"What now?" Leo asked.

Liza looked bemused. "How can Black Jack screw up the town's streets?"

"He can screw up just about everything except running his mill," I replied. "In fact, Bob Sigurdson's running it for him. Jack left town."

Liza tugged at her husband's sleeve. "We *can* walk, Leo. We could stop and eat dinner along the way at the diner."

Leo put his arm around her. "I warned you about winter in Alpine. I should've bought you a fur coat for Christmas."

"It's not snowing that hard now," Liza said. "Let's start hiking and you can tell me why Jack Blackwell's the town villain. We'll walk you to the sheriff's office, Emma. Maybe we can get arrested for bitching about the local weather and one of the deputies will take us home in a squad car."

Alison had already made her escape. I assumed she was riding home with her roommate, Lori. The two young women lived in the same complex as the Walshes, and had I known that Leo and Liza would be worrying about driving home, I would have asked Alison if they could ride along. But that was hindsight. Making sure that Kip was also gone, I turned off all the lights and locked the front door behind us. With a fond glance at my snow-covered Honda, I trudged alongside Leo and Liza to cover the short distance between the newspaper and the sheriff's headquarters.

"I've never been so cold in my life," Liza declared, glancing at her husband. "You didn't tell me how wretched the winters are."

Leo shrugged. "You knew we had snow here. Some years we haven't had any. Frankly, I don't remember it ever being this cold." He nodded at the temperature sign by City Hall across the street, which showed that it was twenty-five degrees, then looked at me. "Do you recall the temp ever being this low before I came here?"

I shook my head. "At the worst it hovered around thirty, maybe high twenties. It'd snow for a day or two, the temp would stay around freezing, then it'd warm up and turn to rain or else the clouds would go away and we'd have sun."

"That *sounds* good," Liza murmured, but she didn't look as if she believed me.

Doe Jamison was behind the front desk. Liza hadn't yet met her, so Leo introduced them. I scooted behind the counter and headed for the sheriff's office. The door was open. Milo was on the phone. He motioned for me to sit down.

"Look, LaVerne," he said, passing a hand over his forehead, "we're doing all we can by putting out the APB. Nobody's called to say they've seen your daughter-in-law or Mickey . . . ." Milo paused, and I could hear LaVerne screaming at him. I only caught "you big dumb bastard" and "I'll have your fucking badge!"

My husband took a deep breath. "You'll have to ask Blackwell to fire me. If you'd calm down, maybe you could figure out where Sofia is. I'm hanging up now." Which he did just after I overheard a few more outraged words from LaVerne.

Milo shook his head. "She hasn't even gotten around to picking up the little kid from the courthouse. They closed at five. Maybe if she gets her ass over there in a hurry, they'll let her take home Clodo or whatever the poor little kid's name is."

"Chloe," I said. "Are you ready to leave? We're giving the Walshes a ride home. Leo's car doesn't handle snow or ice."

Milo scanned the notes he'd made on his yellow legal-sized tablet. "Okay, let's do it."

The Walshes were impressed by the Yukon. Neither had ever ridden in one before. My husband told them his SUV could seat eight. "But," he added, "I never haul more than four perps at a time. Emma doesn't like the clean-up duty."

"Milo!" I exclaimed. "You've never asked me to clean the Yukon! *You* clean it."

He glanced at me before pulling out into traffic. "Not always. Sometimes I make my deputies do it."

"It's very comfortable," Liza said. "Do you ever let Emma drive it?"

"She can't," Milo replied. "It's partially paid for by the county. I don't want her using it to run down a pissed-off reader in a crosswalk."

Both Walshes laughed, but I kept my mouth shut. At least Milo was being congenial. I'd been afraid he might be in a bad mood after the rigors of his day at work. We were now turning onto Alpine Way. The condos were a few blocks up the hill just this side of Fir, our own street.

After we dropped off Leo and Liza, I asked Milo if he had any idea where Mickey and Sofia might have gone.

"How the hell do I know?" he retorted. "Maybe Mickey stole another car."

"Has anybody around here reported a stolen car?"

Milo shook his head. "No such reports this week except for Ralph Gunderson, who called back about ten minutes later to say his wife told him their fourteen-year-old kid took it for a joyride. Ralph's lucky the kid got it back in one piece, especially with snow on the ground."

As we slowed down to approach our driveway, I noticed there was a light on in the Nelson house. I couldn't see LaVerne's pickup. The parking area was hidden by the snow-covered trees near the street. My heart went out to little Chloe. I hoped she still wasn't in the Children's Protective Services shelter at the courthouse. Even being with her feckless grandmother was better than that.

Milo headed off to change while I stared into the fridge's freezer compartment to decide what we should have for dinner. We were getting low on groceries. I hadn't shopped during the week, but I found a package of halibut cheeks and put them in the microwave to thaw. Fried potatoes, green beans, and what was left of an Upper Crust apple pie would complete the meal.

Milo entered the kitchen, where he made our drinks. I waited until we were seated in the living room to tell him about Patti's failed attempt to visit her Montana inheritance.

My husband held his head. "Damn! Blackwell's probably looking for her. It's a good thing she's using a phony name. Do you think the motel people hid her car?"

"I don't know. I gather Jack hasn't been heard from since he took off?"

"The only one he'd talk to is Bob Sigurdson if there was a problem that came up at the mill. Blackwell doesn't exactly have a lot of buddies around here." Milo paused, rubbing his chin. "I can't ask Snohomish County to keep an eye on the motel, but I could have Heppner swing by to see if the car's out of sight."

"Couldn't he go in to find out if Patti's still there?"

"You said she's using a phony name. What is it?"

I made a face. "She didn't tell me."

Milo heaved a big sigh. "Okay, you call the motel. Describe Patti and ask if she's still alive."

"Okay." I reached inside the end table to get out the Monroe directory. But after I found the motel's number, I looked at Milo. "You should be doing this. You're the sheriff. They may not tell me anything."

I could see my husband start to protest, but apparently he thought better of it. "You're right. What's the number?"

I tapped the directory and told him the room number. Just as he was tapping in the digits on his cell, the landline rang. I stood up, grabbed the receiver, and hurried into the kitchen. Vida's voice resounded in my ear. "I'm not going home until tomorrow. Dr. Sung was very unreasonable. These younger practitioners don't realize that older people aren't as feeble as they think."

"He probably wants to be sure you can take care of yourself," I pointed out. "He knows you live alone."

"Yes, and I've been doing it rather well for thirty years," Vida huffed. "But I *will* be released tomorrow at eleven. Ted is picking me up. The first thing I'm going to do is call Nordby Brothers about getting another car, a used one. Maybe another Buick, if they have one on the lot. I think I saw one the last time I drove by."

I flinched, but realized it was useless to argue. Vida was actually a good driver. The accident had been an anomaly. "Call me after you get home," I said. "If it warms up tomorrow and the snow melts, I may be able to come see you."

"That would be lovely," Vida responded. "I should have a decent night here now that I have the room to myself."

I was surprised. "What happened to Mrs. Smith?"

"She died at four o'clock. Just as well. Here comes an orderly to take my tray. I'll be glad to get home to my own cooking. Good night, Emma."

I didn't know what puzzled me more — Vida's predilection for what she considered edible food or that Mrs. Smith was dead. She certainly had appeared to be in dire straits, but there was something about the poor old lady that had bothered me. Then I remembered her frail husband. I felt sorry for both of them. Before leaving the kitchen, I said a prayer for both of them.

But for some weird reason, I couldn't get her "wa-wa-wa" out of my head. Looking back now, I realized that I should have known.

I'd given Milo Patti's room number, and after I hung up with Vida, I went over to sit on the arm of the easy chair to listen in on his call. He identified himself as the Skykomish County sheriff but added that this was a personal inquiry, not an official one. He knew the guest in room 420 and was concerned about her health. Had she received medical attention? Rose, the woman I'd spoken to earlier, was apparently off duty, and her replacement didn't know. She asked if the sheriff wanted to speak to Ms. Hardin.

I saw Milo's puzzled expression before he said he did. We waited as the call was put through. But it rang at least eight times before the woman at the desk informed us that Ms. Hardin had either gone out or was asleep. Milo and I exchanged puzzled looks.

"Okay," he finally said. "But would you

mind checking on her when you get a chance? She just got out of the hospital. You can call me back at this number. Thanks."

Milo pocketed the cell. "What's with this Ms. Hardin bit?"

"That's the name of the Montana town where Patti inherited her money," I replied, sliding off the easy chair's arm. "I knew she was using a phony name, but she didn't tell me what it was."

"Great. I wonder if Blackwell found out where she'd gone and hauled her out of the motel. Heppner can check the motel while he's on patrol this evening, even if it's out of our jurisdiction. Are we ever going to eat tonight or are you trying to starve me?"

"Give me five minutes. You haven't finished your drink." I headed back to the kitchen. Luckily, the halibut cheeks had been on simmer and hadn't suffered from my neglect. I melted more butter in the skillet and flipped them over. Milo strolled into the kitchen just as I was making sure the potatoes were browning in the skillet. After I dished up the food, I asked him what was going on with Rachel's murder investigation.

"We're stuck," my husband admitted. "I still wonder about Will Pace taking off for Mexico. But I can't see that jerk strangling a guest. It's not good for an innkeeper's reputation."

"Maybe," I suggested, "he's not coming back."

Milo pondered while chewing some halibut. "We could try to extradite him. But we have no evidence except as a witness. I did ask Blackwell if he knew Rachel, and he swore he didn't. I can usually tell when somebody's lying, but I don't think he was."

"Maybe she knew *of* Jack, but didn't actually know him."

"Maybe," my husband said with the lift of an eyebrow, "I almost know what you mean."

I decided to drop the subject.

Around eight-thirty, I got a call from the motel. Ms. Hardin had left. No one had seen her go, but the blue Nissan was still parked out front. Someone from the clinic had come by around seven to check on her and found the room empty. She'd paid cash in advance, so they weren't out any money. Yes, her belongings were gone, too.

"Blackwell?" Milo asked when I related the message.

"Probably. Her car was still at the motel."

"I'll ask Sam to swing by there while he's on patrol. I'll have him get the Nissan towed back to Patti's house. The motel people probably won't be able to tell him any more than they told you, but sometimes a uniform can make a difference."

I agreed. But I couldn't help worrying about Patti.

Sam Heppner never got to the motel that night. Although the snow wasn't as deep on Highway 2, there was still enough to cause yet another bad accident. A school bus carrying students from a basketball game in Sultan had skidded off the road and hit a guardrail near Baring. No one was seriously injured, but the bus was undrivable. Sam had to direct traffic until it could be towed away. Then he had to deal with the stalled vehicles going both ways. It was almost midnight before the highway was cleared, and by then Sam was officially off duty. Milo had stayed by the phone to keep in contact with his deputy. I was sound asleep by the time he came to bed.

By morning, the snow had turned to rain. We both slept in, though Milo was up before eight-thirty. When I staggered into the kitchen at nine-fifteen, he'd finished breakfast.

"Any news on Patti?" I asked, fumbling with a coffee mug.

He shook his head. "De Groote's on highway patrol this morning. I asked her to check out the motel if she had a chance. Why don't you give Consi a call later on when you're actually awake?"

"I *am* awake," I declared.

"Then why did you just pour coffee on your bathrobe?"

"Oh!" I grabbed a dishtowel and dabbed at my sleeve. "I can call her. But wouldn't it be better if you talked to her? You're her boss."

Milo sighed. "So I am. Maybe I will, but not until later. Consi may not get down to Monroe until she's almost ready to come off duty at five."

I decided to let go of the subject and sat down at the table. That was when I realized I hadn't gotten anything to eat. Maybe Milo was right and I really wasn't fully awake. But I *was* hungry. Cereal was probably a safe choice. If I cooked something, I might set my bathrobe on fire. It was that kind of morning.

I settled for Cheerios. They should be safe. I hoped that Patti was.

After I got dressed and felt fully conscious, I looked outside where the rain was still falling. All I could see was slush and gray skies. I'd planned to grocery shop, but realized my Honda was still parked at the office.

Milo had gone to the den that had been added beyond the kitchen when we remodeled the cabin the previous year. It was, in effect, his home office. I found him studying some notes he'd made on Rachel's murder. It was supposed to be my office, too, but I rarely used it. There was only one chair, so I perched on the edge of the desk.

"We'll have to get my car today," I announced, "or we may run out of food. I haven't done any grocery shopping all week."

"We can do that," he said in a rather distracted manner.

"Okay. It's really slushy out there now." I peered at the notes. "Rachel?"

"Yeah." He leaned back in the chair. "Why the hell did she come here? Have you heard of anybody besides Jason Campbell who knew she even existed?"

I shook my head. "I suppose she was looking for her roots. There has to be some connection. Alpine isn't exactly a tourist destination, especially this time of year."

"I'd like to nail Blackwell, but damnit, I believe what he told me about never having heard of her. The only other dink I can come up with is Will Pace. Maybe she went to the motel because he's her father, and then he did her in. I'm kind of leaning toward that idea. It'd explain why Pace left town in such a hurry. But extraditing him from Mexico is a pain in the ass. We'd have to find him first, and that means bringing in the feds. If Pace is really on the run, he could be in Brazil by now."

I nodded in a vague way. "He claimed to have come here from Alaska, but hadn't he lived for a time in California?"

"So we heard," Milo agreed, "but his background was always vague."

"Did you ever do any research on him?"

"No. He had all his legal stuff in order. It was up to the county commissioners to check out his background. That was back when we had those three old coots who never did much of anything."

I made a face. "I never thought to have my reporter — I think that was still Scott Chamoud — do any investigating about his background. I thought we should interview Pace, but he turned us down. He said he was too busy getting the motel up and running. That made sense at the time."

"It was probably true," Milo allowed. "I do remember that he hired somebody from out of town to build the motel. A lot of folks resented that, but nothing came of it."

I left Milo to his tasks. Part of my Saturday

was usually devoted to minor housekeeping chores, and by two o'clock I was finished. After lunch Milo had gone through his fishing tackle in the hope of the river dropping enough so he could go steelhead fishing Sunday morning. The sun had come out and the slush had finally disappeared. He told me we could get the Honda so I could grocery shop.

The phone rang just as we were putting on our jackets. Vida's voice was so irate it almost sent me reeling across the living room. "I only got home just now," she announced. "Not only did it take Dr. Sung until past the noon hour to sign the discharge papers, but Ted couldn't pick me up right away because Amy was in the shower and somehow she flooded part of their bathroom. Really, there are times when I don't think I raised my daughters properly. Whatever became of *common sense*?"

"It went down the drain?" I said.

"That's not amusing," Vida declared. "I wanted Ted to take me to Nordby Brothers to look at cars, but he had to get home to Amy. She's afraid to stay alone. Imagine!"

I actually could. "I'm going grocery shopping," I told her, noting the impatient expression on Milo's face as he stood by the door to the garage. "Why don't I pick you up and you can go with me? There must be things you need from the Grocery Basket. Then we can go to the car dealership."

"That's very generous of you, Emma. Yes, just honk when you get here. I would have asked Buck, but this weekend he's entertaining one of his Air Force chums, Alex, who has been visiting his children in Everett. I believe he retired to Florida. Can you imagine a winter with nothing but sun and alligators?"

I had to admit that I couldn't, but said I'd see her in about five minutes.

I explained her problem to Milo. "I think that Amy and Ted feel she shouldn't drive anymore, but this is the first accident of any kind she's ever had. You know that. I'm sure something distracted or upset her, but she's not letting on what it was."

Milo backed out of the garage and onto Fir Street. "Maybe the wreck caused her to lose her memory about it. Shock can do that."

"True." We went down Fourth Street and turned right onto Front, which wasn't all that busy on a Saturday afternoon. I could see my Honda sitting like a forlorn orphan at a family party. There were no cars parked on either side. Milo pulled into the parking space on the driver's side and told me he'd stay to see if the engine started right away.

It did. I gave him a thumbs-up sign, then waited for him to pull out after a gray pickup carrying a load of firewood went by. Vida lived on Tyee between Sixth and Seventh Streets. The Nordby Brothers dealership was just down the hill. I pulled up in front of the modest but well-maintained Craftsman house and honked. Vida appeared like a genie from a magic lamp. I noticed that she took the five steps rather slowly and placed a gloved hand on the wrought-iron rail. I thought of asking if she needed help getting into the car but decided against it. I was sure that Vida's pride was intact, even if three of her ribs had been broken.

"Such a silly predicament," she declared after settling into the passenger seat and adjusting her taupe turban. Apparently she saw me staring at the turban's bronze-and-rhinestone star. "I'm wearing this to cover my hair. I must call the salon Monday and ask Stella for a shampoo-and-set appointment. My hair is a disaster."

Like the hair's owner, it had a mind of its own. My chestnut mop did too, so I sympathized. I also asked if she wanted me to wait to make certain she could get a rental car. But she had called ahead and been assured that the Nordby boys — as she called them, despite Skunk and Trout being older than I am — had a very nice secondhand Buick Skylark waiting for her.

"Did you end up with another roommate before you were able to leave?"

"No, thank goodness, but I heard they were admitting more patients. Actually, I was dressed and waiting at the nurses' station. Astrid Overholt told me that Mrs. Wa-wa-wa's husband was very distraught. I suppose he is, poor man, though he never came to see her after she was put in with me. Maybe he couldn't bear it."

I allowed that could be the reason. We had arrived at the dealership. I saw a green and silver Buick parked near the entrance. "There's your ride," I said, stopping as close as I could get to the dealership's double doors. "Should I wait to make sure everything's in order?"

Vida had already opened the car door. "It better be," she said with a gleam in her eyes. "If not, I'll make a fuss."

I wished her good luck, watched her enter the building, and waited just long enough to make sure that Trout and Skunk Nordby weren't taking flight.

The Grocery Basket was busy. Shoppers were obviously restocking their shelves after being housebound by the snow. After running up a bill of over $120, I arrived home to find Milo pacing in the living room with the cellphone in his hand.

"Right, right," he was saying to whoever was on the other end. "You can't reason with Roy. He's convinced his mama is still alive after damned near twenty years."

I stayed in the kitchen to unload the groceries. Myrtle Everson had been only sixty-two when she disappeared. The last thing I heard Milo say was to tell Roy that we'd gone out of town for the weekend and wouldn't be back until Monday. Then he apparently rang off. Just as I emptied the first grocery bag, my husband entered the kitchen.

"Damn!" he exclaimed, still looking irked. "Why can't Roy give up on his mama? Now he claims the bucket's gone. He told Jamison the old lady came back to get it. His goofy wife, Bebe, probably used it for something and forgot where she put it. Is it too early for me to start drinking?"

I glanced at the clock on the kitchen stove. "It's four-fifty. Just take your time pouring the booze for both of us."

Milo's expression changed to what looked like concern. "Are you okay?"

I smiled. "Yes, but I've been busy. I think

we both need to crash. You make the drinks while I put away the rest of the groceries."

I saw my husband's broad shoulders slump. "Why did you marry me?" He came over to where I was standing by the counter and hooked his right arm around my neck. "Mulehide refused to hear anything about my job."

"So you've told me. But your job is a big news source for my job. It's too bad I can't include Roy's latest theory about poor Myrtle." I frowned. "Maybe I should use it. After I took over the *Advocate* we never ran any of his wacky theories about her still being alive." I eased out of Milo's embrace. "Do you remember how Marius Vandeventer handled the story? Myrtle's disappearance must have been reported to your office."

"It was," Milo agreed, opening the door to the liquor cabinet. "I'm sure it was in the paper because it would've been in the log."

"I should check it out on Monday," I said. "There was probably a follow-up. Maybe more than one."

Milo set two glasses on the counter. "You want to start a new search for the old girl?"

"No, but it's a human-interest feature. The only problem is that I don't know what kind of effect the coverage would have on Roy.

He's already been hospitalized at least once when he got himself into a tizzy. Do you remember what year Myrtle disappeared?"

"Not offhand," Milo replied, handing me my Canadian Club as we went into the living room. "It was in August, because that's when the wild blackberries would have been ripe for picking."

"Kip will know," I said as I sat down on the sofa. "He was in high school back then, and he and some of his classmates formed a search party for Myrtle. No luck, of course."

Milo leaned back in his easy chair and put his feet up on the ottoman. "I had my deputies do some searching, too. Back then there were more places around here where the wild berries could grow. The last big timber harvest was in the late seventies, before the environmentalists moved in with their propaganda. That's when the smaller mills were forced to close."

I recognized the hint of bitterness in my husband's voice. His father had been a logger, but he'd been injured in the woods and forced to take a desk job. Neither Milo nor his older brother, Clint, had wanted to follow in his footsteps. Logging, my husband had once told me, is brutal work.

I agreed. "When I moved here," I said, "Alpine was still pretty bleak. I wondered for a while if I'd made the right decision. Then the community college started up and things began to change."

Milo chuckled. "Now you're stuck here with me. Say, are you trying to starve us to death? I don't see anything on the stove."

"Dinner will be simple fare," I said in a formal voice. "Rib-eye steak, mashed potatoes, and fresh broccoli. No, I don't know where the Grocery Basket gets fresh vegetables this time of year, but they do. Yes, I'll return to the kitchen in about ten minutes. It's only ten after five."

"It seems later." Milo picked up the TV sports listing for the day. "Guess I'll see who's beating the crap out of who on ESPN."

"You do that," I said, getting off the sofa and making a detour to kiss the top of his head.

I was putting the peeled potatoes in a pot of water when a phone rang. I paused to hear whether it would keep ringing, but Milo answered. "What kind of bug does Engelman have up his ass now?" he asked in an irritated voice.

Curiosity overcame me. I plunked the last of the potatoes into the pot and returned to the living room. The college basketball game on TV had been muted.

"I haven't any idea where Blackwell has gone, either," my husband said. "All I know is that he left town. He could be anywhere. Why is Fred looking for him? . . . If he won't tell you, that's on him . . . . Right. It's not our problem, Sam. Take it easy. Sorry you have the desk tonight, but Gould should be back, maybe even tomorrow." He rang off.

"Let me see," I said, fingering my chin. "Fred can't find Blackwell. But after selling the poached timber to somebody in Forks, why wouldn't he want to avoid Jack?"

"How do I know?" Milo replied. "I hope Jack didn't find Patti and do some more damage to her. She's using an alias, but if her car was still parked out in front of the motel, he'd recognize it. Damn!"

"Maybe Fred poached some more trees," I suggested. "He may want to do business with Jack."

"Fred should've been arrested for doing that, but the timber was on federal government property," Milo said in a musing voice. "I suppose at that level, they have to go through a bunch of damned channels. Maybe Fred should have followed the trees to Forks over on the Olympic Peninsula to avoid the law."

I thought about Fred's wife, Janie. She was, as Vida once described her, "a twittering ninny." No help there. I considered calling Janie, but decided that was a bad idea. Or was it? Maybe it was a job for Vida.

CHAPTER 22

I called Vida after dinner to check on her status. She informed me that she was feeling fine and had made a casserole for the Hibberts.

"I just talked to Ted," she went on, "and he told me that Amy only picked at her meal, but he'd enjoyed it very much. She still feels puny. Ted especially liked the sardines I'd added."

Even just imagining what it would have tasted like, I almost felt as if my own stomach was about to rebel. "Amy should perk up by tomorrow." I changed the subject to the Engelmans and asked Vida why Fred would be trying to find Blackwell.

"Well now," she said in a musing tone, "something to do with timber, I suppose. They have nothing else in common. Isn't Fred taking over Will Pace's duties at the motel? Of course, Will probably won't be gone very long. I don't recall him ever leaving town until now. Curious, really."

"Maybe Will doesn't like snow. It cuts down on visitors to Alpine."

"The skiers should make up for that," Vida pointed out. "If they can get here, of course. I think that . . . Oh! There's someone at the door. It's Buck. I must let him in. Take care, Emma." She hung up without giving me a chance to talk to her about visiting with Janie Engelman.

The phone rang in my hand before I could put it down. Buddy Bayard's voice was at the other end. "Hey, Emma, I wanted to let you know I took some pretty darned good snow photos the last few days. You may want to use one of them in the paper this week."

"I will," I said. "Bring them in Monday morning. Mitch hasn't done anything spectacular except for a shot of Front Street."

"I used both color and black and white," Buddy replied. "Say, what's the deal with Will Pace taking off? Did having a murder at his motel scare him all the way to Mexico?"

"Maybe," I ventured. "Though he strikes me as a bit on the callous side. But I suppose even Will needs to take a break once in a while."

"I think it's a first for him," Buddy said. "Roseanna wondered if he was fleeing the country."

"I doubt it. He must make a decent living off of the motel."

"Oh, I'm sure he does. It's a no-frills kind of place. Cuts down on overhead. See you Monday." Buddy rang off.

Milo looked up from the *Sports Illustrated* he'd been reading. "Are you going to gab on the phone all night?"

"I hope not," I replied — just as the blasted thing rang again. This time it was Roseanna Bayard.

"Buddy forgot to tell you about Will Pace's ticket," she said with a reprimand in her voice. "It was one-way. I saw it."

I glanced at Milo. "You mean Will doesn't intend to come back?"

"So it seems," Roseanna replied. "Maybe he killed that poor woman."

"Anything's possible," I allowed. "Will's a jerk, but I assume he didn't even know her. The only reason I can think of for him fleeing the country is tax evasion."

"Well . . ." Roseanna hesitated. "Now I wish I'd ask him about the ticket. But I can't stand the guy, so I kept quiet."

"I don't blame you. Any response from Will would've been rude."

"You're right." Roseanna uttered a truncated laugh. "I said good morning to him one day on Front Street and he growled back, 'What's good about it? Morning's a good time to commit suicide.' I'll let you go, Emma. Buddy wants to play some chess."

I wondered if that was a euphemism for something more erotic. "Have fun," I said, and hung up.

Milo had put aside the magazine. "What was that all about?"

"Will Pace's ticket was one-way," I replied. "You already wondered if it might be. You were right."

Milo heaved a big sigh. "Yeah, I did. I'm not surprised. But why?" My husband didn't wait for an answer. "I'm calling Fred Engelman at the motel."

I watched Milo as the phone apparently rang several times. "The sonuvabitch isn't picking up." He shoved it in his shirt pocket. "I'll head over there right now and find out what's going on. And no, you can't come with me. Stay put."

I stood up. "No. This could be a story for the paper. I'm coming with you. If you won't let me get in the Yukon, I'll take my own car."

The sheriff was already putting on his jacket. He started to say something, then stopped. "Okay. I'm armed. Let's do it."

Milo usually carried a smaller weapon than the King Cobra Magnum he had in his hip holster. A Ruger was attached above his right ankle. Fortunately, I didn't have to be armed for my job, though there were times when I wished I had a baseball bat to drive off nasty readers who wanted to run me out of town.

The rain had definitely turned to snow, though it wasn't coming down very hard. The drive to the motel would take less than five minutes.

"I can't believe you're letting me ride along," I said as we pulled onto Fir Street.

"It beats leaving you alone. I can keep you from getting into trouble."

"It's my job, you big jerk."

Milo turned left onto Old Service Road, which ran alongside the cemetery. It had literally been a service road until it was paved a few years ago. The previous dirt road had been merely called the Service Road, but the trio of doddering county commissioners had added "Old" to the name. I'd assumed that was because they were all . . . old. But I didn't mention that in my news coverage.

We had reached the Alpine Falls Motel, a cluster of small, rather depressing units on Front Street. Limited parking was available by each room, with the door to the office somewhere in the middle. Obviously, planning hadn't been Will Pace's strong suit. Nor was the motel anywhere close to Alpine Falls.

Milo barely had room to park the Yukon. "I don't know what Engelman drives, but there's a light on in the office. Try not to hurt yourself getting out of the vehicle. I have a feeling that Pace isn't much good at groundskeeping."

My husband was right. The first thing I spotted on the mangy grass was an empty bottle of cheap wine. That seemed to set the tone for the motel.

"The damned place is locked," Milo said, then pounded on the door in a way that suggested a sledgehammer.

I couldn't hear any sound from inside, but less than a minute passed before Fred Engelman opened up. "Sheriff?" His tone was wary. "What's wrong?"

"Nothing as far as you're concerned, Fred," Milo assured him as we entered the small but surprisingly tidy office. "Go ahead, sit down. This won't take long."

Fred backtracked to the front desk. "You're here about that poor woman who was killed, right? I don't know anything about her. Will didn't talk about . . . what happened."

"No," Milo replied. "I want to know when Pace is coming back to town. We haven't finished our interviews with him."

"Gosh." Fred grimaced. "He didn't really give me a date. Will knew I wasn't working steady."

"Did you see him just before he took off?"

"You mean like when he left the motel?"

"Right."

Fred frowned, stroking his short, graying beard. I noticed his hairline had receded a bit farther since I'd last seen him. "No. He had an early flight to California and then was going to go on from there to Mexico. I think he took off in the middle of the night because he told me to show up here around five-thirty the first day. Some guests check out real early, like before six."

"Did he pay you in advance?"

"Will set it up so I could get paid by the day," Fred replied. "What I do is I have Janie stop by to take the payments to the bank and bring me back fifty bucks in cash for every day I work here. It's a pretty good deal. I mean, it's easier than working as a logger."

"It is," Milo agreed. "Okay, Fred, that's all I need. But if you hear from Will, let us know, okay?"

"Sure," Fred agreed, looking relieved. "I suppose you like to keep up with folks from around here who might get into trouble in some of those foreign countries. Those foreigners can be real dangerous."

Milo didn't comment. But I knew he was thinking that Will Pace might be more dangerous than the foreigners.

"How," Milo asked when we were back in the Yukon, "did you keep from asking any questions? Are you sick?"

I put on my most innocent face. "You were on the job. As it turned out, there was no story for the paper. We don't *speculate* in print."

"So on Monday," Milo said as we pulled out of the parking lot, "you or Laskey will pay a call on Fred?"

"I haven't thought that far ahead," I replied with a straight face. "It *is* the weekend, after all."

The sheriff didn't comment.

By Sunday morning the snow had stopped, though the temperature was holding just below freezing. Milo offered to drive me to St. Mildred's, but after checking Fir Street, he thought my snow tires would keep me safe. I left Milo at home reading the Sunday

Seattle Times.

Most of the parishioners had braved the cold weather. I saw Buddy and Roseanna Bayard, several Bourgettes, Jack and Nina Mullins, Marisa Foxx, and all seven of the Bronskys. Father Kelly announced before the homily that there would be no coffee and doughnuts after the liturgy. The bad weather had somehow affected the coffeemaker, but an electrician was due to show up early Monday morning. I almost expected Ed to stand up and ask Father Den if he'd ordered the doughnuts anyway.

Milo was watching the NFL pregame show. The Seattle Seahawks would play for the NFC championship against the Carolina Panthers with a one o'clock kickoff at Qwest Field in Seattle.

"Can you imagine what those tickets cost?" Milo almost bellowed as I was hanging up my jacket. "But they'll fill the place and half of those sixty-seven thousand suckers will be too sauced by the end of the game to know who won. I'd hate to be working security for a game like that."

I came behind his chair, put one hand on his shoulder, and felt his forehead. "You don't seem to be running a fever. Why should you care what the suckers pay to see a big game?"

He hit the mute button. "Why don't you sit on my lap while I tell you?"

"I'm not sitting on your lap," I declared. "In fact, I'm going to call Vida to see how she's getting along. I was afraid she might have overdone it yesterday."

"She probably did," Milo agreed. "Are you going to gab on the phone in here or take it somewhere else so I can hear the pregame bullshit?"

I'd moved across the room to the end table. "She may've gone to church. Her Presbyterians start at ten like we do, but go on much longer."

"So do these so-called pro football experts," Milo grumbled. "They speculate almost as much as you do."

"Jerk," I said under my breath as Vida's phone rang — and kept on ringing. I hung up before I got her long-winded message to leave every bit of my information, including the last time I had heartburn.

I went into the kitchen to pour a mug of coffee. Back on the sofa, I went through the Sunday paper. As usual, Milo had read only the first section, with local, national, and international news, and the sports section. He had no interest in the rest of the paper, which was devoted to arts and entertainment, articles about the Seattle area, business, technology, and a couple of others that even I never leafed through. But I did read the obituaries to see if I knew anyone who had died. Sometimes I did. It was a reminder that we are all mortal.

Apparently bored with the pregame commentary, Milo informed me he was going outside to check for possible damage the recent snowfall might have caused. I hadn't noticed any in the front of our log cabin, but that didn't mean there might not be some out back, where our yard sloped upward on the face of Tonga Ridge.

When Milo returned twenty minutes later, he reported that there had been a few branches blown down, but nothing serious. He'd put them in the wood box to use as fireplace kindling.

A little after eleven-thirty, I figured Vida should be home from church. I was about to call her when she called me.

"Honestly," she began in obvious dismay, "the service was overly long today. We had a visiting minister and he talked forever! But I did have an opportunity to chat with Jean Campbell. She was very concerned about Jason's visit to Alpine. He called on them and ended up staying overnight at their house. But Jean still can't understand why he bothered to come up here in the first place. She wonders if perhaps they cared more for each other than she realized."

As she paused for breath and Milo glared at me for hampering Jim Nantz's assessment of the two NFC teams, I moved into the kitchen. I suggested to Vida that it was natural for Jason to be curious about his girlfriend. "And imagine yourself in Jean's place. Wouldn't you be concerned if one of your relatives was involved?" I asked in an artless tone.

"My family members — foolish as some of them may be — don't get mixed up with murder victims," Vida huffed. "Jean felt it was in poor taste to travel all the way to Alpine to get information about the victim. She also told me that some of our fellow Presbyterians had been asking her why he'd do such a thing. Jason's visit struck them as curious, even prurient. I'm surprised that she didn't add 'suspicious.' "

I was a bit surprised as well, knowing how Vida and her congregation thrived on gossip. "It isn't as if Jason lives here," I pointed out. "He went back to California and may not visit here again for years. Frankly, Jean's attitude about him coming to Alpine may've hurt his feelings."

"Perhaps," Vida allowed. "Jean and Lloyd had visited Jason when they were in California a few years ago. They tried to coax him into moving up here, but for some strange reason, he preferred the Bay Area. I can't think why. She even had a nice girl picked out for him, one of my Gustavson relations, Dana. But Jean hasn't been feeling well lately. You probably never knew that she went through the change rather late and had a miserable time. When she told me that she was feeling poorly, I asked her — tactfully, of course — if she was otherwise in good health. After all, I'd been in the hospital. But she dismissed the question, reminding me that we're all getting older. Of course we are! But she's not nearly as old as I am." The words were spoken with a sense of pride.

"It isn't as if the Campbells are immune to a murder investigation," I said. "One of the suspects in a homicide was living with them years ago."

"True," Vida agreed. "But the young woman was innocent. Oh, I must go! Amy is calling on my other line."

I returned to the living room. Milo was getting up from the easy chair and had muted the TV. "Let's eat lunch. The game doesn't come on until one. I'm tired of listening to so-called experts speculating."

We were just finishing our meal when

Milo's cell rang. "Now what?" he muttered. He answered with his usual "Dodge here" and then listened with a growing expression of dismay. "Okay, Consi. We'll have to extend the APB for Blackwell. Let me know when you find out what airline he's on. I'll be at home for the rest of the day. Thanks."

My eyes probably looked huge. "Blackwell's left the area?"

Milo rubbed his forehead. "So it seems. His car was parked in a lot adjacent to Sea-Tac. Where the hell would he go? And why?"

"Patti may be with him," I said. "Maybe she wanted to see her daughter in L.A. Dani had to cancel her Christmas trip here, as you may recall."

"Yeah, I know that." He sighed. "Hell, maybe they went to Mexico to party with Will Pace. This whole mess just keeps getting crazier and crazier. Consi's going to find out what airline Blackwell was on. That shouldn't take too long."

Milo's deputy didn't report back until after the football game had started. He muted the TV and I watched his face go from stoic to aggravated. "How the hell could Blackwell's car be at the airport but he wasn't listed as a passenger on any of the damned planes?" He paused to wait for an answer. "Right, Consi, I don't get it, either.

Maybe he stowed away in the baggage compartment. Or Patti smuggled him aboard. Did you give airport security her name, too?" Another pause. "Okay, the good news is Jack's not here in Alpine. If you find out anything else, let me know. I'm not going anywhere." He rang off.

"Maybe," I said, "Jack and Patti flew wherever they were going on a magic carpet."

Milo glared at me. "You're no help." He turned the TV sound back on.

I shut up.

CHAPTER 23

Except for the Seahawks' victory, which put the team in the Super Bowl, the rest of Sunday was quiet. Deputy De Groote reported back that she couldn't find any confirmation of Blackwell and Patti taking a flight out of Sea-Tac. Milo and I wondered if they'd parked there but had been forced to stay in a nearby motel because of Patti's shaky health.

Monday brought heavy rain with temperatures teetering on forty degrees when I arrived at the office. I can deal with rain, having grown up in Seattle, but melting snow in our mountains could cause flooding in the Skykomish River. The first thing I did when I got to the office was to check in with Kip. We'd have to keep in touch with the weather service so we could post warnings on our website.

Mitch was already standing by the coffee urn, waiting for it to finish perking. "Sorry I missed work Friday," he said by way of greeting. "But the visit with Troy was really worth it. He seemed in good spirits, and that made Brenda feel much better. She started weaving again yesterday."

"I'm glad to hear that," I replied. "My son, Adam, is being transferred to Michigan's Northern Peninsula. Have you ever been to Gaylord?"

Mitch shook his head. "No reason to go there. My beat was Detroit. Who's in charge of the pastries?"

So much for my son's news. I poured my own coffee and retreated to my cubbyhole. After everyone was assembled, I made my assignments for the special issue. Vida hadn't yet arrived, but she might be catching up with Maud Dodd at the retirement home. I was convinced that even some people who hadn't yet become golden-agers read Vida's column with Maud's ramblings. Of course, at least half of the town was probably related to the oldsters.

Around nine-thirty, Alison brought me an obituary. "A Mrs. Overby from Leavenworth brought this in just now. She's the daughter of the deceased and on her way to comfort her father. He's very distraught."

"Understandable," I said, and lowered my

voice. "Have you hatched a plan to visit Troy?"

Alison's eyes sparked. "I'm working on it."

"Good for you. Mitch told me he was in good spirits. But you really should talk to him first before you take on his son."

"You think?" Alison made a face. "He might tell me it's a bad idea."

"Well . . ." I paused. "You know how touchy Mitch is."

"I'll figure out something," Alison said. "I'm fairly resourceful."

"So you are." I grinned at her. "Go get 'em, Lindahl."

She grinned back. "I intend to." With a flip of her blond hair she returned to the front office through the newsroom.

I opened the business-letter-sized envelope and stared at the deceased's name: Julia Anne Roberts Danforth. She had been eighty-one years old, born in Nooksack, Washington, moved with her family later to Bellingham, where she attended Western Washington College, taught elementary school in Blaine, then quit to raise her two daughters. She and her husband had retired first to Long Beach, Washington, but later moved to Baring on the Stevens Pass Highway to be closer to her elder daughter's family. The survivors, including the two daughters, their spouses, and the grandchildren were listed by name. So, of course, was her husband, Waldo Danforth, also of Baring. Services were pending.

Suddenly I wondered if that was why Vida had wrecked her car.

Mitch returned from his rounds around ten-thirty. "Not much news from the sheriff's office except for weather-related problems on the road," he informed me. "What's going on now with your Nelson neighbors?"

"You mean LaVerne and little Chloe?"

My reporter nodded. "LaVerne came into headquarters while I was there. She wanted to see the sheriff, but he was out. She's in a flap because she doesn't know where Sofia is."

"Milo doesn't know, either," I said. "Sofia and Mickey O'Neill have gone to ground."

Mitch fingered his chin. "So the prison authorities haven't tracked down O'Neill?"

I shook my head. "Obviously not, or they'd have notified the sheriff. You may recall the car Mickey stole was found downstream in the river."

"You think they may be in Alpine?"

"If they are," I replied, "nobody's reported seeing them. They weren't at the O'Neill house, which is about to fall down. Maybe it has by now with all the snow we've gotten."

Mitch looked thoughtful. "I should check that out. It's off Disappointment Avenue, right? Don't you think it'd make a good photo?"

I considered the idea. "Go ahead. It depends on how it looks. The county may've condemned the property. You can ask at the courthouse. But beware of squatters. It's been vacant for a while, and a bum or two from the trains may be staying there."

"I'm from Detroit, Emma," Mitch said with an ironic expression. "There's not much I haven't seen in the way of squalor. But I'm glad to hear that things are looking up back there these days."

As always, Mitch's gloom lifted temporarily when he faced a challenge. Meanwhile, I brooded about the Danforth obituary. Vida still hadn't shown up. I began to worry that she'd overdone things and had a relapse. But my deeper concern was how she'd react to seeing the obit that included Waldo as a survivor. Whatever effect the name had had on her, it was deeply disturbing. Shortly before noon, I decided to call Vida and ask if she was coming to the office, but just as I was about to pick up the phone, Alison showed up to tell me that Vida had called while I was talking to Mitch.

"Mrs. Runkel won't stop by today," Alison said. "She's nursing her daughter back to health. Is Amy some kind of wuss?"

"Yes," I replied. "I think all three of her daughters are on the wussy side. I only know Amy, but while they resemble Vida physically, they lack what their mother would call gumption."

"I get it," Alison said with a wistful smile. "I often wonder if I'd've turned out differently if my birth mother had raised me. She sounded kind of overwhelming, too. I was much better off with my adoptive parents. They were great people. They still are. Oh — I didn't get a chance earlier to tell you Jan and I hung out together yesterday with a couple of his buds from Anacortes. He wasn't on call for a change. I thought he might be because of it being a weekend and the weather was sort of iffy."

"That sounds like you two really get along. Guys are sometimes reluctant to introduce a new girl to their friends."

"They were both cool," Alison said. "They're fishermen and spend the summer up in Alaska. The rest of the year they work on keeping up their boats. Or should I say ships?"

"That depends on the size of the craft," I said. "It's dangerous work. There's a memorial in Seattle at the fishing boat docks in Ballard to all of the fishermen and crabbers who've been lost at sea."

Alison looked aghast. "Really? That's awful!"

My phone rang again. With Alison in my cubbyhole, I had to take the call. She scooted off as I picked up the receiver.

"What's with the woman who croaked in the hospital?" Janet Driggers demanded. "She dies here, but nobody notifies Al? I assume you got the obit. 'Fess up, Ms. Publisher."

I counterattacked. "I assume you're talking about Mrs. Danforth. So how do you know about it if someone from the family hasn't contacted you or Al?"

"I have my ways," Janet said slyly. "Oh, crap, Al found out from Nell Blatt, who called to thank Al for the fine job he did on her in-law, Melva Pierce. Trust me, it wasn't easy for Al, given that Melva didn't look that good even when she was younger. I guess Nell knew the Danforths a zillion years ago. It's a wonder she remembered. Her memory went down the drain a long time ago."

I decided not to mention that Vida had

been in the same hospital room when Julia Danforth died. The last thing I wanted was to make any connection between the two women. Janet couldn't be trusted to keep anything to herself. If any of the older folks remembered the Danforths, by the time the gossip mill finished grinding, someone might start a rumor that Vida had done in Waldo's wife.

"Sorry you missed out on the job," I said.

"No big deal," Janet assured me. "There's always a next time, especially in the winter. Business picks up. Al's got his eye on several old coots who are on shaky ground. Got to go. It's quiet around here now, so maybe Al and I can have a quickie in the curtained family mourning room."

On that relatively mild if semi-explicit note, Janet rang off.

Mitch returned a little after eleven. "So I went up to the O'Neill house," he said, sitting down in one of the visitor chairs and handing me three photos. "The place is almost literally falling down. I couldn't get around to the back because everything was overgrown. Too bad we didn't get these shots in October for Halloween. It may collapse before October rolls around again."

"We could save them." I studied the black-and-white pictures. One was of the front and the other two had been taken on either side of the house. The roof was severely damaged. "The inside must be full of mold. The county should condemn it as a health hazard." I peered more closely, noticing a white blob in one of the windows. "Is that mold or a hole in the window?"

Mitch studied the picture. "That's odd. I didn't notice it at the time. I was too focused on the house itself. Frankly, I didn't want to spend any more time there than it took to snap off those shots. I remember what you told me about the O'Neills being massacred by the Hartquists. That was where it happened, right?"

I nodded. "It was an ambush. The two families had a long-standing feud. The Hartquists brought the bodies to the meat locker." Even after seven years, the memory of the O'Neill corpses still sickened me. "It probably *is* mold. Let's not dwell on what that house looks like inside. I was actually inside shortly after the O'Neills were killed. Back then, it wasn't as bad as you might imagine."

"I'll try not to," Mitch said. "But I've probably seen worse in Detroit's inner city."

I didn't doubt him. Mitch went back to his desk while I pondered my editorial. Given the winter weather and the recent vehicular accidents, I decided to urge all drivers in the county to be prepared, especially when they ventured onto Highway 2. Black ice was a potential killer. I shuddered when I thought how Vida had skidded on it and wrecked her Buick. She was lucky she hadn't been killed. I wouldn't mention her accident in print, but I would refer to the number of casualties, including the fatalities.

At ten minutes before noon, my phone rang. The woman's strained voice sounded familiar, but I didn't recognize it until Kay Burns identified herself. "Can you come to see me on your lunch hour?" she asked. "I have to talk to you. By the way, I'm not at RestHaven. I'm at my town house."

"Are you sick?" It was a knee-jerk question.

"No. But I need privacy for what I have to tell you. I'm sorry to bother you, but . . . Do you mind coming up here? I can make sandwiches."

"No, I'll be there in ten minutes. Is there anything I can bring?"

Kay's laugh was mirthless. "I'm afraid not. There's nowhere in Alpine where you can get a set of new nerves. See you soon." I heard a clattering noise as she disconnected. Maybe Kay had dropped the phone.

Five minutes later, I turned off the Icicle Creek Road and pulled up in front of Kay's town house. She must have been watching for me, as the front door opened before I set foot on the stone walkway. The wind was coming down from Tonga Ridge, blowing in from the east. That could mean more snow.

But I hadn't called on Kay to talk about the weather. My first reaction was that she'd aged since I'd last seen her just a week or two ago. I wondered if that was because of Iain Farrell. She'd always been protective of him. Maybe they really had been lovers. But I questioned her taste in men, seeing as she'd married Jack Blackwell in her younger years. I'd never blamed Kay for leaving Alpine after that disaster. Her previous union with Dwight Gould had been even briefer. Milo had said it hadn't lasted a year.

"Thank you for coming," she said, ushering me into the well-appointed living room. "Can I offer you something to drink?"

"I'm fine," I assured her.

"I'm not," she said, indicating that we were both going to sit on the handsome green leather sofa. I noticed an opened bottle of red wine but couldn't see the label. Not that it mattered. I'm ignorant when it comes to any distinction beyond red and white. Kay took a quick sip before speaking again. "It's about Iain. He's gone."

I was surprised. "You mean he left before his official resignation date at the end of the month?"

Kay nodded and sipped more wine. "I hadn't seen him for a few days, but that's not unusual. Iain's always kept to his office during the workday. He's not a social sort of person."

No kidding. I thought back to my first encounter with him when RestHaven opened. He'd been rude from the start and moved on to insulting. I ended up walking out on him. That had been one of my all-time worst — and briefest — interviews.

Kay sipped more wine before continuing. "When I mentioned Iain to Dr. Woo this morning, he told me that Iain had left his practice at RestHaven last Wednesday and apparently left town the next day. Dr. Woo is very discreet, so he gave me no details. I waited until Friday to call Iain, but his phone had been disconnected. I found out this morning that he'd paid his rent at Clemans Manor through the end of the month but gave immediate notice." She paused to refill her glass. "I'm worried about him. He's a lone wolf, but over time we'd established a budding friendship. At least," she went on with a sad little smile, "I thought we had."

"Maybe," I suggested, "he had a family problem. Did he still have relatives back in the Midwest?"

"If so, he never mentioned them." Kay frowned into her wineglass. "He did go into Seattle on rare occasions. He enjoyed chamber music concerts. But I think he went alone."

"Sad," I remarked. Something about Farrell's official — and brief — RestHaven biography niggled at the back of my brain, but I couldn't figure out what. "Do you think he might keep in touch with you?"

Kay shrugged. "I don't know. Perhaps. We sometimes had dinner together after work, either here or at the ski lodge. Goodness," she said, turning away, "I'm tearing up. I think I must be missing him already. Silly of me, really."

"No, not if you liked him," I assured her. "I still miss my former reporter Scott Chamoud and his wife, Tamara."

"Yes, but . . ." Kay paused. "I'm worried about Iain. I think something terrible must have happened." She looked me in the eye. "I'm sure Dr. Woo would never tell any of the staff why Iain left in such a rush, but you're the press. I know you run articles about people who come here to take jobs and those who move on to somewhere else. Could you call on Dr. Woo?"

I hesitated. "I'll send Mitch Laskey. I won't mention your name, not even to Mitch." That was a lie, but my reporter understood discretion when it came to news sources. "Even if you hadn't told me, word would get out about Farrell's departure. That's a story in itself, as his replacement will be when the job is filled."

Kay put her hand on my arm. "Oh, Emma, thank you! I appreciate your understanding. Are you sure I can't make you some lunch?"

"Actually," I said, "I'd planned to meet Milo for lunch." Another lie, but maybe I would see if he was at the Burger Barn. "Please keep in touch, okay? Maybe we can have lunch later this week."

Kay removed her hand, and I stood up. "I'd like that," she said. "I thought it was so nice that you and the sheriff got married. I didn't realize you were even dating."

I tried not to show my surprise. But Kay had only returned to Alpine a year ago, when RestHaven opened. Apparently she wasn't tuned in to the local gossip grapevine. "Milo and I were always good friends," I said. That was lame, but Kay didn't seem to notice. She had other matters on her mind.

So did I. And one of them that we now shared was Iain Farrell.

Chapter 24

There was no sign of Milo in the Burger Barn. I went to the take-out area and asked the curly-haired young man behind the counter if the sheriff had placed an order. I was informed that he had and it would be ready for pickup in about ten minutes. I told him to make it a double order but hold the cheese on mine. I'd deliver the burgers, the fries, and even the slice of cherry pie he shouldn't have with lunch.

Lloyd Campbell was entering the restaurant. He was looking a little lost, so I called his name and asked how Jean was getting along. His expression changed to disturbed.

"Emma," he said, and paused. "Are you eating here?"

"No, I'm doing takeout for the sheriff and me."

Lloyd indicated a vacant booth toward the front. "Do you mind sitting for a few moments?"

I told him I didn't because I'd just put in the order. We sat down after Lloyd appeared to check out the nearby booths. I assumed he was making sure there was no one who would want to eavesdrop.

"I know Jean came to see you a few days ago," he said. "I also know you met Jason. He's a fine young man. But since he came here, poor Jean has gone into what I can only call a slump. Depression might be a better word. I've urged her to make an appointment with Doc Dewey, but she refuses. I guess I'm telling you this because I wondered if you saw any indications of her being overly stressed."

I decided to skip the earlier menopausal trauma. It'd be indiscreet to acknowledge the Presbyterians' propensity for gossip. Over the years, I'd felt that most men believed menopause was a woman's excuse for being crabby about the aging process. I'd had my own problems. I was going through the change when Tom was killed. It took me fifteen months to recover, thanks to Paxil — and Milo.

"She was upset about Jason's loss of his girlfriend," I said. "Jean didn't think they were that serious when they were dating, but maybe she misjudged their feelings."

"Yes," Lloyd replied, still with one eye on

the café's door. "That's the sense we got from him. But making the trip up here seemed very important to him. Of course, Jason's a serious type of person. But still . . ." He held up his hands in a helpless gesture.

"I can understand," I responded. "My impression was that Rachel was a bit of a loner. That is, she had no family nearby. It was probably like a pilgrimage for Jason."

Lloyd frowned. "I suppose you could look at it that way. He told us that he'd make the arrangements for Rachel's burial. Frankly, I felt that should be left to Alameda County. In fact, I told him so, but Jason had made up his mind."

An image of a tight-fisted, thrifty Scotsman flew through my mind's eye. Not wanting to picture Lloyd Campbell in a kilt, I remarked that it was very generous of Jason. "He seems like a good guy."

"He is," Lloyd said, then brightened and waved his hand. "Here comes my lunch companion."

Simon Doukas had entered the Burger Barn. He was down at the bottom of the list of people I wanted to see. "I'll give you two some privacy," I said, sliding out of the booth. "Enjoy your lunch."

I took the long way around to get back to

the take-out area. Just seeing Simon almost spoiled my appetite. But I wondered why he and Lloyd were having lunch. Of course, they could be friends. On the other hand, I'd heard that despite being retired, Simon still took on a case now and then — especially for friends. I wondered if there was a reason Lloyd Campbell might be consulting a lawyer.

"What's with those new owners at the Burger Barn?" Milo demanded as he removed the top of the bun and stared at the hamburger. "They're cheating on the amount of meat they hide under bigger buns. I should cite them for defrauding their customers."

"Does SkyCo have a law about that?" I asked in an innocent voice.

"If we don't, I'll make one up," Milo declared. "Mullins told me they're going to put out new menus and add some new stuff. They damned well better not screw with their basics."

I diverted my husband by telling about my encounter with Lloyd Campbell. Milo wasn't impressed. "So? Maybe he and Doukas are old pals. They're about the same age. They probably went to high school together."

"You're right," I conceded. "You're younger than they are. They would've been out of high school by the time you got there. Now tell me about LaVerne Nelson's temper tantrum."

"I wasn't there," Milo replied. "I locked myself in my office when I saw her truck pull up in front of headquarters."

"You can't blame her for wondering where her daughter-in-law is," I said. "Did she have the little girl with her?"

"Yeah, she did." Milo paused to scarf down some of his burger. "The poor little twerp looked woebegone. I figure she was traumatized by being left in the courthouse shelter. Some of those kids can be ornery."

"I suppose," I allowed. "I gather LaVerne hasn't heard from Sofia?"

Milo shook his head. "Hell, I don't blame her. Mickey's on the lam, so maybe he stole another car and he's taken Sofia out of state. Nothing new with the APB for him or for Blackwell and Patti. The weather's against us, too. Doe says there's more snow on the way. I tend to believe her. Those Muckleshoot instincts of hers are usually accurate. Her people have lived around here for two thousand years." He grabbed four of my fries.

"I have some news for you," I said. "Iain

Farrell has left town."

"So? I wasn't planning on giving him a going-away party."

"I think the staff might've." I gave my husband a steely-eyed look. "Dr. Woo believed Farrell would be staying on until the end of the month."

"That's Woo's problem," Milo said, stealing three more of my fries. "Farrell's another horse's ass. But unlike Blackwell, I've never really had to tangle with him. He gave me some lip once, but I shut him down. What's for dinner?"

"Soup."

"Get serious."

I stood up. "You've eaten part of my lunch. That's a meal and a half. And you don't need pie for dessert. Do you want to gain back the weight you lost last year helping nurse Tanya back to health after she got shot?"

"I've stayed at that weight," Milo asserted. "Ditch the soup."

I'd reached the door. "I'll think about it." I blew him a kiss before moving on. As I walked back to my office, I realized Milo hadn't reimbursed me for his lunch. Maybe I *should* serve him soup for dinner. But I wouldn't. Having eaten barely half of a lunch, I'd be starving by six o'clock. Maybe a stop at the Grocery Basket on the way home was in order.

Just as I was about to enter the front office, I heard Alison call to me as she came past the Venison Inn.

"I skipped lunch," she announced as we went inside. "Jan called and asked me out to dinner tomorrow night. I went to Francine's Fine Apparel to get something new to wear. She didn't have the sweater I wanted in my size, but she checked with the outlet in Seattle and they'll have it here by late morning."

"Wow!" I exclaimed with a smile as we went inside. "Things are heating up."

"I hope so. Oh — Marlowe Whipp came by just as I was leaving. He forgot to give me a postcard for you from somebody in Montana. Now where did I . . . Ah! Here it is. I hope you can read the handwriting. I can't."

The glossy picture on the front was of cows grazing in a big green pasture. "Greetings from Hardin, Montana" was printed in a script font at the top. I turned it over and understood why Alison had a problem with the handwriting. The only thing I could read was the sign-off at the bottom: "XXX OOO Patti."

"Maybe I need glasses," I muttered, peering more closely at Patti's erratic handwriting. She might have written the postcard while she was drinking. My name had been spelled as "Emma Lard" and the message was relatively short. I finally made out the first sentence and read it aloud: " 'We are here in Hardin on my ranch.' " The next two lines were indecipherable. I passed the postcard back to Alison. "See if you can figure it out. I give up."

"Wow!" Alison exclaimed. "Is this really from Patti Marsh?"

"The very same," I assured her. "She inherited a big chunk of land in Montana."

Alison sat down at her desk and got a magnifying glass out of the drawer. "Let's see if this helps," she murmured. "Omigod! Patti and Jack got married! Can you believe it?"

I started to say I couldn't, but realized I had to. "Read it to me — if you can. I do believe it. Blackwell wouldn't pass up the chance to prevent Patti from keeping all that land for herself. Washington is a community-property state."

"It *is* hard to make out," Alison said. "Translated into actual English, the gist is that she and Jack are honeymooning on the ranch. Patti doesn't spell very well."

"No surprise there," I said, wondering

how Milo would react to the news. Suddenly the personals ad we'd run came back to me. I reminded Alison about it. "Patti always went by her exhusband's last name, Marsh. They divorced, but she kept his last name because of their daughter, Dani Marsh, the actress. But now I recall that her maiden name was Erskine. I hadn't thought of that in ages." I couldn't help but wonder about the other Erskines who had popped up.

"I wanted to meet Dani when she was supposed to come here at Christmas," Alison said wistfully. "I've never met a movie star. But then she had to cancel. I was really bummed."

"Dani's nice. At least she was back then. That was over fifteen years ago."

"I've seen her in a couple of movies," Alison said, handing the postcard to me. "Something on TV, too. She still looks good."

I glanced outside. The rain was coming down very hard and the temperature sign now read thirty-three degrees. That suggested we were in for more snow. I wanted Milo to see the postcard, but I preferred not to get drenched in the process. I decided that common sense was better than valor, so I'd give him a call. But before I could do that, my phone rang.

"Emma," Kay Burns said in a stilted voice, "Dr. Woo just heard from Iain Farrell. He's in Helena, Montana, and he just got married."

I was momentarily speechless, though if Jack and Patti could finally get married, why not Iain Farrell? But all I could say was, "He did?"

"Yes," Kay paused. "If you recall from his résumé, he worked in Montana for a few years. With children, I think. His wife is one of the patients he had while he was there. She must be considerably younger." The last words smacked of disapproval.

I still wasn't sure what to say. "Isn't Iain about fifty?"

"I believe so. He was a bit cagey about his age."

Pot, meet kettle. Kay had always been. "I've held off putting anything about Farrell's resignation in the paper." The truth was, I'd forgotten about it. "Do you want me to go public?"

"No, not yet," Kay replied. "It may take some time to find a replacement. I wouldn't want RestHaven to sound understaffed. It might upset our patients."

"Understandable," I agreed. Their patients were already sufficiently upset, which was why they were patients. With an exchange of pleasantries, we rang off. I made a few notes, then finally called the sheriff's headquarters.

Lori answered. "The boss man can't talk to you right now," she informed me. "He's just leaving."

"For where?" I asked.

"There's a situation at the Alpine Falls Motel."

"What kind of situation?"

"I honestly can't say. Dustin and Consi went with him. Really, I'm sorry, but I'm not sure except that it must be . . . serious. All I know is that Fred Engelman called for help, but didn't say why. I think he got cut off."

I paused long enough to hear sirens. "Okay. We'll check it out. Thanks, Lori."

Looking into the newsroom, I could see Mitch walking toward his desk. I hurried off to tell him that there was some kind of dustup at the Alpine Falls Motel. "The sheriff and a couple of deputies are on the way there now. I hate to send you out in this kind of awful weather, but we have to know what's going on."

Mitch grimaced as he grabbed his all-weather coat. "This is nothing. I'm from Detroit, remember?"

One of the problems with Mitch was that he could never forget to remind me.

CHAPTER 25

Liza was the only person still in the newsroom. "What's going on?" she asked after Mitch had hurried away.

I explained that the sheriff and two deputies apparently had been summoned by Fred Engelman to the Alpine Falls Motel. "Fred's the temporary manager while Will Pace is in Mexico."

Liza rolled her eyes. "How long will it take me to figure out who everybody is in this town? Isn't the motel just a couple of blocks from here?"

"Right," I replied, seeing a curious Alison in the doorway. "And no," I added for the benefit of both my employees, "I haven't a clue about what's going on."

Liza shrugged. "I recognize Pace's name. Leo complains about how hard it is to get him to pay for his postage-stamp-sized ad in the paper. I'll bet he has hookers at his motel. Will strikes me as a real sleazebag."

"The description is apt," I assured her.

Alison was nodding in agreement. "He came into the office once when I was the only one here except for Kip, who was in the back shop. He seemed like a total perv. I was afraid he was going to try to touch me. He leaned so close over the desk that I could smell his awful breath. I told him I wasn't able to answer whatever his question was and he should talk to Kip. But he just shrugged and went away."

"Typical," Liza remarked. "That kind of guy is basically a coward."

I was getting antsy. There had been two sirens, one of them the familiar *ga-goo-ga* sound from Milo's Yukon, and the other from a SkyCo cruiser. That struck me as more than a drunken motel guest raising hell. I considered calling Mitch to find out what was going on, but my reporter could be prickly when I appeared to interfere with him doing his job.

A glance through the window above Liza's desk showed that the rain had definitely turned to snow. If I sneaked out the back way, it would take me only a couple of minutes to get to the motel. Alison had gone back to the front office and Liza was making a phone call. I returned to my cubbyhole, grabbed my jacket, and went out through the newsroom's rear door. Kip was studying something high-tech that I wouldn't understand even if he tried to explain it to me.

"Don't rat me out," I said to him. "I'm on a secret mission."

Kip grinned at me. "Sneaking off to Francine's Fine Apparel?"

"That's my cover story," I said, and went out the back door, pulling my hood up over my head. The snow was picking up momentum.

Despite the weather, the Yukon and the cruiser had attracted the attention of at least a dozen other people. Milo and his deputy had obviously gone inside. I couldn't see Mitch. Maybe he'd followed them. I considered doing the same thing, but now another half-dozen curious Alpiners barred the way.

Then I remembered that there was a second entrance in the little courtyard off the parking area. I scooted around the corner and collided with Lloyd Campbell.

"Emma!" he exclaimed, looking very red in the face. "What are you doing here?"

"My job," I replied. "There's some kind of trouble going on here."

Lloyd suddenly looked conflicted, and took a deep breath before he spoke. "Yes. I'm here to help. Why don't you go back to your office?"

"My reporter is already inside," I said, wondering why Lloyd had made such a strange request. "Why are you here?"

Lloyd seemed to shrink into himself and couldn't look me in the eye. "Please, Emma," he finally said. "I have to save Jean." He brushed past me, almost staggering across the open space to the motel door.

If he was going inside, so was I. To the surprise of us both, the door opened before we reached it. Mitch gaped at me as Lloyd almost knocked him down and barreled his way into the motel.

"Is that Campbell, the Alpine Appliance owner?" he asked as I crossed the threshold.

"Yes." I paused to catch my breath. "What's going on?"

Mitch closed the door. "Craziest thing I ever ran into, even in Detroit. His wife — Jean?" He paused, and I nodded. "She just confessed to killing Rachel Douglas. The sheriff is taking her to headquarters."

Almost an hour later, Mitch, Spencer Fleetwood, and I sat in Milo's office. According to Fred Engelman, a distraught Jean Campbell had come to the motel office and told him she'd killed a guest. Jean was so upset that he didn't know if she was talking about the present or the past. He tried to calm her down, but she got more frantic, starting to tear at her clothes and her hair. That was when Fred called the sheriff.

"She'd passed out before we got here," Milo explained. "When Jean came around, she was incoherent. I had Consi take her to the ER. I hope they can keep her there at least overnight. I'll make sure there's a deputy on duty. What I'm really afraid of is she might try to off herself."

I asked if Lloyd could stay with her, but Milo felt that was a bad idea. "He's tapped out," my husband replied. "She'd already told Lloyd about killing Rachel. She swears it was an accident. Jean had met Jason's previous girlfriend on a trip to the Bay Area and thought she'd make their nephew a good wife. Somehow she got it into her head that Rachel had broken up that romance and was hell-bent on marrying Jason. Jean went to the motel to tell her to back off. Rachel denied it, but Jean thought she was lying. She started shaking Rachel and lost control. Jean told Lloyd she blacked out after that and didn't remember how she left the motel or got back home."

"She really isn't of sound mind," I said, more to myself than to Milo or Mitch. "How very sad."

Milo nodded. "Lloyd was so worried about what Jean might do next, maybe even to herself, that he consulted Simon Doukas about having her certified as legally insane."

"She must be." I looked at Mitch. "This is your story. All of it."

Spence spoke up for the first time. "Jean needs to be admitted to RestHaven. Rosalie will try to help her. And Lloyd." He glanced at me. "As you know, Rosalie traveled that rocky road with a mentally ill spouse before he finally died."

Milo sat back in his chair. "I'll have to charge her," he said in a reluctant voice. "Jean has already confessed, at least informally. But she'll never make it to trial. The plea will be that she's of unsound mind."

Mitch and Spence merely nodded.

Back at the office, my reporter was busy writing the story, and I wondered if I should let Vida know what happened. As a member of the Presbyterian church, she might have already heard. There had been enough of a crowd at the motel that the news Mitch would post online in a few minutes probably had already spread from Alpine Baldy to Mount Sawyer.

But Alison hadn't heard of the tragedy. She'd spent her lunch hour at Stella's Styling Salon getting highlights for her hair in preparation for her date with Jan. While Stella was usually a major source for gossip, the salon was far enough away from the motel that the news hadn't yet traveled there. Alison was briefly agog, but she quickly changed the subject, asking me what color eye shadow she should use for her evening with Jan. I suggested mauve before fleeing to the peace that was my cubbyhole.

What was left of the workday wound down without incident. I tried to call Vida, but her line was busy. Even while taking care of Amy, she couldn't give up her need to know all things Alpine. I wondered how she'd react when she saw the Danforth obituary. Maybe I shouldn't run it. But that would be wrong. The family obviously wanted it to appear in the *Advocate.* I owed it to the readers along the Highway 2 corridor to learn of Julia Danforth's death.

Milo called me five minutes before quitting time. "I don't want you driving home in eight inches of snow. I'll pick you up in ten minutes." He hung up before I could say anything.

By the time I was standing at the front door a few minutes after five, my entire staff had left. I saw Liza's car still parked two spaces down from my Honda, but no sign of Leo's Toyota. Obviously he, too, didn't want his wife risking a nasty accident. Liza had probably never seen snow this deep except on Christmas cards. And it was still coming down.

Milo pulled in a couple of minutes later. "Try to get in without falling on your cute little ass, okay?"

"Try to act like you're glad to see me," I snapped, struggling to get my feet planted on the snow-covered ground. "At least you closed a case today."

"A damned pitiful case," Milo muttered as he pulled into what was fairly light traffic in our slower-than-big-city rush hour. "I've never felt this crappy about charging somebody with homicide. What's worse is that poor Jean had no intention of killing Rachel."

"You go by the book, Sheriff," I reminded him. "You have to. The real fault lies with Lloyd for not getting help for Jean before she went completely around the bend."

"I can't charge him for willful neglect," Milo replied. "He may not have realized how . . ." The beeper on his cell went off. "Grab that thing off the dashboard. I have to keep both hands on the wheel going up the hill."

I said hello. There was a pause; I heard voices in the background. "Emma?" Sam

Heppner said as I heard a siren. "Are you with the boss?" I said I was. "We've got a situation at the O'Neill house. It's on fire and there may be somebody inside. Got to go." Another siren could be heard in the distance.

"Damn!" Milo had been able to get the gist of Sam's information. "You're going to have to come with me. But don't even think about getting out of the Yukon. I mean it."

He turned on the siren and the flashing red lights before executing a U-turn in the middle of Front Street that almost gave me a heart attack. It was probably only one of the few byways in town that wasn't totally covered in snow. I could hear tires squealing like so many hungry pigs. But I didn't worry about the Yukon getting hit. It was built so solidly that any other vehicles would probably bounce off of it.

We turned onto Disappointment Avenue, where there was less traffic. The O'Neill house was in what I would describe as a cul-de-sac, for lack of a better term. It was still snowing a bit, so all I could see at first were the emergency vehicles. A fire truck, an ambulance, and a sheriff's cruiser blocked part of the view. I could see some flames but couldn't tell exactly where in the house they were coming from.

Milo pulled in behind the cruiser. "I'm locking you in, so don't even think about trying to get any closer."

Obviously, my husband remembered the time I'd done just that on a previous occasion. As he got out, I called Mitch on my cell. We had to have photos, and the story — whatever it might be — was his.

"Good thing Brenda doesn't have dinner ready yet," he said. "I won't give her any details. She might worry herself into a knot if she thought I was in danger."

I'd lost sight of Milo beyond all the parked vehicles. I could see streams of water being poured on the house, though the flames didn't seem to be dying down yet. Less than a minute passed before I heard a siren and the ambulance rushed past the Yukon toward the hospital. *Who?* I wondered. Could this be a repeat of Mickey O'Neill holding Sofia Nelson hostage? He'd done it once before. I was starting to feel giddy, thinking about Mickey having a lack of imagination.

A couple of minutes later, the flames flickered out. But now it was hard to see through all the smoke and the increasing snowfall. I'd gotten a grip on my emotions by the time Milo emerged from what seemed like a dense fog. He unlocked the

Yukon's door on the driver's side and got in.

"Your reporter just pulled up," he said. "He can talk to me in my office. I have a report to fill out. You might as well come along to figure out what you want to put online."

"Who was in the ambulance?" I asked as he reversed the Yukon.

"Sofia Nelson," he replied. "She's got two black eyes and a bunch of other injuries. Mickey O'Neill beat the crap out of her."

I let out something between a sigh and a groan. "I assume you've arrested him."

Milo shook his head. "I can't. Sofia grabbed a butcher knife and stabbed him through the chest. Mickey's dead."

Chapter 26

As we headed down Disappointment Avenue, I asked Milo if Sofia would be charged.

"Hell, no," Milo replied. "It was self-defense. She's so banged up that she may need surgery. I doubt Sofia even knew where she was putting the knife into him. She's going to have two shiners along with her other injuries. She probably couldn't see very well."

"Poor girl," I murmured. "I suppose the house is destroyed."

"The roof may have caved in by now. I don't know how long they've been holed up in there. Maybe since the stolen car went in the river after it ran out of gas. Mickey didn't want to be seen, so they bummed a ride from somebody who dropped them at the turnoff to Alpine. It was dark by then, so I'm guessing they took a route up to the house where they wouldn't be noticed. Blatt and Jamison couldn't find them in the house, so maybe he'd hauled Sofia outside and hid in all that overgrowth. He told her if she tried to ask anyone for help, he'd kill her on the spot."

I shuddered, remembering the spot I'd seen in Mitch's photo of the house. Maybe it was Sofia, trying to get help. Mickey had threatened to do that to his previous girlfriend, which was what had sent him to prison in the first place. Alison had taken Vonnie Mertz under her wing and she eventually recovered.

"How did the fire start?"

"Mickey tried to get the old wood-burning stove started," Milo replied. "He put in too much fuel and the flames touched off the kitchen curtains. You can imagine how rotted everything was inside that dump."

Unfortunately, I could. It had been deteriorating when I'd been inside six years ago after the O'Neills were massacred by the Hartquists. But despite my antipathy for the Nelsons, I felt sorry for Sofia. I'd never really gotten to know her. In fact, I couldn't remember ever having spoken to Sofia. She was related to the family only by marriage. Maybe I shouldn't paint her with the same brush that I'd used on the rest of the Nelsons.

"You mean they went all that time without

eating?" I asked.

"No idea," Milo replied. "I figure Mickey went to the house before he grabbed Sofia. He may have had food on hand, but stuff you wouldn't need to cook on the stove. Mickey never struck me as a gourmet kind of guy."

We pulled into our garage. I made up my mind that I'd go to see Sofia in the morning. But I wouldn't mention that to my husband. I had a feeling he wouldn't approve.

We dropped the subject after we went inside our log cabin. Milo needed to unwind, and eat. I needed to cook.

After dinner we watched the Gonzaga Bulldogs beat the University of San Francisco on the Dons' home court. Milo asked me how a squirty little school in Spokane could field a nationally ranked team. I told him it was because they were a Catholic university. He told me I was nuts. I told him the Pope rooted for the Zags. Milo shook his head and wandered off to the bedroom.

The snow had stopped during the night, but it hadn't started to melt yet. Having worked late, Milo was in no rush to get to headquarters, so it was no problem for him to drive me to work first, since my Honda was still parked outside of the office.

Most of my staff was on hand when I arrived. Only Kip hadn't yet shown up, but it was pub day and he'd be working into the night. Naturally, they pelted me with questions. Even Mitch wondered if anything else had happened after he left the O'Neill house, which had been shortly before Milo and I did. I told him I didn't think so or the sheriff would have heard about it. I poured a mug of coffee before retreating into my cubbyhole. I still felt emotionally and physically drained.

Five minutes later, a grim-looking Spencer Fleetwood all but charged through my door. "How," he demanded, "could I have missed the big news last night? But I did. Rosalie wanted to see a movie that was playing in Monroe. My fill-in at the station never heard the sirens. Help me out here. I need to at least include the basics in the hour-turn break at nine, then do a big follow-up in prime time this evening."

I wasn't sufficiently awake to give him a hard time. Keeping my account brief, I filled Spence in. "Obviously, I don't know the condition of the Nelson daughter-in-law yet. Feel free to scoop me if you find out before I do."

"Call now and I'll give up scooping you," Spence said. "You can post it online before

I do the hour-turn."

"You're a sport," I declared, picking up the phone. "Let's hope I get one of the nurses who isn't a . . ."

Just then Olga Overholt answered. She was one of the few nurses who was usually pleasant. I posed my question about Sofia.

"I don't know," Olga replied. "She's still in the ICU. I understand her condition is still listed as critical. But that's probably because Doc Dewey hasn't yet seen her this morning. Call back after ten, Emma."

I promised I would. In fact, if the snow was melting, I'd go to the hospital. After posting that the survivor of the fire at the O'Neill house was still in the ICU, I went through my mail and found nothing of interest except a couple of letters asking Vida's advice. Just before ten o'clock, I saw that the snow on the nearby streets had been cleared enough that I could drive to Alpine Memorial. Maybe I could catch Doc Dewey before he finished rounds and headed to the clinic.

I entered the underground garage and saw his car parked in its usual spot. I took the elevator to the second floor, where I found Doc standing by the reception desk talking to Olga. He saw me, and after finishing his conversation, he met me halfway.

"I've been up all night, Emma," he said. "Between what happened at the O'Neill house last night and all the accident victims we've had the last few days, Elvis Sung and I are worn out. I need coffee or I won't be able to drive home without falling asleep at the wheel. I'm heading for the cafeteria. If you want to ask me any questions, come along."

Neither of us spoke on the brief ride down. In fact, Doc rested his balding head against the back of the elevator and stared upward. I felt guilty for bothering him, but if I didn't, somebody else would. There's always someone around who espies a doctor at apparent ease and has to seek an explanation for whatever symptoms he or she is currently experiencing.

Luckily, only a handful of people were in the cafeteria. They were all employees, judging from their hospital attire. I insisted that he sit down while I collected our coffee. Doc looked almost boyish when he asked me to bring him a glazed doughnut. I guessed that he hadn't eaten since the previous day.

It took me under five minutes to present Doc with his coffee and doughnut. "This is on me, Doc. You should be on your way home."

He nodded a faint assent before we settled down to business. "That poor young woman," he said with a sigh. "She'll pull through, but she took quite a beating. The Nelsons live near you, right?"

"Unfortunately, yes," I agreed.

Doc shook his head. "Having Milo as their neighbor hasn't improved their behavior. Anyway, Sofia suffered multiple injuries while she was being held hostage by Mickey O'Neill. She may even require some plastic surgery." He turned grim. "Mickey was the product of bad blood. That's not a medical condition, but up here." He tapped his head. "Maybe it's just as well he's dead. Better Mickey than Sofia. She has a child to raise."

"I think her husband, Luke, gets out of prison sometime this year," I said.

"But his father, Doyle Nelson, got a longer sentence," Doc responded. "Different situation." He took a sip of coffee before continuing. "How's Vida getting along? I found out she had a fainting spell a few days before the car accident. I asked her what she thought had caused it, but she dismissed it as something to do with the cold weather. I didn't believe her, but I knew it was useless to argue." He took another bite of doughnut.

I thought back to what we'd been talking about before Vida collapsed. "She'd been asking if anyone knew who was living in the cabin at Baring. Vida had driven by there recently and had seen smoke coming out of the chimney. Milo had told me that the person living there was named Waldo Danforth. When I told her the name, she passed out."

Doc frowned thoughtfully. After a few moments he said, "You may know that a Mrs. Danforth passed away while Vida was in the hospital. She was registered as Mary Smith, however, because her family didn't want her illness publicized in the *Advocate*. I assume Waldo Danforth was her spouse?"

"Yes," I told him. "A relative brought in the obituary. But do you know of any reason why his name would cause Vida to faint?"

Doc started to shake his head, but stopped. He gave me a bemused look. "Funny how things you haven't remembered in years can come back to you. My father knew the Danforth family. They were his patients. And yes, they had a son named Waldo." He took off his glasses and rubbed at his left eye. "My God, Emma," he said, blinking at me before he put his glasses back on, "I remember now. When I first started my practice, Vida came to see me for her annual checkup because Dad was away at a conference. She seemed kind of put out about it." He paused to take a sip of coffee.

"That sounds like Vida," I remarked with a smile. "She's never liked change. She thought your father was the greatest doctor on the planet and you were an upstart."

Doc nodded. "Later Dad told me something about her. When Vida was about twenty, she fell in love with a young man from Sultan. She'd met him at a dance in Skykomish. Apparently they went out together on the sly, or so rumor had it. Dad never paid attention to gossip. But Vida suddenly became ill and her mother insisted on having her hospitalized. Dad knew better than to argue with Muriel Blatt. He diagnosed Vida as having a nervous breakdown. She poured her heart out to him. The young man she'd been seeing was already married and her heart was broken." He paused. "Yes, he was Waldo Danforth." Doc ate the last of his doughnut.

It took me a few seconds to take in the notion of Vida with a broken heart. "No wonder she fainted. I assume that was the real reason the Danforths used a phony name. They'd moved away a long time ago, according to their daughter, and they finally moved back to the area to be closer to family members in Leavenworth. Vida never realized that she was sharing a hospital room with Waldo's wife."

Doc agreed. "They knew Vida checked in with the hospital to find out who she could send get-well wishes to in her column. Of course, they never expected Vida to end up in the same room with Mrs. Danforth. Julie Canby told me that Mr. Danforth had a very successful career with the Weyerhaeuser timber company south of Seattle. But if Vida saw him, she probably wouldn't have recognized him. He's been suffering from ill health for some time."

"Poor man," I murmured. No wonder Vida had always been so encouraging about my relationship with Tom. She'd been reliving her own broken romance. Sadly, I shook my head. "And now he's lost his wife." I gave Doc a stern look. "Go home. I don't want you to become the next patient."

"And I don't want to add to Elvis's workload," Doc replied. "You won't be able to see Sofia Nelson in the ICU, so we'll walk out together. You may have to prop me up."

Back at the office, I went over the additional copy Mitch had written on our lead stories. As usual, he'd done a good job, and I told him so.

He shrugged. "Lots of practice from working in Detroit. I once covered three separate murders in a single day. But things seem to be improving back there." He looked a little wistful.

We then turned to meeting Tuesday's deadline. I decided to skip lunch and sent Alison to get me takeout from the Burger Barn. I thought about asking Milo to join me, but I knew he was as busy as I was. A little after one, he called me.

"I made that APB on Blackwell nationwide," he said in a weary voice. "Nothing so far. I even called the cops in Hardin, Montana. No luck there either. Hell, it's a small town. If they'd seen the names Blackwell or Marsh, they'd recognize them as strangers."

"They would," I agreed. "Look how everybody in Alpine starts yakking about anyone who . . ." I stopped. "Try Erskine."

"Irksome?" Milo sounded puzzled. "Those two are way beyond . . ."

"No," I interrupted, and spelled out Erskine. "It's Patti's maiden name."

"Damn," my husband said softly. "You're right. I'd forgotten that. I'll change the APB right away." He banged down the phone.

An hour later, Alison came into my office holding a piece of paper. "That Mrs. Overby came by again with another obituary. She's like the Grim Reaper. Here."

I scanned the page and actually wasn't shocked to see who had passed away. "It's for Waldo Danforth, the man whose wife died last week."

Alison shrugged. "I guess he couldn't live without her. That's kind of sweet."

"It is," I said vaguely, scanning Mrs. Overby's information about her deceased father. "They were the same age, born exactly a month apart."

"Soulmates," Alison said in a dreamy voice. "I wonder if I'll ever find someone like that."

"You've got Jan for now," I reminded her.

"But maybe not for always." She sighed. "Oh, well."

I watched her walk away, her shoulders slightly slumped.

It was almost four o'clock when Vida showed up. I'd been worrying about her, but she looked fine except for being a bit pale. Most of all, I dreaded how she'd react to finding out that Waldo Danforth had died. I hoped she wouldn't pass out again.

She paused to greet Liza, Leo, and Mitch, then tromped into my office. "So wet and chilly this afternoon," she said before plunking herself into a visitor chair. "However, I suspect we haven't seen the last of the snow.

Amy's feeling better, thank goodness. I gave her a good dose of gumption last night. She needs to be up and doing."

"Can Ted cook?" I asked, hoping that Vida hadn't gotten anywhere near the Hibberts' stove.

"Simple fare," she said with a shrug. "How many died since last week?"

"Three," I replied. "Someone named Conrad Carson, but he lived in Skykomish. The other two people were from Baring."

"Yes," she said, her voice tightening. "The Danforths. Doc called to ask how Amy was getting along. He mentioned that they'd died. I won't put any of them in my column. None of them lived in Alpine."

"True," I agreed, keeping a poker face.

"So sad about Jean Campbell," Vida remarked. "She was such a blessing to the rest of us Presbyterians. It's going to be hard for our pastor to find anyone who can replace her. I hope her mind is at rest. I must find out where she's recuperating."

I shrugged. Vida was obviously dismissing the idea that Jean had killed someone. "Don't ask me. I'm not a member of your church."

"That's your loss." Vida stood up and adjusted the plastic rain bonnet she wore over her purple pillbox. "I must be off. I've yet to make the casserole for Amy and Ted. I'll insist that she eat some of it to get back her strength. It should turn out well. I added some prunes to provide more flavor. How could anyone resist?"

I could if you made it, I thought, feeling a little queasy, but I merely offered my best wishes for Amy's recovery.

Still, I wondered how she'd reacted to Waldo's death when Doc broke the news. I considered calling to ask him, but he might still be asleep. Maybe he'd keep mum, citing patient privacy. It occurred to me that I really didn't want to know. Losing her first love had broken her heart, and in middle age she'd lost her husband, Ernest. In the last year she'd been forced to take off her blinders when her spoiled grandson Roger had been sent to prison. Most women would have grown bitter with age. Vida had been off her feed for a while — and embarrassed, but she'd recovered. Vida's strength of character had carried her through life's heartaches. I mentally saluted her. If I told her how I felt, she'd call me a sentimental fool. I smiled as I heard her voice in my head.

I'd been home for only ten minutes when Milo came in from the garage. "Blackwell and Patti aren't in Hardin, Montana," he said after kissing me. "Maybe they heard about the APB and got the hell out of Hardin."

"Eventually they'll have to come back here. Jack's not going to give up his mill. But if Patti drops the charges, you have to cancel the APB."

Milo nodded as he reached for the Scotch and the Canadian Club. "I'll find out tomorrow at the courthouse." Obviously, he wasn't going to change out of his uniform until he'd fortified himself with a dose of MacNaughton's.

"You look tired," I said. "You should've slept in even longer this morning."

"It's a good thing I didn't," he replied, pouring my Canadian Club into a glass. "I was lucky to get out of the office before five-fifteen. Fred Engelman called just before five. Will Pace isn't coming back to Alpine. Fred got a postcard from him saying he's decided to stay in Mexico."

"I'm not surprised. I remember Roseanna Bayard saw it was a one-way ticket."

"Right." Milo headed into the living room, where he settled into the easy chair. I sat down on the sofa. "What I suspected turned out to be right," he went on. "Pace not only rented rooms to hookers, but recruited them via a network of pimps operating in the western part of the state. I couldn't get a search warrant because there were no reported violations. Pace obviously kept a lid on what was going on behind his motel's closed doors."

"You never mentioned that to me!" I was practically shouting. "You should've told me what you thought he was doing."

Milo shook his head. "It was what you call 'speculating.' You know I don't like to do that."

I was still irked. "But you did it. You know I would never run anything about your speculating in the paper."

"Hell, Emma," Milo said with a wry expression, "can you honestly tell me that if you'd known what I was thinking, you wouldn't have nagged me to do something about it even though I didn't have any evidence?"

I grudgingly allowed that my husband was probably right. "Is Pace putting the motel up for sale?"

"No, he'll keep it. He told Fred to stay on, and he'll pay him a regular salary that will come out of the monthly rentals. Pace is opening a bank account in Honduras. Maybe that's his new home."

"That's good news for Fred," I allowed.

"But he can't live there like Will did. He and Janie have a house."

Milo shrugged. "They'll work it out. Meanwhile, I'll have to decide if it's worth trying to extradite Will Pace. I'm guessing Fred won't encourage the hookers. He strikes me as a straight arrow when it comes to his morals."

"Fred's fundamentally sound," I agreed as Milo's cell went off.

"Damn! Now what? . . . Dodge here."

I watched as his expression changed from annoyance to disbelief to anger and then to resignation. "Okay, Sam. There's nothing we can do about it from here. They can't stay away forever." He put the cell back in his shirt pocket. "That was Heppner. Blackwell and Patti took a plane to Chicago and left from there for a Paris honeymoon."

I was speechless. But Milo's expression was wry. "Are you jealous because we've never had a honeymoon?" He stood up. "Want to have one now?" He nodded toward the hallway.

Awkwardly I got to my feet. "Yes."

Later, after we emerged from the bedroom, I felt rejuvenated. The tragedies, frustration, and crises of the past two weeks melted like the snow that had covered Alpine. There was a cure for the ills of the world. In middle age, Milo and I had found it.

We called it Love.

ABOUT THE AUTHOR

Mary Richardson Daheim started spinning stories before she could spell. Daheim has been a journalist, an editor, a public relations consultant, and a freelance writer, but fiction was always her medium of choice. In 1982, she launched a career that is now distinguished by more than sixty novels. In 2000, she won the Literary Achievement Award from the Pacific Northwest Writers Association. In October 2008, she was inducted into the University of Washington's Communication Alumni Hall of Fame. Daheim lives in her hometown of Seattle and is a direct descendant of former residents of the real Alpine, which existed as a logging town from 1910 to 1929, when it was abandoned after the mill was closed. The Alpine/Emma Lord series has created interest in the site, which was named a Washington State ghost town in July 2011. An organization called the Alpine Advocates has been formed to preserve what remains of the town as a historic site.

marydaheimauthor.com

The employees of Thorndike Press hope you have enjoyed this Large Print book. All our Thorndike, Wheeler, and Kennebec Large Print titles are designed for easy reading, and all our books are made to last. Other Thorndike Press Large Print books are available at your library, through selected bookstores, or directly from us.

For information about titles, please call:
(800) 223-1244

or visit our website at:
gale.com/thorndike

To share your comments, please write:
Publisher
Thorndike Press
10 Water St., Suite 310
Waterville, ME 04901